SO-ASU-259

BREED
TO COME

by
Andre Norton

ace books
A Division of Charter Communications Inc.
1120 Avenue of the Americas
New York, N.Y. 10036

It was Ha-Hang, one of the Elders of the Western tribe who spoke—"There are Rattons in the lairs, and Demons. If they have indeed returned, it is best to let them have the lairs. Those of our kind saved their lives before by taking to the wilds."

Foskatt spoke for the first time. "Only just, Elder. It was only because the Demons fought among themselves that they escaped. These Demons are neither sick nor fighting among themselves. If they come in strength, how long will it be before they hunt us again?"

A sharp growl arose among the tribes, ears flattened and tails lashed. The warriors rose, their claws ready for battle. . . .

With appreciation for their invaluable aid in research, my thanks to my resident people-in-fur (in order of seniority)

Timmie
Punch
Samwise
Frodo
Su Li

and to the valiant memory of

Thai Shan
Sabina
Samantha

who were with us for far too short a time

Man is old enough to see himself as he really is—a mammal among mammals . . . He is old enough to know that in the years to come he may be crowded out like the prehistoric monsters of the past, while life breaks out in some ascendant form that is better suited to survive. . . .

—Homer W. Smith, *Kamongo*

What monstrous folly, think you, ever led nature to create her one great enemy—man!

—John Charles Van Dyke

1

There was a light breeze, just enough to whisper through the leaves. Furtig lay belly down on the broad limb of the tree, hunter-fashion, but his claws were still in his belt loop, not strapped on. No sniff of that breeze brought any useful scent to his expanded nostrils. He had climbed the tree not for a base from which to make a good capture-leap, but to see what lay beyond. However, now he knew that he must climb higher still. The leaves were too thick a screen here.

He moved with sinuous grace. Though his ancestors had hunted on four legs, Furtig now went on two, save when time pressed and he had to take to a fast run. And he was very much at home in the treetops. For those ancestors had also been climbers, just as their active curiosity had led them into exploration. Now he drew up from his perch into smaller branches, on which he balanced with inborn skill.

At last he gained a crotch, and there he faced

through an opening what he had come to see. He had chosen a tree on a small hill, and the expanse before him was clear.

The first nips of frost had struck the country, though by day a gentle warmth returned. Tall grass rippled between him and those distant, monstrous shadows. The grass was brown, and it would not be long before the cold season. But first came the Trials of Skill.

Furtig's black lips pulled tight, and he opened his mouth on a soundless battle snarl. The white curve of tearing fangs showed their pointed tips. His ears flattened in folds against his rounded skull, the furred ridge along his back lifted, and the hair on his tail puffed.

To those who had known his ancestors, he would be a grotesque sight; for a body once well fitted to the needs of its owner had altered in ways strange to nature. Rounded forepaws had split into stubby fingers, awkward enough but able to accomplish much more in the way of handling. His body was still largely furred, but there were places where the fur had thinned to a light down. There was more dome to his skull, just as the brain beneath was different, dealing with thoughts and conceptions earlier unknown. In fact it was that brain which had altered most of all. Feline, Furtig's ancestors had been. But Furtig was something which those who had known those felines could not have accurately named.

His people did not measure time more than by certain rites of their own, such as the bi-yearly Trials of Skill when a warrior gave the best evidence of his prowess so that the females could pick a mate. One noted the coming of winter cold, and the return of spring, summer's heat when one drowsed through the days and hunted by night. But the People did not try to count one year apart from the rest.

Though it was said that Gammage did things none other of the People thought of doing. Gammage—

Furtig studied the bulk of buildings on the other side of the fields, lairs of the Demons. Yet Gammage feared no Demon. If all the stories were true, Gammage lived yonder in the heart of the lost Demon world. It was the custom for first-rite warriors to speak of "going to Gammage." And once in a long while one would. Not that any returned—which argued that the Demons still had their traps at work, even though no Demon had been seen for generations.

Furtig had seen pictures of them. It was part of the regular scout training to be taught to recognize the enemy. And, while a youngling could be shown one of the Barkers, a Tusked One, or even a vile Ratton in the flesh, he had to depend solely upon such representations of Demons for identification.

Long ago the Demons had gone from their lairs, though they had left foul traces of their existence behind them. The stinking sickness, the coughing death, the eaten-skin ills—these had fallen on the People too in the past, for once they had been imprisoned in the Demons' lairs. Only a small handful of them had escaped.

The memory of such deaths had kept them away from the lairs for many lifetimes. Gammage had been the first to dare to return to live in the Demons' forsaken shells. And that was because his thirst for knowledge had taken him there. Gammage came of a strange line differing yet again from many of the People.

Absently Furtig brought his hand to his mouth, licked the fur on it clean of an itch-causing leaf smear. He was of Gammage's own clan line, and they were noted for their boldness of curiosity and their differences in body. In fact they were not too well regarded. Once more his lips wrinkled, his tail twitched a little. Warriors of his family did not find it easy to take a mate, not even when they won in the Trials. Their restlessness of spirit, their habit of questioning old ways, of exploring, was not favored by any prudent cave mother who wished security for future younglings.

Such would look in the opposite direction when Gammage's kin padded by. And Gammage himself, awesome as he was, had little repute nowadays. Though the clans were willing enough to accept the infrequent, but always surprising, gifts which he had sent from the lairs in times past.

The hunting claws, which clicked softly as Furtig shifted his weight, were one of Gammage's first gifts to his people. They were made of a shining metal which did not dull, break, or flake with the passing of years as did the shards of metal found elsewhere. Set in a band which slipped over the hand, they snapped snugly just above the wrist, projecting well beyond the stubby fingers with tearing, curved hooks, like the claws one grew, but far more formidable and dangerous. And they were used just as one used one's natural defenses. A single well-placed blow could kill one of the deer or wild cows Furtig's people hunted for their staple food.

In war with one's kind they were forbidden. But they could be worn to face the Barkers, as those knew only too well. And with the Rattons—one used all and any weapons against those evil things. While with the Tusked Ones there were no quarrels, because of a truce.

Yes, the claws were from Gammage. And from time to time other things came from him, all designed to lighten the task of living in the Five Caves. So that the clans were respected and feared. There were ruors that another tribe of the People had settled lately to the north of the lairs, but so far none of Furtig's people had seen them.

The lairs—Furtig studied those blots on the landscape. They formed a long range of mountains. Was Gammage still there? It had been—he began to count seasons, tapping them off with a finger—it had been as many as fingers on his one hand since any word or gift had come from Gammage. Perhaps the Ancestor was dead.

Only that was hard to believe. Gammage had already lived far past the proper span of any ordinary warrior. Why, it had been Furtig's great-great-grandfather who had been Gammage's youngling in the last of the families born before the death of his mate and his departure for the lairs. It was also true that Gammage's blood lived longer than most. Fuffor, Furtig's father, had died in a battle with the Barkers, and he was then the only one of his years left at the Five Caves. Nor had he seemed old; his mate had had another pair of younglings that very season, and she was the fourth mate he had won during the passing of seasons!

If it was not that so much of Gammage's blood now ran in the tribe there might be trouble. Once more Furtig snarled silently. Tales grew, and dark tales always grow the faster and stronger. Gammage was in league with Demons, he used evil learning to prolong his life. Yet for all such mewling of stories in the dark, his people were eager enough to welcome one of Gammage's messengers—take what he had to offer.

Only, now that those messengers came no more, and one heard nothing from those who had gone to seek Gammage, the stories grew in force. At the last Trials Furtig's older brother of another birth time had won. Yet he had not been chosen by any mate. And so he had joined the far scouts and taken a western trail-of-seeking from which he had never returned. Could it be any better for Furtig? Perhaps less—for he was not the warrior-in-strength that Fughan had been, being smaller and less powerful, even though his rivals granted him speed and agility.

He supposed he should be in practice now, using all those skills for the Trials, not wasting time staring at the lairs. Yet he found it hard to turn away. And his mind built strange pictures of what must lie within those walls. Great had been the knowledge of the Demons, though they had used it ill and in a manner which later brought them to defeat and death.

Furtig remembered hearing his father discuss the dim history of those days. He had been talking with one of Gammage's messengers about some discovery the Ancestor had made. That had been when Gammage had sent his picture of a Demon; they were to beware any creature who resembled it.

Before they had died, the Demons had gone mad,

10

even as sometimes the Barkers did. They had fallen upon one another in rage, and were not able to mate or produce younglings. So without younglings and with their terrible hatred for one another, they had come to an end, and the world was the better for their going.

Gammage had learned this in the lairs, but he also feared that someday the Demons might return. From death? Furtig wondered. Great learning they had had, but could any living creature die and then live again? Perhaps the Demons were not rightly living creatures such as the People, even the Rattons. Someday—someday he would go to Gammage to learn more.

But not today, not until he had proven himself, shown all the Five Caves that the blood of Gammage was not to be ill-considered. And he would waste no more time in spying on the dead lairs of Demons either!

Furtig swung out of the tree, dropping lightly. This was the outpost of a small grove which angled back to become an arm of the forest country, the hunting territory of the Five Caves. Furtig was as at home in its shade as he was in the caves.

He stopped to tuck his hunting claws more tightly into his belt so that no small jangle would betray his passing, and then flitted on, his feet making no sound on the ground. Since he wanted to make speed he went to all fours, moving in graceful bounds. The People stood proudly upright when it was a time of ceremony, thus proving that the Demons who always walked so were no greater, but in times of need they fell back upon ancestral ways.

11

He planned to approach the caves from the north, but at first his course was west. That would take him by a small lake, a favorite feeding place of plump ducks. To return with an addition to the cave food supplies was always the duty of a warrior.

Suddenly a whiff of rank scent brought Furtig to a halt, crouching in the bushes. His hand whipped to his belt, reached for the claws, and he worked his hands into them with practiced speed.

Barkers! And more than one by the smell. They were not lone hunters like his own people, but moved in packs, centering in upon the kill. And one of the People would be a kill they would enjoy.

Courage was one thing, stupidity another. And Furtig's people were never stupid. He could remain where he was and do battle, for he did not doubt that the Barkers would speedily scent him (in fact he wondered fleetingly why they had not already done so). Or he could seek safety in the only flight left—aloft.

The hunting claws gave him a firm grip as they bit into tree bark, and he pulled himself up with haste. He found a branch from which he could view the ground below. Deep in his throat rumbled a growl he would not give full voice to, and with flattened ears and fur lifted on his spine, he watched, eyes aslit in a fighting face.

There were five of them, and they trotted four-footed. They had no one such as Gammage to supply them with any additions to the natural weapons of fangs. But those were danger enough. The Barkers were a third again as large as Furtig in size, their strong muscles moving smoothly under hides which were some as gray as his own, others blotched with black or lightened on belly and chest with cream.

They wore belts not unlike his, and from three of these dangled the limp bodies of rabbits. A hunting party. But so far they had found only small prey. If they kept on along that way though (Furtig's soundless growl held a suggestion of anticipation), they were going to cross the regular ranging ground of the Tusked Ones. And if they were foolish enough to hunt *them*—Furtig's green eyes glistened. He would back the Tusked Ones against any foe—perhaps even against Demons. Their warriors were not only fierce fighters but very wily brained.

He hoped that the Barkers would run into Broken Nose. In his mind Furtig gave that name to the great boar leader. The People could not echo the speech of the Tusked Ones, any more than they could the sharp yelps of the Barkers—though no reasonable creature could deem those speech. At the rare times of truce communication, one depended on signs, and the learning of them was the first lesson of any youngling's education.

Furtig watched the Barkers out of sight and then worked his way around the tree, found a place where he could leap onto the next, and made that crossing skillfully.

He was still growling. To see Barkers invading the hunting territory of the Five Caves was a shock. He would waste no time duck-stalking. On the other hand he must make sure that those he had seen were not outscouts for a larger pack. There were times when packs changed hunting territories, driven out by larger packs or by lack of game.

If such a pack were coming into the woods, then Furtig's warning would carry a double impact. He must back trail on those he had seen for a space.

For a time he kept to the trees, where he left no trail to be sniffed out even though, unlike the Barkers and the Tusked Ones, his people had no strong body odor. They hunted by sight and hearing and not by scent as did their enemies.

As a final precaution Furtig opened a small skin pouch made fast to his belt. Within was a wad of greasy stuff; its musky smell made his nose wrinkle in disgust. But he resolutely rubbed it on his feet and hands. Let a Barker sniff that and he would get a noseful as would send him off again, for it was the fat of the deadly snake.

Down again on the ground, Furtig sped along. As he went he listened, tested the air, watched for any sign that the home woods had been invaded in force. But he could not find anything save traces of the small party he had seen.

Then— His head jerked around, his nose pointed to a tree at his left. Warily he moved toward it. Barker sign left there as a guide, but under it—

In spite of his disgust at the rankness of the canine scent, Furtig made himself hold his head close, sniff deeper. Yes, beneath that road sign of the enemy was another, a boundary scent—of the People, but not of his own clan.

He straightened to his full height, held his arms overhead as far as he could reach. Scratches, patterned scratches, and higher than those he could make with his own claws. So the stranger who had so arrogantly left his hunting mark there had been larger, taller!

Furtig snarled aloud this time. Leaping, he slashed with his claws, managing to reach and dig into the other's sign, scouring out that marking, leaving the deeper grooves he had made. Let the stranger see that! Those deep marks crossing the first ought to be a warnoff to be heeded.

But the forest was getting far too crowded. First a hunting party of the Barkers, now a territory marking left by a stranger, as if Five Caves and its clans did not exist at all! Furtig abandoned his back trailing. The sooner the People learned of these two happenings, the better.

However, he did not throw away caution but muddled his trail as he went. If any scout tried to sniff out the reptile scent, he would be disheartened by these further precautions. But this took time, and Furtig had to make a wider circle to approach the caves from a different direction.

It was dusk and then night. Furtig was hungry. He rasped his rough-surfaced tongue in and out of his mouth when he thought of food. But he did not allow himself to hurry.

A sudden hiss out of the night did not startle him. He gave a low recognition note in return. Had he not sounded that he might well have had his throat clawed open by the guard. The People did not survive through lack of caution.

Twice he swung off the open trail to avoid the hidden traps. Not that the People were as dependent on traps as the Rattons, who were commonly known to have raised that defense to a high art in the lairs. For, unlike the People, who distrusted and mainly kept away from the Demon places, the Rattons had chosen always to lurk there.

The Five Caves were ably defended by nature as well as by their inhabitants. None of them opened at ground level. High up, they cut back from two ledges with a straight drop below. There were tree-trunk ladders rigged to give access to the ledges. But these could be hauled up, to lie along ledge edge, another barrier to attack. Twice the caves had been besieged by packs of Barkers. Both times their defenses had been unbreakable, and the attackers had lost more pack members then they had slain in return. It was during the last such attack that Furtig's father had fallen.

Within, the caves cut deeply, and one of them had a way down to where water flowed in the ever-dark. Thus the besieged did not suffer from thirst, and they kept always a store of dried meat handy.

Furtig's people were not naturally gregarious. Younglings and their mothers made close family units, of course. But the males, except in the Months of Mating, were not very welcome in the innermost caves. Unmated males roved widely and made up the scouts and the outer defenses. They had, through the years, increased in numbers. But seldom, save at the Trials of Skill, were they ever assembled together.

They had a truce with another tribe-clan to the west, and met for trials with them that they might exchange bloodlines by intermating. But normally they had no contact with any but their own five families, one based in each of the caves.

Furtig's cave was at the top and north, and he

swung up to it quickly, his nose already sorting and classifying odors. Fresh meat—ribs of wild cow. Also duck. His hunger increased with every sniff.

But as he entered the cave, he did not hurry to where the females were portioning out the food but slipped along the wall to that niche where the senior member of the clan sat sharpening his hunting claws with the satisfaction of one who had recently put them to good use. So apparent was that satisfaction, Furtig knew Fal-Kan had been responsible for the cow ribs.

Though his people's sight adjusted well to partial darkness, there was light in the cave, a dull glow from a small box which was another of Gammage's gifts. It did not need any tending. When the first daylight struck into the mouth of the cave it vanished, coming alive again in the dusk of evening.

Gammage's bounty, too, were the squares of woven stuff that padded the sleeping ledges along the walls. In summer these were stowed away, and the females brought in sweet-scented grasses in their places. But in the cold, when one curled up on them, a gentle heat was generated to keep one warm through the worst of winter storms.

"Fal-Kan has hunted well." Furtig squatted several paces away from his mother's eldest brother, now sitting on his own sleep ledge. Thus Furtig was the prescribed respectful distance below him.

"A fat cow," Fal-Kan replied as one who brings home such riches each morning before the full heat of the sun. "But you came in haste, wearing trail destroyer—" He sniffed heavily. "So what danger have your eyes fastened on?"

Furtig spoke—first of the Barkers and then of the strange boundary sign. With a gesture Fal-Kan dismissed the Barkers. They were what one could expect from time to time, and scouts would be sent to make sure the Barkers were not pack forerunners. But at the story of the slash marks Fal-Kan set aside his claws and listened intently. When Furtig told of his counter-marking, the Elder nodded.

"That was well done. And you say that these slashes were not deep. Perhaps no more deeply set than these could do?" He held out his hand, extending his natural claws.

"So it looked." Furtig had long ago learned that caution was the best tone to take with Elders. They were apt to consider the opinions of the young as misled and misleading.

"Then this one did not know Gammage."

Furtig's open astonishment brought him to the discourtesy of actually interrupting an Elder.

"Know Gammage! But he is a stranger—not of the Five Caves—or of the western People. Gammage would not know him."

Fal-Kan growled softly, and Furtig, in confusion, recognized his error. But his surprise remained.

"It is time," Fal-Kan said in the throat-rumbling voice used for pronouncements against offenders of cave custom, "that one speak clearly about the Ancestor. Have you not wondered why we have not been favored by his attention lately, during this time of your growing—though it would seem by your actions that you have not in truth progressed far beyond a youngling?"

Fal-Kan waited for no answer but continued without a pause.

"The fact is that our Ancestor"—and he did not say Honored Ancestor or use any title of respect—"is so engrossed by this fear of returning Demons which has settled in his head that he raises voice to unite all People—as if they were of one family or clan! All People brought together!" Fal-Kan's whiskers bristled.

"All warriors know that the Demons are gone. That they slew each other, and that they could not make their kind any more, so they became fewer and fewer and finally there were none. Whence then would any come? Do old bones put on flesh and fur and come alive again? But the Ancestor has this fear, and it leads him in ways no prudent one would travel. It was learned the last time his messenger came that he was giving other People the same things he had sent here to the caves.

"And—with greater folly—he even spoke of trying to make truce with the Barkers for a plan of common defense, lest when the Demons returned we be too scattered and weak to stand against them. When this was known, the Elders refused the gifts of Gammage and told his messenger not to come again, for we no longer held them clan brothers."

Furtig swallowed. That Gammage would do this! There must be some other part of the story not known. For none of the People would be so sunk in folly as to share with enemies the weapons they had. Yet neither would Fal-Kan say this if he did not believe it the truth.

"And Gammage must have heard our words and understood." Fal-Kan's tail twitched. "We have not seen his messengers since. But we have heard from our truce mates in the west that there were truce flags set before the lairs in the north and strangers gathered there. Though we do not know who those were," Fal-Kan was fair enough to add. "But it may well be that, having turned his face from his own kin when they would not support his madness, Gammage now gives to others the fruits of his hunting. And this is a shameful thing, so we do not speak of it, even among ourselves, unless there is great need.

"But of the hunting sign on the tree, that we must speak of—all warriors together. For we are not so rich in game that we can allow others to take our country for their own. And we shall also tell this to the western kin. They come soon for the Trials. Go and eat, warrior. I shall take your words to the other cave Elders."

2

The visitors had been in sight of the cave scouts since midafternoon, but their party did not file into their usual campsite until after nightfall. This was the alternate season when the western clans came to the caves. Next season Furtig's people would cross country for the Trials.

All the young unmated warriors who were to take part in the coming contests scattered along the inroad (unless their Elders managed to restrain them with other duties). Though it was ill mannered to stare openly at their guests, there was naught to prevent their watching the travelers from cover, making comparisons between their champions and those marching in the protect circle about the females and younglings, or, better still, catching glimpses of their Choosers.

But to Furtig none of those were as attractive as Fas-Tan of the cave of Formor. And his interest was more for probable rivals than for the prizes of battle the other tribe could display. Not, he reflected ruefully, that he had much chance of aspiring to Fas-Tan.

Through some trick of heredity which ran in her family, she had odd fur coloring which was esteemed, along with the length of that fur, as beauty. The soft fur about her head and shoulders was nearly three times the length of that sprouting from Furtig's own tougher hide, and it was of two colors—not spotted or patched as was often the case but a dark brown shading evenly to cream. Her tail, always groomed to a silken flow, was also dark. Many were the fish-bone combs patiently wrought and laid at the message rock to the fore of Formor's cave, intended by the hopeful to catch the eye of Fas-Tan. And to know that she used the work of one's clumsy hands was enough to make a warrior strut for a day.

Fas-Tan would certainly have first choice, and with her pride, her selection of mate would be he who proved himself best. Furtig had not the least chance of catching her golden eyes. But a warrior could dream, and he had dreamed.

Now another thought plagued him. Fal-Kan's revelations concerning the folly, almost the treachery of Gammage, hung in his mind. He found himself looking not at the females of the westerners, but at the fringe of warriors. Most had hunting claws swinging at their belts. However, Furtig's eyes marked at least three who did not wear those emblems of manhood, yet marched with the defenders. A warrior could gain his claws in two ways, since they no longer came from Gammage. He could put on those which had been his father's if his sire had gone into the Last Dark, or he

22

could challenge a claw wearer and strive for a victory that would make them his.

Furtig's claws had been his father's. He had had to work patiently and long to hammer their fastenings to fit his own hands. If he were challenged tomorrow by one of the clawless and lost— He dropped his hand protectingly over the weapons at his belt. To lose those—

However, when he thought of Fas-Tan there was a heat in him, a need to yowl a challenge straight into the whiskered face of the nearest warrior. And he knew that no male could resist the Trials when the Choosers walked provocatively, tails switching, seeming to see no one, yet well aware of all who watched.

And he was the only contender from the cave of Gammage this year. Also, since his brother Fughan had brought home no mate, he was doubly held to challenge. He wriggled back into the brush and headed for the caves.

As he pulled up into his own place, he gave a small sigh. Trials were never to the death; the People were too few to risk the loss of even one warrior. But a contender could be badly mauled, even maimed, if the Ancestors turned their power from him.

Only Gammage, Furtig's most notable Ancestor, was not here, even in spirit. And it seemed, after he had listened to Fal-Kan, that Gammage had fallen from favor with his own kind. Furtig squatted by the lamp box and lapped a mouthful or two of water from his bowl as he thought about Gammage.

Why did the Ancestor fear the return of the Demons? It had been so long since the last one had been seen. Unless—Furtig's spine hair raised at the thought—deep in the lairs they still existed. And Gammage, creeping secret ways there, had learned more of their devilish evil than he had shared. But if that were true—no, he was certain Gammage would have sent a plain message, one which might even have won some of the People to join in his wild plans.

Elders sometimes took to living in the past. They spoke to those who had gone into the Last Dark as if such still stood at their sides. It came to them, this other sight, when they were very old. Though few lived so long, for when a warrior grew less swift of thought, less supple of body, he often died suddenly and bloodily by the horns and hoofs of hunted prey, from the coughing sickness which came with the cold, of a hundred other perils which always ringed the caves.

Only such perils might not haunt the lairs. And Gammage, very old, saw Demons stalking him in the shadows of their own stronghold. Yes, that could be the answer. But you could not argue with one who saw those gone before. And Gammage, moved by such shadows and master of the lair wonders—why, he could even be a menace to his own People if he continued in his folly of spreading his discoveries among strangers! And even—as Fal-Kan had said—among his enemies! Someone ought to go to Gammage in truth, not just in the sayings of young warriors, and discover what he was doing now. For the good of the People that should be done.

Going to Gammage—it had been four trials ago that the last one who said that had gone, never to return. Foskatt of Fava's cave. He had been bested in the contests. Furtig tried to recall Foskatt and then wished he had not. For the image in his mind was too like the one he had seen of himself the last time he had looked down at the other-Furtig in the smooth water of the Pool of Trees.

Foskatt, too, had been thin, narrow of shoulder and loin. And his fur was the same deep gray, almost blue in the sun. He also had been fond of roving on his own and had once shown Furtig something he had found in a small lair, one of those apart from the great ones in which Gammage lived. It was a strange thing, like a square box of metal, and in its top was a square of other material, very smooth. When Foskatt pressed a place on the side of the box, there appeared a picture on the top square. It was Demon-made, and when the cave Elders saw it they took it from Foskatt and smashed it with rocks.

Foskatt had been very quiet after that. And when he was beaten at the Trials, he had gone to Gammage. What had he found in the lairs?

Furtig fingered his fighting claws and thought about what might happen tomorrow; he must forget Gammage and consider rather his own future. The closer it came to the hour when he would have to front an opponent chosen by lot, the less good that seemed. Though he knew that once a challenge was uttered, he would be caught up in a frenzy of battle he would neither want to avoid nor be able to control. The very life force of their kind would spur him on.

Since it was not the custom that one tribe should stare at another in their home place, those of the caves went to their own shelters as the van of the visitors settled in the campgrounds, so Furtig was not

alone for long. In the cave the life of his family bub-
bled about him.

"There is no proper way of influencing the drawing
of lots." Fal-Kan and two of the lesser Elders drew
Furtig aside to give him council, though he would far
rather have them leave him alone. Or would he?
Which was worse, foreseeing in his own mind what
might happen to him, or listening to advice delivered
with an undercurrent of dubious belief in their champion? Fal-Kan sounded now as if he *did* wish there
was some way to control the selection of warrior
against warrior.

"True." Fujor licked absentmindedly at his hand,
his tongue rasping ever against the place where one
finger was missing, as if by his gesture he could regrow the lacking member. Fujor was hairier of body
than most of the cave and ran four-footed more often.

"There are three without claws," Fal-Kan continued. "Your weapons, warrior, will be an added in-
ducement for any struggle with those. Some will fight
sooner for good weapons than a mate."

Furtig wished he could pull those jingling treasures
from his belt and hide them. But custom forbade it.
There was no escape from laying them on the challenge rock when he was summoned. However, he
dared speak up out of a kind of desperation. After all,
Fal-Kan and Fujor had been successful in their own
Trials. Perhaps, just perhaps, they could give him
some manner of advice.

"Do you think, Elders, that I am already defeated,
that you see the claws of my father on the hands of a
stranger? For if this is so, can you not then tell me
how the worst is to be avoided?"

Fal-Kan eyed him critically. "It is the will of the Ancestors who will win. But you are quick, Furtig. You know all we can teach you. We have done our best. See that you do also."

Furtig was silenced. There was no more to be gotten out of these two. They were both Elders (though Fujor only by right of years, not by any wisdom). Fe-San, the other Elder, was noted for never raising his voice in Fal-Kan's presence.

The other males were younglings, too young to do more than tread the teaching trails by day. Lately they had had more females than males within the cave of Gammage. And after every Trial the females went to the victors' caves. The family was dwindling. Perhaps it would be with them as it had been with the cave of Rantla on the lower level, a clan finally reduced only to Elders and to Choosers too old to give birth. Yet Gammage had founded a proud line!

Now Furtig ate sparingly of the meat in his bowl, scrambled onto his own ledge, and curled up to sleep. He wished that the morning was already passed and the outcome of his uncertain championship decided. Through the dark he could hear the purring whispers of two of his sisters. Tomorrow would be a day of pride for them, with no doubts to cloud their excitement. They would be among the Choosers, not among the fighters.

Furtig tried to picture Fas-Tan, but his thoughts kept sliding in more dismal directions—he pictured a belt with no claws and an inglorious return to his cave. It was then he made up his mind. If he was a loser he was not going to take the solitary trail his brother had followed, or remain here to be an object

27

of scorn for the Elders. No, he was going to Gammage!

The morning cry woke Furtig from dreams he could not remember. Thus they had not been sent by any Ancestor to warn him. And Furtig, as he dropped from his sleep place, felt no greater strength. The thought of the coming day weighed heavily on him, so much so that he had to struggle to preserve the proper impassive manner of a warrior on this day of days.

When they gathered on the pounded-earth flooring of the Trial place, Furtig had to join the line of Challengers as confidently as if he were San-Lo himself, there at the other end. San-Lo was easily counted the best the caves could produce. His yellow fur with its darker brown striping was sleek and well ordered, seeming to catch the morning sun in a blaze, foretelling the glory which would soon rest on him in the sight of both caves and westerners.

Furtig had no illusions; of that company he was certainly the least likely to succeed. There were ten of them this year, with a range of different fur coloring making a bright pattern. Two brothers of the gray-with-black-striping, which was the commonest; a night black, a contrast to his two black-and-white brothers, a formidable trio who liked to hunt together and shared more companionship than others of their age group. Then came a stocky white with only ears and tail of gray; two more yellows, younger and lighter editions of San-Lo; a brown-striped with a white belly; and last Furtig in solid gray.

Their opponents were more uniform, having originally come from only two families, according to tradition. They were either all black, or black-and-white in various markings.

The Choosers were lying at languid ease on top of the sun-warmed rocks to the east of the combat field, while the Elders and the mated gathered north and south. Now and then one of the Choosers would wantonly utter a small yowling call, promising delights for him she would accept. But Fas-Tan did not have to attract attention so. Her superb beauty already had registered with them all.

Ha-Ja, who was the Eldest of the Westerners, and Kuygen, who held the same status at the caves, advanced to the center of the field. At a gesture each brought forward the first warrior in each line, holding a bowl well above the eye level of the contestants. Those raised their hands and drew, keeping their choices as concealed as they could. So it went, two by two, until Furtig had his chance. He groped in the bowl, felt the two remaining slips of wood, and pulled but one.

Once they had all drawn, each contestant smoothed a small patch of earth and dropped his choose-stick on it. Ha-Ja called first:

"One notch end."

San-Lo showed his fangs and gave a low snarl of assent.

Kuygen gestured to the westerners. The duplicate lay at the feet of a powerfully built all-black, whose tail was already twitching. At least, by the look of him, San-Lo would be fairly matched.

Both advanced to the center rock, tossed their hunting claws with a jangle of metal on the stone. At least in this battle there would be no forfeiture of weapons.

Together Ha-Ja and Kuygen made signal. The warriors went to full ground-crouch, their tails alash, ears flattened, eyes slitted. And from their throats came the howls of battle. They circled in one of the customary challenge moves, and then the black sprang.

Their entanglement was a flurry of such fast tearing, rolling, and kicking with the powerful hind feet that the spectators, accustomed as they were to such encounters, were hardly able to follow the action before the warriors parted. Tufts of fur blew from the battle site, but they were yowling again, neither seeming the least affected by the fury of their first meeting.

Again that attack, vicious, sudden, complete. They rolled over and over on the ground and fur flew. The emotion spread to the spectators. Waiting warriors yowled, voicing their own battle cries, hardly able to restrain themselves from leaping at each other. Even the Elders added to the general din. Only the Choosers held to their studied languor, though their eyes were very wide, and here and there a pink tongue tip showed.

San-Lo won. When they separated the second time, the black had lowered tail and backed from the field, raw and bleeding tears on his belly. The champion of the caves strutted to the rock to pick up his claws, dangling them in an arrogant jingle before he returned to his place in line.

The fights continued. Two of the cave warriors surrendered to the visitors. Then there were three straight wins for Furtig's clan. But his apprehension was growing. The matching of pieces was leaving another warrior on the western side as formidable in size as the one who had stood up to San-Lo. If the favor of the Ancestors was against Furtig—

And it was. His neighbor on the cave line bested—but just—his opponent. Furtig must face the powerful warrior. Also—no claws swung from the other's belt, so he had to face the thought of not only one defeat but two.

Dreading what was to come, yet knowing it must be faced, he went dutifully to the rock, tossed his claws there with a reluctance he hoped was not betrayed.

At least he could make the black know that he had been in a fight! And he yowled his challenge with what strength he could muster. When they tangled, he fought with all the skill he had. Only that was not enough. Sheer determination not to give in sent him twice more to tangle with those punishing clawed legs, fangs which had left wounds. It was a nightmare to which there was no end. He could only keep fighting—until—

Until there was blackness and he was lost in it, though there were unpleasant dreams. And when he awoke in the cave, lying on his own pallet, he first thought it *was* all a dream. Then he raised his swimming head and looked upon the matted paste of healing leaves plastered on him.

Almost hoping, he fought pain to bring his hand to his belt. But there were no claws there. He had plainly lost, and those weapons which had been Gammage's good gift to Furtig's father were gone with all his hopes of ever being more in the caves than Fu-Tor of the missing hand.

31

They had patched him up with the best of their tending. But there was no one in the cave. He craved water with a thirst which was now another pain, and finally forced his aching and bruised body to obey him, crawling through the light of the night lamp to the stone trough. There was little left, and when he tried to dip out a bowlful his hand shook so that he got hardly any. But even as he had fought on when there was no hope of victory, he persisted.

Furtig did not return to his ledge. Now that he was not so single-minded in his quest for water, he could plainly hear the sounds of the feasting below. The Choosing must be over, the winners with the mates who had selected them. Fas-Tan—he put her out of his mind. After all she had been only a dream he could never hope to possess.

His clawless belt was the greater loss, and he could have wailed over that like a youngling who had strayed too far from his mother and feared what might crouch in the dark. That he could stay on in the caves now was impossible.

But to go to Gammage armed and confident was one matter. To slink off as a reject from the Trials, with his weapon lost as spoils of victory— In some things his pride was deep. Yet—to Gammage he must go. It was his right, as it had been his brother's, to choose to leave. And one could always claim a second Trial—though at present that was the last thing he wanted.

However, Furtig had no intention of leaving before he proclaimed his choice. Pride held him to that. Some losers might be poor spirited enough to slink away in the dark of night, giving no formal word to their caves—but not Furtig! He crawled back to the ledge, knowing that he must also wait until he was fit for the trail again.

So he lay, aching and smarting, listening to the feasting, wondering if his sisters had chosen to mate with victorious westerners or within the caves. And so he fell asleep.

It was midday when he awoke, for the sun was shining in a bright bar well into the cave mouth. The ledges of the Elders were empty, but he heard noises in the parts within. As he turned his head one of the younger females almost touched noses with him, she had been sitting so close, her eyes regarding him un-winkingly.

"Furtig." She spoke his name softly, putting out a hand to touch a patch of the now dried leaf plaster on his shoulder. "Does it hurt you much?"

He was aware of aches, but none so intense as earlier.

"Not too much, clan sister."

"Mighty fighter, in the cave of Grimmage—"

He wrinkled a lip in a wry grimace. "Not so, young-ling. Did I not lose to the warrior of the westerners? San-Lo is a mighty fighter, not Furtig."

She shook her head. Like him she was furred with rich gray, but hers was longer, silkier. He had thought Fas-Tan was rare because of her coloring, but this youngling, Eu-La, would also be a beauty when her choose-time came.

"San-Lo was chosen by Fas-Tan." She told him what he could easily have guessed. "Sister Naya has taken Mur of Folock's cave. But Sister Yngar—she

33

took the black warrior of the westerners—" Eu-La's ears flattened and she hissed.

Furtig guessed. "The one I battled? He is a strong one."

"He hurt you." Eu-La shook her head. "It was wrong for Sister Yngar to choose one who hurt her brother. She is no longer of the cave." Once more she hissed.

"But of course she is not, sister. When one chooses, one is of the clan of one's mate. That is the way of life."

"It is a bad way—this fighting way." She chewed one claw tip reflectively between words. "You are better than San-Lo."

Furtig grunted. "I would not like to try to prove that, sister. In fact it is a not-truth."

She hissed. "He is strong of claw, yes. But in his head—does he think well? No, Fas-Tan is a fool. She should pick a mate who thinks rather than one who fights strongly."

Furtig stared at her. Why, she was only a youngling, more than a season away from her own time of choice. But what she said now was not a youngling kind of thing.

"Why do you think so?" he asked, curious.

"We"—her head went up proudly—"are of the cave of Gammage. And the Ancestor learned many, many things to help us. He did not so learn by fighting. He went hunting for knowledge instead of battles. Brother, females also think. And when I grow trail-wise I shall not choose—I shall go to Gammage also! There I shall learn and learn—" She stretched forth her thin furred arms as if she were about to

34

gather to her some heaping of knowledge, if knowledge could be so heaped and gathered.

"Gammage has grown foolish with time—" He spoke tentatively.

Once more she hissed, and now her anger was directed at him.

"You speak as the Elders. Because some do not understand new things they say that such are stupid or ill thought. Think instead on what Gammage has sent us, and that these may only be a small part of the great things he has found! There must be much good in the lairs."

"And if Gammage's fears are the truth, there may also be Demons there."

Eu-La wrinkled a lip. "Believe in Demons when you see them, brother. Before then take what you can which will aid you."

He sat up. "How did you know I was minded to go to Gammage?"

She gave a soft purr of laughter. "Because you are who you are you can do no other, brother. Look you." She brought out from behind her a small bag pulled tight by a drawstring. Furtig had seen only one such before, that being much prized by the females. It had been made, according to tradition, by Gammage's last mate, who had had more supple fingers than most. But it had not been duplicated since.

"Where got you that?"

"I made it." Her pride was rightly great. "For you—" She pushed it into his hand. "And these also."

What she produced now were as startling as the bag, for she had a pair of hunting claws. They were not the shining, well-cared-for ones which had been his. There were two points missing on one set, one on the other, and the rest were dull and blunted.

"I found them," Eu-La told him, "in a place between two rocks down in the cave of waters. They are broken, brother, but at least you do not go with bare hands. And—this I ask of you—when you stand before the Ancestor, show him this—" She touched the bag. "Say to him then, shall not a female of the cave of Gammage not also have a part in the learning of new things?"

Furtig grasped both bag and claws, astounded at her gifts, so much more than he could have hoped for.

"Be sure, sister," he said, "that I shall say it to him just as you have said it to me."

3

Furtig crept forward. It was not yet dawn, but to his eyes the night was not dark. He had chosen to cross the wide expanse of open space about the western fringe of the Demons' lair by night—though a whole day of watching had shown no signs of life there. Nor had he, during this patient stalk across the grass-covered open, discovered any game trail or sign that aught came or went from the buildings.

But the closer he approached the lairs, the more awe-inspiring they were. From a distance he had been able to judge that their height was far greater even than that of the cliff which held the Five Caves. However, he had had no idea how high they were until he neared their bases. Now he had almost to roll on his back to see their tips against the sky.

It was frightening. Furtig felt that to venture in among those banks of towering structures would be to set foot in a trap. As Gammage had? Was it death and not the reception afforded his unwelcome ideas which had kept the Ancestor silent these past seasons?

Though his sense of smell was no way near as keen as a Barker's, Furtig lifted his head higher and tried to distinguish some guiding odor. Did Gammage's people mark the boundaries of their territory here as they would forest trees, though with scent not scratches? He could detect the scent of the dying grass, got some small whiffs of the inhabitants of that flat land—mice, a rabbit. But nothing seemed to issue from the lairs, though the wind blew from there, rippling the grass in his direction.

On all fours, Furtig advanced with the stealth of a hunter creeping up on unwary prey, alert to sounds. There was a swishing which was the wind in the grass, some rustlings born of his own movements, which could not be helped unless one could somehow tread air above the blowing fronds. A frantic scurrying to his left—rabbit.

The grass came to an end. Before him was a stretch of smooth stone—almost as if the lairs had opened a mouth, extended a tongue to lap him in. There was no hiding place beyond. He would have to walk across the open. Reluctantly, Furtig rose on hind feet.

It was well enough to creep and crawl when one had the excuse of keeping to cover. But he did not intend to enter the lairs so. There was something in him which demanded boldness now.

He paused only to slip the claws over his hands. They were inferior, and did not fit his hands smoothly, but he had worked them into the best condition he could. And, while he never ceased to regret the loss of

his own fine weapons, he was deeply grateful to Eu-La
for her gift. Armed, he was now ready.

A quick dart took him across into the shadow by
the first wall. There were regular breaks in that, but
set so high he could not reach any. Surely there must
be some guide to Gammage, some trail markings to
lead in a newcomer. For it was well known that Gammage welcomed those who came to him.

Furtig continued to sniff for such a marker. There
was a smell of bird. He could see streaks of droppings
on the walls. But nothing more than that.

With no guide he could only work his way into the
heart of the lairs, hoping to pick up some clue to those
he sought. However, he went warily, making use of all
shadows he could.

And, as he went, awe of those who had built all this
grew in him. How had they piled up their cliffs? For
these erections were not natural rock. What knowledge the Demons had had!

Sunrise found him still wandering, at a loss for a
guide. He had come across two open spaces enclosed
by the buildings. They were filled with tangles of vegetation now seared by fall. One surrounded a small
lake in which water birds suddenly cried out and rose
with a great flapping of wings.

Furtig crouched, startled. Then he realized that he
could not have been the reason for that flight. Then—
what had?

At that moment he caught the hot scent, rank,
overpowering. And he snarled. Ratton! There was no
mistaking its foulness. Rattons—here? They clung to
the lairs of Demons, that was true, yet it was thought
they had not spread far through those.

Furtig edged back into the hollow of a doorway. At his back the door itself was a great unbroken solid slab, and it was closed. As it was about six times his own height and gave the appearance of strength, he had no hope of opening it. And if he were sighted, or scented, in this place he would be cornered.

The Rattons did not fight as the People did but more like the Barkers, sending many against one. Though Furtig was much larger than any of their kind, he could not hope to stand up to a whole company of them. His tail twitched sharply as he watched the bushes about the lake and used his nose and ears to aid his eyes in locating the foe.

Though most of the water birds had flown, at least three of their flock were in difficulty. For there was a beating of wings, harsh cries at the far end of the lake. Furtig could not see through the screen of bushes, and he was not about to advance into what might be enemy territory. Suddenly the squawking was cut off, and he thought the hunters must have finished their prey.

His own plans had changed. To go into Ratton-held lairs—no! And he imagined now what might have been Gammage's fate—well-picked bones!

But could he withdraw without being hunted? Furtig was not sure whether the Rattons hunted by scent or by ear and eye. His only recourse was to befuddle his trail as well as he could. And in the open he could not do that.

Furtig tried feverishly to remember all he had heard concerning the Rattons. Could they leap, climb, follow the People so? Or were they earthbound like the Barkers? It seemed he was soon to prove one or the other.

On either side of the door behind him was a panel in the wall. These were set higher than his head, even when he stretched to his full height. The one to his right was intact. But the other had a break in its covering, leaving only shards of stuff in the frame.

Furtig crouched and leaped. His fighting claws caught on the edge of those shards and they splintered. He kept his hold and kicked his way in. He found himself on a ledge above a dusky floor. It was narrow, but he could balance there long enough to survey what lay beyond.

There were objects standing here and there, a heavy dust covering the floor. He surveyed that with disappointment. Not a track on it. When he dropped he would leave a trail the most stupid tracker could follow. Furtig teetered on the ledge, undecided. The dead air made his nose wrinkle, and he fought the need to sneeze. His half plan now seemed rank folly. Better to stay in the open— He turned his head to look out. There was a flash of movement in the bushes near the door.

Too late! They were already closing in. He needed speed now to reach a place where he could wedge his back as he turned to face his attackers.

He made a second leap from the ledge to the top of one of the objects standing on the floor. His feet plowed into the soft dust and he skidded nearly to its far end, pushing the dust before him, before his claws held fast.

The room had two doors, both open arches, neither barred. What he wanted now was to get to the very top of this lair, and out into the open, where he would perhaps have a bare chance of leaping to the next lair, just as he would leap from tree to tree to escape ground-traveling enemies.

There was little choice between the doors, and in the end he took the nearest. This gave onto a long passage from which opened other doorless rooms— rather like the caves. Save that these promised no security.

Furtig wasted no time exploring, but ran at top speed past those doorless openings to the end of the hall. Here was a door and it was closed. He tried to insert claw tips in the crack he could see and was answered by a slight give. Enough to set him tearing frenziedly at the promise.

When it did open far enough for him to slip his body through, he gave a convulsive start backward. For, opening at his feet, was a deep shaft. There was nothing beyond the door but a hole that might entrap a full-sized bull. In his fear Furtig spat, clawed at the edges of the door.

It was too late. The momentum of his assault on that stubborn barrier pitched him out into empty space. He had closed his eyes in reflex as he went, fear filling him, forcing out sense and reason—

Until he realized that he was not falling like a stone pitched from one of the cave ledges, but drifting downward!

Furtig opened his eyes, hardly aware even now that he was not on his way to a quick death. It was dark in the shaft, but he could see that he was descending, slowly, as if he rested on some solid surface that was sinking into the foundations of the lair.

Of course it was well known that the Demons commanded many powers. But that they could make thin air support a body! Furtig drew a deep breath and felt his pounding heart lessen its heavy beat a fraction. It was plain he was not going to die, at least not yet, not so long as this mysterious cushion of air held. Thinking about that, he grew fearful again. How long *would* it hold?

He wondered if he could aid himself in some way. This was almost like being in water. One swam in water. Would the same motions carry one here? Tentatively Furtig made a couple of arm sweeps and found himself closer to the wall of the shaft. He reached it just in time to see the outline of another door, and tried to catch at the thin edge around it with his claws. But those scraped free and he was past before he could make any determined effort. Now he waited, alert to another such chance as he drifted down. Only to be disappointed.

A sound from above! The faint squeal echoed in the shaft. Rattons up there! Probably at the door he had forced open. Would they take to the air after him? Furtig flexed his fingers within the fastening of the claws. He had no liking for the prospect of fighting in mid-air. But if he had no choice he had better be prepared.

However, it seemed that those above were not ready to make such a drastic pursuit. Perhaps if they could not sight him they would believe that he had plunged to death. Unless they, living in the lairs, knew the odd properties of the shaft. If so, would they ambush him on landing?

Alarmed at the thought, Furtig kicked out and

thrust closer to the wall, searching as he drifted down for any signs of an anchorage he could use. But he must have waited too long. The walls here were uniformly smooth. And, though he drew the claws despairingly along, hoping to hook in some hole, he heard only the rasping scrape of those weapons, found nothing in which they could root.

He could not judge distance, and time seemed strange too. How long, how far, had he fallen? He had entered the lair at ground level, but this descent must be carrying him far under the surface of the earth. Though he knew security in caves which reached underground, yet this was something else, and the fear of the unknown was in him.

He was falling faster now! Had that cushion of air begun to fail? Furtig had only time to ready himself for what might be a hard landing before he did land, on a padded surface.

The dark was thick; even his night sight could not serve him. But he could look up the shaft and see the lighter grayish haze of what lay beyond the door he had forced.

Furtig tested the air for Ratton stench but was only a fraction relieved at its absence. There were other smells here, but none he could identify.

After a moment he straightened from the instinctive crouch into which he had gone and began to feel his way around the area. Three sides, the scrape of his claws told him, were walls.

His whiskers, abristle on his upper lip, fanned out above his eyes, gave him an additional report on space as they were intended to. The fourth wall was an opening like the mouth of a tunnel. But Furtig, re-

membering his error at the door above, made no quick
effort to try it.

When he did advance, it was on all fours, testing
each step with a wide swing of hand ahead, listening
for the sound of the metal claw tips to reassure him
about the footing.

So he crept on. The tunnel, or hall, appeared to run
straight ahead, and was the width of the shaft. So far
he had located no breaks in its walls, at least at the
level of his going. Now he began, every five paces, to
rise and probe to the extent of his full reach for any
openings that might be above.

However, he could find none, and his blind progress
continued. He began to wonder if he were as well
trapped by his own recklessness as the Rattons could
have trapped him by malicious purpose. Could he
somehow climb up the shaft if he found this a dead-
end way?

Then his outthrust hand bumped painfully against
a solid surface. At the same time there was a lighten-
ing of the complete dark to his right, and a sharply
angled turn in the hall led him toward it.

Furtig's head came up, he drew a deep breath, testing that faint scent. Ratton—yes—but with it a more
familiar, better smell, which could only come from one
of his own people! But the People and the Rattons—
he could not believe any such combination could be a
peaceful one. Could Gammage have carried his madness so far as to deal with *Rattons!*

The Ratton smell brought an almost noiseless
growl deep in his throat. But the smell of his own kind
grew stronger, and he was drawn to it almost in spite
of himself.

Furtig discovered the source of the light now, a slit set high in the wall, but not so high that he could not leap and hook claws there, managing to draw himself up, despite the strain on his forearms, to look through.

All that short glimpse afforded him was the sight of another wall. He must somehow find the means of remaining longer at the slit. Whatever was there must lie beyond eye level, and the odor of the People was strong.

Furtig had his belt. Slowly he pulled the bone pin which held it about him, unhooked the pouches of supplies, and laid the belt full length on the floor. He shed the claws and clumsily, using his teeth as well as his stubby fingers, made each end of the belt fast to the claws, testing that fastening with sharp jerks.

Then he looped the belt around him, slipped the claws on lightly, and leaped once more for the slit. The claws caught. He jerked his hands free, and the belt supported him, his powerful hind legs pressed against the wall to steady him.

He could look down into the chamber. His people—yes—two of them. But the same glimpse which identified them showed Furtig they were prisoners. One was stretched in tight bonds, hands and feet tied. The other had only his hands so fastened; one leg showed an ugly wound, blood matted black in the fur.

Furtig strained to hold his position, eager to see. The bound one—he was unlike any of the People Furtig knew. His color was a tawny sand shade on his body; the rest of him, head, legs, tail, was a deep brown. His face thinned to a sharply pointed chin and his eyes were bright blue.

His fellow prisoner, in contrast to the striking color

combination of the blue-eyed one, was plain gray, bearing the black stripes of the most common hue among the People. But—Furtig suppressed a small cry.

Foskatt! He was as certain as he was of his own name and person that the wounded one was Foskatt, who had gone seeking Gammage and never returned.

And if they were prisoners in a place where there was so strong a stench of Ratton, he could well guess who their captors were. If he had seen only the stranger he would not have cared. One had a duty to the caves and then to the tribe, but a stranger must take his own chances. Though Furtig hesitated over that reasoning—he did not like to think of *any* of the People, stranger or no, in the hands of the Rattons.

But Foskatt had to be considered. Furtig knew only too well the eventual fate of any Ratton captive. He would provide food for as many of his captors as could snatch a mouthful.

Furtig could hold his position no longer. But he took the chance of uttering the low alerting hiss of the caves. Twice he voiced that, clinging to the claw-belt support.

When he hissed the second time, Foskatt's head turned slowly, as if that effort was almost too much. Then his yellow eyes opened to their widest extent, centered on the slit where Furtig fought to keep his grip. For the first time Furtig realized that the other probably could not see him through the opening. So he called softly: "Foskatt—this is Furtig."

He could no longer hold on but slid back into the tunnel, his body aching with the effort which had kept him at that peephole. He took deep breaths, fighting to slow the beating of his heart, while he rubbed his arms, his legs.

His tail twitched with relief as a very faint hiss came in answer. That heartened him to another effort to reach the slit. He knew he could not remain there long, and perhaps not reach it at all a third time. If Foskatt were only strong enough to—to what? Furtig saw no way of getting his tribesman through that hole. But perhaps the other could supply knowledge which would lead Furtig to a better exit.

"Foskatt!" It was hard not to gasp with effort. "How may I free you?"

"The caller of Gammage—" Foskatt's voice was weak. He lay without raising his head. "The guard-has-taken-it. They-wait-for-their-Elders—"

Furtig slipped down, knew he could not reach the slit again. He leaned against the wall to consider what he had heard. The caller of Gammage—and the Ratton guard had it—whatever a caller might be. The guard could only be outside the door of that cell.

He picked up his belt, unfastening the claws. Now—if he could find a way out of this tunnel to that door. It remained so slim a chance that he dared not pin any hopes on it.

He stalked farther along the dark way. Again a thin lacing of light led him to a grill. But this one was set at an easier height, so he need not climb to it. He looked through into a much larger chamber, which was lighted by several glowing rods set in the ceiling.

To his right was a door, and before it Rattons! The first live ones he had ever seen so close.

They were little more than half his size if one did not reckon in the length of their repulsive tails. One of them had, indeed, a tail which was only a scarred stump. He also had a great scar across his face which had permanently closed one eye. He leaned against the door gnawing at something he held in one paw-hand.

His fellow was more intent on an object he held, a band of shining metal on which was a cube of glittering stuff. He shook the band, held the cube to one ear. Even across the space between them Furtig caught the faint buzzing sound which issued from that cube. And he guessed that this must be Gammage's caller—though how it might help to free Foskatt he had no idea. Except he knew that the Ancestor had mastered so much of Demon knowledge in the past that this device might just be as forceful in some strange way as the claws were in ripping out a Ratton throat.

Furtig crowded against the grill, striving to see how it was held in place, running his fingers across it with care so as not to ring his weapon tips against it. He could not work it too openly with Rattons on guard to hear—or scent—him.

The grill was covered with a coarse mesh. He twisted at it now with the claw tips, and it bent when he applied pressure. So far this was promising. Now Furtig made the small chirruping sound with which a hunter summons a mouse, waiting tensely and with hope.

Three times he chirruped. There was a shadow rising at the screen. Furtig struck. Claws broke through the mesh, caught deep in flesh and bone. There was a muffled squeak. With his other hand Furtig tore furiously at the remaining mesh, cleared an opening, and wriggled through, hurling the dead Ratton from him.

On the floor lay the caller. The scarred guard had fled. Furtig could hear his wild squealing, doubtless sounding the alarm. It had been a tight fit, that push through the torn mesh, and his skin had smarting scratches. But he had made it, and now he caught up the caller.

He almost dropped it again, for the band felt warm, not cold as metal should. And the buzzing was louder. How long did he have before that fleeing guard returned with reinforcements?

Furtig, the caller against his chest, kicked aside the bars sealing the door and rushed in. He reached Foskatt, hooked a claw in the other's bonds to cut them. But seeing the extent of his tribesman's wounds, he feared the future. It was plain that with that injury Foskatt could not walk far.

"The caller—give it to me—" Foskatt stared at the thing Furtig held. But when he tried to lift a hand it moved like a half-dead thing, not answering his will, and he gave an impatient cry.

"Touch it," he ordered. "There is a small hole on the side, put your finger into that!"

"We must get away—there is no time," Furtig protested.

"Touch it!" Foskatt said louder. "It will get us out of here."

"The warrior is mad," growled the other prisoner. "He talks of a thing coming through the walls to save him. You waste your time with him!"

"Touch it!"

Foskatt made no sense, yet Furtig found himself

turning the caller over to find the hole. It was there, but when he tried to insert a finger, he discovered that his digit was far too thick to enter. He was about to try the tip of a claw when Foskatt batted clumsily at his arm, those deep ridges in his flesh, cut by the bonds, bleeding now.

"No—don't use metal! Hold it closer—hold it for me!"

Furtig went to his knees as Foskatt struggled up. Foskatt bent forward, opened his mouth, and put forth his tongue, aiming its tip for the hole in the cube.

4

Foskatt's head jerked as if that touch was painful, but he persisted, holding his tongue with an effort which was manifest throughout his body. At last, it seemed, he could continue no longer. His head fell back, and he rested his limp weight against Furtig's shoulder, his eyes closed.

"You have wasted time," snarled the other prisoner. "Do you leave us now to be meat, or do you give *me* a fighting chance?" There was no note of pleading in his voice. Furtig had not expected any; it was not in their breed to beg from a stranger. But he settled Foskatt back, the caller beside him, and went to cut the other's bonds.

When those were broken, he returned to Foskatt. The stranger had been right. There was no chance of escape through these burrows, which the Rattons knew much better than he. He had wasted time. Yet Foskatt's urgency had acted on him strongly.

The stranger whipped to the door. Even as he

53

reached it, Furtig could hear the squealing clamor of gathering Rattons. He had failed. The only result of his attempt at rescue was that he had joined the other two in captivity. But he had his claws at least, and the Ratton forces would pay dearly for their food when they came at him.

"Fool," hissed the stranger, showing his fangs. "There is no way out now!"

Foskatt stirred. "The rumbler will come—"

His mutter, low as it was, reached the stranger, and his snarl became a growl, aimed at them both.

"Rumbler! He has blatted of none else! But his wits are wrong. There is no—"

What he would have added was forgotten as he suddenly whirled and crouched before the door, his bare hands raised. However, for some reason, the Rattons did not rush the prisoners at once, as Furtig had expected. Perhaps they were trying to work out some method whereby they could subdue their captives without undue loss on their part. If they knew the People at all, they must also realize that the Rattons on the first wave in would die.

Furtig listened, trying to gauge from sounds what they were doing. He did not know what weapons the Rattons had besides those nature had given them. But since they frequented the lairs, they might have been as lucky as Gammage in discovering Demon secrets. Foskatt pushed at the floor, tried to raise himself. Furtig went to his aid.

"Be ready," his tribesman said. "The rumbler— when it comes—we must be ready—"

His certainty that something was coming almost convinced Furtig that the other knew what he was talking about. But how that action of tongue to cube could bring anything—

The stranger was busy at the door. He had pulled some litter together, was striving to force into place rusty metal rods as a bar lock. Even if that worked, it could not save them for long, but any action helped. Furtig went to aid him.

"This should slow them—a little—" the stranger said as they finished as well as they could.

He turned then and padded across the room to stand beneath the wall grill high overhead. "Where does that lead? You were behind it when you signalled—"

"There is a tunnel there. But the opening is too narrow."

The stranger had kept one of the pieces of metal, too short to be a part of their barrier. Now he struck that against the wall in a rasping blow. It did not leave more than a streak of rust to mark its passage. There was no beating their way through that wall.

He strode back and forth across the cell, his tail lashing, uttering small growls, which now and then approached the fury of battle yowls. Furtig knew the same fear of being trapped. He flexed his fingers, tested the strength of his claw fastenings. In his throat rumbled an answering growl. Then the stranger came to a halt before him, those blue eyes upon Furtig's weapons.

"Be ready to cut the net with those." His words had the force of an order.

"The net?"

"They toss nets to entangle one from a distance. That was how they brought me down. They must have taken your comrade in the same fashion. He was already here when they dragged me in. It is only because they were awaiting their Elders that they did not kill us at once. They spoke among themselves much, but who can understand their vile chittering? One or two made signs—there was something they wished to learn. And their suggestion"—the hair on his tail was bushed now—"was that they would have a painful way of asking. Die in battle when they come, warrior, or face what is worse."

The Rattons were trying to force the door now. How long would the barrier hold?

Furtig tensed, ready to face the inpour when the weight of those outside would break through. Foskatt pulled himself up, one hand closing upon the caller, raising it to his ear. His eyes glowed.

"It comes! Gammage is right! The rumblers will serve us! Stand ready—"

Then Furtig caught it also, a vibration creeping through the stone flooring, echoing dully from the walls about them. It was unlike anything he had experienced before, though it carried some tones of storm thunder. It grew louder, outside the door, and once more the enemy squealed in ragged chorus.

"Stand back—away—" Foskatt's husky whisper barely reached Furtig. The stranger could not have heard it, but, so warned, Furtig sprang, grasped the other's arm, and pulled him to one side. The stranger rounded on him with a cry of rage, until he saw Foskatt's warning gesture.

As if some supreme effort supplied strength, Foskatt was sitting up, the caller now at his mouth, his tongue ready, extended as if he awaited some signal.

Then—there was a squealing from the Rattons which became a hysterical screeching. These were not battle cries but rather a response to fear, to a terrible, overpowering fear.

Something struck against the wall with a force that certainly the Rattons could not exert. Thudding blows followed, so close on one another that the noise became continuous. The door broke, pushed in, but that was not all. Around its frame ran cracks in the wall itself; small chunks flaked off.

Together Furtig and the stranger backed away. No Ratton had sprung through the opening. The prisoners could see only a solid, dark surface there, as if another wall had been erected beyond. Still those ponderous blows fell, more of the wall broke away.

Yet Foskatt, showing no signs of fear, watched this as if it were what he expected. Then he spoke, raising his voice so they could hear over the sounds of that pounding.

"This is one of the Demons' servants from the old days. It obeys my will through this." He indicated the caller. "When it breaks through to us we must be ready to mount on top. And it will carry us out of this evil den. But we must be swift, for these servants have a limit on their period of service. When this"— again he brought the caller their notice—"ceases to buzz, these servants die, and we cannot again awaken them. Nor do we ever know how long that life will last."

There was a sharp crash. Through the wall broke what looked to be a long black arm. It swept around, clearing the hole. Instantly, at its appearance, Foskatt thrust his tongue into the opening in the cube.

The arm stopped its sweeping, was still, as if pointing directly to them. Behind it they could see the dark bulk of the rumbler, solid as a wall.

"We must get on it—quick!" Foskatt tried to rise but his weakened body failed him.

Furtig, at his side, turned to face the stranger.

"Help me!" He made that an order. The other hesitated. He had been heading for the break in the wall. But now he turned back, though it was plain he came reluctantly.

Together they raised Foskatt, though their handling must have been a torment, for he let out a small mewling cry at their touch. Then he was silent as they somehow got him through the broken door, raised him to the back of the boxlike thing.

It had more than one of those jutting arms, all of them quiet now. And it was among their roots that they settled their burden. How the thing had arrived they could not determine, for they could see no legs.

But that it had come with ruthless determination was plain by the crushed bodies of the Rattons lying here and there.

Once on top, Furtig looked to Foskatt. How did they now bring to life this Demon rumbler? Would it indeed carry them on?

"Brother!" Furtig bent over his tribesman. "What do we do now?"

But Foskatt lay with closed eyes, and did not answer. The stranger growled.

"He cannot tell you. Perhaps he is near death. At least we are free of that hole. So—I shall make the most of such freedom."

Before Furtig could hinder him, he jumped from

the top of the servant and ran in long leaping bounds into the dimness beyond. But, greatly as he was tempted to follow, the old belief that one ought not to desert a tribesman held Furtig where he was.

He could hear distant squealing. More Rattons must be gathering ahead. Now he no longer believed that the stranger had made the best choice. He could well be heading into new captivity.

As would happen to them unless—Furtig pried at Foskatt's hold on the caller. Tongue tip had gone in there, and the servant had come. Again tongue tip, and the rumbler had stopped beating down the wall. Therefore the caller ordered it. If that were so, why could Furtig not command it now?

He brought it close to his mouth. How had Foskatt done it? By some pressure like the sign language? Furtig knew no code. All he was sure of was that he wanted to get the rumbler away from here, back to Gammage, if that was where it had come from.

Well, he could only try. Gingerly, not knowing whether the caller might punish a stranger without learning for attempting to use it, Furtig inserted his tongue and tried to press. A sharp tingling sensation followed, but he held steady.

There was an answering vibration in the box on which he crouched. The arms pulled back from the wall, and the thing began to move.

Furtig caught at Foskatt lest he be shaken loose as the rumbler trundled back from the wall and slewed around, so that the arms now pointed toward the broken door of the room.

They did not move fast, no faster than a walk, but the rumbler never paused. And Furtig knew a new feeling of power. He had commanded this thing! It might not take them to Gammage as he wished it to do, but at least it was bearing them away from the Ratton prison, and he believed that those slinkers would not dare to attack again as long as Foskatt and he rode this servant.

Foskatt's warning of the uncertain life span of the Demons' servants remained. But Furtig would not worry about that now. He was willing to take what good fortune was offered in the present.

They slid away from the light of the Ratton-held chambers. But now the rumbler provided light of its own. For two of those arms extended before it bore on their ends small circles of radiance.

This was not a natural passage like the cave ways; the Demons had built these walls. Furtig and the wounded Foskatt rumbled past other doorways, twice taking angled turns into new ways. It would seem that for all the sky-reaching heights of the lairs aboveground, there was a matching spread of passages beneath the surface.

Furtig's ears pricked. They had not outrun, probably could not outrun, pursuit. Behind he heard the high-voiced battle cries of the Rattons. At least he was well above their heads on the box and so had that small advantage.

Hurriedly he used Foskatt's own belt to anchor him to the arms of the rumbler, leaving himself free for any defense tactics needed. With the claws on his hands, he hunched to wait.

Strange smells here. Not only those natural to underground places, but others he could not set name to. Then the rumbler halted in front of what seemed a blank wall, and Furtig speedily lost what small confidence had carried him this far. They were going to be trapped; all this servant of Gammage had bought them was a little time.

But, though the rumbler had halted, its outthrust arms moved. They were doing nothing Furtig could understand, merely jerking up and down, shining round spots of light on the wall here and there.

There was a dull grating sound. The wall itself split in a wide crack, not such as those arms had beaten in the prison wall, but clean, as if this was a portal meant to behave in this fashion. As soon as the opening was wide enough, the rumbler moved on into a section which was again lighted. Furtig looked back; the wall started to shut even as they passed through. He gave a small sigh of relief as he saw the opening close. At least no Ratton was coming through there!

But the rumbler no longer moved steadfastly; rather it went slower and slower, finally stopping with its arms curled back upon its body. Now it looked— Furtig's woods-wise mind made the quick comparison—like a great black spider dying. When the rumbler ceased to move he lifted the caller to his mouth, readied his tongue. This time there was no tingling response to his probing. It must be as Foskatt had warned—the servant had died, if one might term it so.

There was light here, and they were in another corridor with numerous doors. Furtig hesitated for a long moment and then dropped to the floor. Leaving Foskatt where he was, he went to the nearest opening to look within.

The room was not empty. Most of the floor was covered with metal boxes, firmly based. And there was an acrid smell which made him sneeze and shake his head to banish it from his nostrils. Nothing moved, and his ears, fully alert, could not pick up the slightest sound.

He returned to the rumbler. If that could not carry them farther, and Foskatt could not be transported, what was he to do? When he was the merest youngling, he had learned the importance of memory patterns, of learning the ways of the People's tribal hunting grounds until those became a matter of subconscious recall rather than conscious thinking. But here he had no such pattern as a guide, he had only—

Furtig scrambled up to sit beside Foskatt. There was one thing— If they had in truth been heading toward Gammage's headquarters when this journey began, he could try— He closed his eyes, set about methodically to blank out the thought of what lay immediately around him.

He must use his thoughts as if they were ears, eyes, nose, to point to what he sought. This could be done, had been done many times over, by some individuals among the People. But Furtig had never been forced to try it before.

He had never seen Gammage, but so well was the Ancestor fixed in the mind of all who dwelt in the caves, that he had heard him described many times over. Now he tried to build in his mind a picture of Gammage. And, because the Ancestor was who he was and had been to his tribe a figure of awe and wonder across several generations, doubtless that mind picture was different from the person it represented, being greater than reality.

As he had never tried before, Furtig strove now to

think of Gammage, to discover where in the lairs he could find this leader. So far—nothing. Perhaps he was one of those for whom such searching did not work. Each of the People had his own abilities, his own weaknesses. When the People worked together, one could supply what another lacked, but here Furtig had only himself. Gammage—where was Gammage?

It was like picking out the slightest ripple in the grass, hearing a sound so thin and far away that it was not true sound at all but merely the alerting suggestion of it. But a warm flush of triumph heated Furtig. It was true—he had done it! That sense would lead him now. Lead *him*. He opened his eyes to look at Foskatt.

What of Foskatt? It was plain that the other could not walk, nor could Furtig carry him. He could leave, return later— But perhaps that wall which had opened and closed was not the only entrance. One dared not underrate the tenacity of the Rattons. Long before Furtig could return with help, Foskatt could be captive or dead.

Suppose that somewhere in one of these chambers along this way he could find another of these servants, one which could be activated? It would do no harm to go and look, and it might be their only chance.

Furtig began the search. But he found himself moving slowly, needing to stop now and then to lean against the wall. All of a sudden, now that the excitement of their escape had died, he needed rest. He fed on some of the dried meat from Eu-La's bag. But it was hard to choke down even a few mouthfuls of that without water. And where was he going to find water?

Determinedly Furtig prowled among those metal boxes set in the first chamber, finding nothing useful. Stubbornly he went on to explore the next room.

This was different in that it had tables, long ones, and those tables were crowded with masses of things he did not understand at all. He backed away from one where the brush of his tail had knocked off a large basin. The basin shattered on the floor, and the sound of the crash was magnified a hundred times by echoes.

Furtig's startled jump almost brought him to disaster. For he struck against what seemed a smaller table, and that moved! He whirled around, expecting an attack, snarling. The table went on until it bumped against one of the larger tables.

Warily Furtig hooked his claws lightly about one of its slender legs. Very cautiously he pulled the small table back. It answered so readily, he was again startled. Then he mastered surprise, and experimented.

The surface was high, he could barely touch the top with his chin when he stood at his tallest. There was a mass of brittle stuff lying across it, and when he tried to investigate, it broke and powdered, so that he swept it off, leaving a bare surface.

But he could move the table!

Pushing and pulling, he brought it out of the room, back to the side of the rumbler. Luckily there was only a short space between the two levels, the table being a little lower. He was sure he could get Foskatt from one to the other.

Blood was seeping again from the matted fur about Foskatt's wound by the time Furtig had finished. He settled the unconscious tribesman in the center of the table, hoping he would not roll, as there was no anchorage here.

He fastened his belt to the two front legs of the table and then slung the end over one shoulder. It was a tight fit, the table bumping continually against his back and legs, and if it had not rolled so easily he could not have moved it. Resolutely he set out down the corridor.

There were times following, which could have been night and day, or day and night, since Furtig could no longer measure time so here—times when he believed that he could not go on. He would hunch down, the table looming over him, breathing so hard it hurt his lower ribs. His whole body was so devoted to pulling the table that he was not really aware of anything save that he had not yet reached the place to which he must go.

On and on, and there was no end, from corridor to room, across room, to another hall. The lights grew brighter, the strange smells stronger. He was never sure when the vibration in the walls began. It might have started long before his dulled senses recorded it. There was a feeling of life here . . .

Furtig leaned against the wall. At least there was no smell of Ratton. And they were still heading in the right direction.

Then he really looked about him. The corridor down which they had just come ended at a wall. And if this was like the wall the servant had opened, well, he did not have the ability to get through it. Leaving the table, he shambled forward to examine it better.

What was happening to him? This was the bottom of a shaft, much the same as the one he had fallen down earlier. But now—he was going up! Gently, as if the air itself was pushing him.

Frantically Furtig fought, managed to catch hold of the shaft entrance and pull out of that upward current. As he dropped to the ground, he was shaken out of that half-stupor which had possessed him.

It was plain, as plain as such a marvel could be, that here the shaft reversed the process of the other one. And it was also plain that Gammage—or what his search sense had fastened on as Gammage was above.

Would this mysterious upward current take the table also? He could only try. Pulling, he got it into the shaft. Foskatt's body stirred, drifting up from the surface. So—it worked on him, but not on the table. Wearily Furtig accepted that, kept his hold on his tribesman as they began to rise together.

It took a long time, but Furtig, in his weariness, did not protest that. He watched dully as they slid past one opening and then another. Each must mark a different level of these vast underground ways, even as the caves opened from two ledges. Up and up—

Four levels up and Furtig's search sense gave the signal—this one! Towing the limp Foskatt, he made swimming motions to take them to the opening. And he had just enough strength to falter through, out of the pull of the current, to the floor beyond.

He lay there beside Foskatt, panting, his sides and back aching from his effort. What now? But he was too worn out to face anything more—not now. And that thought dimmed in his mind as his head fell forward to rest on his crooked arm.

5

Furtig came out of sleep, aware even before he opened his eyes that he was not alone. What he sniffed was not the musky scent of Ratton, but rather the reassuring odor of his own kin. With that, another smell, which brought him fully awake—food! And not the dried rations of his traveling either.

He was lying on a pallet not unlike those of the caves. And, waiting beside him, holding a bowl which sent out that enticing fragrance, was a female he had never seen before. She was remarkable enough to let him know he was among strangers. And he gaped at her in a way which should have brought her fur rising, set her to a warning hiss.

Fur—that was it! Though she had a goodly show of silky, silverly fur on her head and along her shoulders, yet on the rest of her body it was reduced to the thinnest down, through which it was easy to see her skin.

And those hands holding the bowl—the fingers were not stubby like his own but longer, thinner. Furtig did not know whether he liked what he saw of her, he was only aware that she was different enough to keep him staring like a stupid youngling.

"Eat—" She held the bowl closer. Her voice had a tone of command. Also it was as different as her body was from those he knew.

Furtig took the bowl and found its contents had been cut into easily handled strips. As he gnawed, and the warm, restorative juices flowed down his throat, he came fully to attention. The female had not left and that disconcerted him again. Among the People this was not the custom—the males had their portion of the caves, the females another.

"You are Furtig of the Ancestor's cave—"

"How did you—"

"Know that? Did you not bring back Foskatt, who knows you?"

"Foskatt!" For the first time since his waking Furtig remembered his tribesman. "He is hurt—the Rattons—"

"Hurt, yes. But he is now in the healing place of the Demons. We"—there was pride in her tone— "have learned many of the Demons' secrets. They could heal as well as kill. And every day we learn more and more. If we are given the chance we shall know all that they knew . . ."

"But not to use that knowledge to the same purposes, Liliha."

Startled, Furtig looked beyond the female. The soft tread of any of his race should not be entirely noiseless, but he had been so intent he had not been aware of a newcomer. And looking up—

"Famed Ancestor!" He set down the bowl with a

bump which nearly shook out what was left of its contents, hastened to make the gesture of respect due the greatest Elder of them all.

But to his pride (and a little discomfort, were the full truth to be known), Gammage hunkered down by him and touched noses in the full acceptance of the People.

"You are Furtig, son of Fuffor, son of Foru, son of another Furtig who was son of my son," Gammage recited as a true Elder, one trained to keep in memory clan and tribe generations through the years. "Welcome to the lairs, warrior. It would seem that your introduction here has been a harsh one."

Gammage was old; the very descent lines he had stated made him older than any Elder Furtig had ever known. Yet there was something about him which suggested vigor, though now perhaps more vigor of mind than of body.

Like the female's fur, though she was clearly young and not old, Gammage's body fur was sparse. And that body was thin, showing more bony underlining than padded muscle.

He wore not just the belt common to all the People but a long piece of fabric fastened at his throat, flowing back over his shoulders. This somehow gave him added stature and dignity. He also had about his neck a chain of shining metal links and from that hung a cube not unlike the one Foskatt had carried. While his hands—

Furtig's gaze lingered. Whoever had he seen among the People with such hands! They were narrower, the fingers longer and thinner even than those of the female. Yes, in all ways Gammage was even stranger than the old tales made him.

"Eat now." Gammage gestured to the bowl. "Within the lairs we need all the strength food can give us. Rattons"—his voice deepened to a growl—"Rattons establishing their own place here! Rattons attempting to gain Demon knowledge! And so little time perhaps before we shall be called upon to face the Demons themselves." Now his voice became a growl without words, the sound of one about to offer battle.

"But of that we can speak later. Furtig, what say they of me now in the caves? Are they still of like mind—that I speak as with the mindless babble of the very young? The truth, warrior, the truth is of importance!"

And such was the compelling force of the Ancestor's tone that Furtig answered with the truth.

"The Elders—Fal-Kan—they say that you plan to give Demon secrets to strangers, even to the Barkers. They call you—"

"Traitor to my kind?" Gammage's tail twitched. "Perhaps in their narrow viewing I might be termed so—now. But the day comes when the People, plus the Barkers, plus the Tusked Ones, will have to stand together or perish. Of the Rattons I do not speak thus, for there is that in them akin to what I have learned of the Demons. And when the Demons return, the Rattons may run with them to overturn all our lives."

"The Demons return?" Listening to the note of certainty in the Ancestor's voice made Furtig believe that Gammage was sure of what he said. And if he truly believed that, yes, would it not be better to make truce even with Barkers against a common and greater enemy?

"Time!" Gammage brought those odd hands of his together in a clap to echo through the room. "Time is our great need and we may not have it. We have so many lesser needs, such as the one which took Foskatt into that section of the lairs we had not fully explored, seeking hidden records. But, though he did not find what he sought, he has alerted us to this new danger, a Ratton base on the very edge of our own territory. Let the Rattons learn but this much"— Gammage measured off between two fingers no more than the width of one of them—"of what we have found here, and they will make themselves masters, not only of the lairs, but of the world beyond. Say that to your Elders, Furtig, and perhaps you will find they will listen, even though they willfully close their ears to a worse threat."

"Foskatt was seeking something?"

Gammage had fallen silent, his eyes on the wall beyond Furtig, as if he saw there something which was as plain to be read as a hunting trail, and yet to be dreaded.

"Foskatt?" Gammage repeated as if the name were strange. Then once more his intent gaze focussed on Furtig. "Foskatt—he was hardly handled, near to ending, when you brought him back to us, warrior. But now he heals. So great were the Demons—life and death in their two hands. But they played games with those powers as a youngling plays with sticks or bright stones, games which have no meaning. Save that when games are played as the Demons play them, they have grim consequences.

"They could do wonderful things. We learn more and more each day. They could actually make rain fall as they pleased, keep the sun shining as they would. There was no great cold where they ruled and— But they were not satisfied with such, they must do more, seeking the knowledge of death as well as of life. And at last their own learning turned against them."

"But if they are all dead, why then do you speak of their return?" Furtig dared to ask. His initial awe at seeing Gammage had eased. It was like climbing a mountain to find the way not so difficult as it had looked from the lowlands. That Gammage could impress, he did not doubt. There was that about him which was greater than the Elders. But he did not use it consciously as they did to overawe younger tribesmen.

"Not all died," Gammage said slowly. "But they are not here. We have tracked them through this, their last lair. When I first began that search we found their bodies, or what was left of them. But once we discovered the knowledge banks we also uncovered evidence that some had withdrawn, that they would come again. It was more concerning that second coming that Foskatt sought. But you will learn, Furtig— There is so much to learn—" Again Gammage gazed at the wall, rubbing one hand on the other. "So much to learn," he repeated. "More and more we uncover Demon secrets. Give us time, just a little more time!"

"Which the Rattons threaten now." Liliha broke into the Ancestor's thoughts, amazing Furtig even more. The fact that she had not withdrawn at Gammage's arrival had surprised him. But that she would

72

speak so to the Ancestor, almost as if to an unlessoned youngling, bringing him back to face some matter which could not be avoided, was more startling yet.

However Gammage appeared to accept her interruption as proper. For he nodded.

"True, Liliha, it is not well to forget today in considering tomorrow. I shall see you again and soon, cave son. Liliha will show you this part of the lairs which we have made our own."

He pulled the fabric tighter about him and was gone with the speed of a warrior years younger. Furtig put down the bowl and eyed the female uncertainly.

It was plain that the customs of the caves did not hold here in the lairs. Yet it made him uncomfortable to be left alone with a Chooser.

"You are not of the caves," he ventured, not knowing just how one began speech with a strange female.

"True. I am of the lairs. I was born within these walls."

That again amazed Furtig. For all his life he had heard of warriors "going to Gammage," but not females. But that they carried on a normal manner of life here was a minor shock. Until he realized the limit of his preconceptions concerning Gammage's people. Why should they not have a normal life? But whence had come their females?

"Gammage draws more than just those of his own tribe," she went on, as if reading his thoughts. "There are others of the People, on the far side of the lairs, distant from your caves. And over the seasons Gammage has sent messengers to them also. Some listen

73

to him more closely than his blood kin seem to." Furtig thought he detected in that remark the natural air of superiority which a Chooser would use on occasion with a warrior.

"There is now a new tribe here, formed from those of many different clans," she continued in the same faintly superior tone. "It has been so since my mother's mother's time. We who are born here, who learn early the knowledge of the Demons, are different in ways from those outside the lairs, even from those who choose to join us here. In such ways as this do the In-born differ." She put forth her hand, holding it in line with Furtig's. Not with their flesh making contact, but side by side for comparison.

Her longer, more slender fingers, were in even greater contrast when held against his. Now she wriggled them as if taking pride in their appearance.

"These"—she waved her hand slightly—"are better able to use Demon machines."

"And being born among those machines makes you so?"

"Partly, Gammage thinks. But there are also places the Demons use for healing, such as that in which Foskatt now lies. When a mother is about to bear her younglings she is taken there to wait. Also, when she first knows she has young within her, she goes to that place and sits for a space. Then her young come forth with changes. With hands such as these I can do much that I could not do—"

She paused, and he finished for her, "With such as mine." He remembered how he had used his tongue, as had Foskatt, in the cube hole. Perhaps, had he had fingers such as Liliha's, he need not have done that.

"Such as yours," she agreed evenly. "Now, Gammage would have you see the lairs, so come.

"We have," she told him, "a thing to ride on. It does not go outside this one lair, though we have tried to make it do so. We cannot understand such limitations. But here it is of service."

She brought forward something which moved more swiftly than the rumbler on which they had ridden out of the Ratton prison. But this was smaller and it had two seats—so large Furtig was certain they had been made to accommodate Demons, not People.

Liliha half crouched well to the front of one seat. Leaning well forward, she clasped a bar in both hands. He guessed that she was uncomfortable in such a strained position, but she made no complaint, only waited until he climbed into the other seat.

Then she drew the bar back toward her. With that the carrier came to life, moved forward smoothly and swiftly.

That there was need for such a conveyance became clear as they swept ahead. And things which astounded Furtig at first became commonplace as he saw other and more awesome ones succeed them. Some, Liliha told him, they did not understand and had found no way to use—though teams of workers, specially trained by Gammage, and at intervals under his personal supervision, still tried to solve such problems.

But the learning machines, those Gammage had early activated. And the food for them was contained in narrow disks wound with tape. When Liliha fitted one of these into a box and pressed certain buttons, a series of pictures appeared on the wall before them.

While out of the air came a voice speaking in a strange tongue. Furtig could not even reproduce most of the sounds.

However, there was another thing, too large to wear comfortably, which Furtig put on his head. This had small buttons to be fitted into the ears. When that was done, the words became plain, though some had no meaning. One watched the pictures and listened to the words and one learned. After a while, Furtig was told, he would not need the translator but would be able to understand without it.

Furtig was excited as he had not been since he had forced himself to face up to the Trials, knowing well he might lose. Only this time it was an excitement of triumph and not of determination to meet defeat. Given time (now he could understand Gammage's preoccupation with time in a way no cave dweller could) one could learn all the Demons' secrets!

He would have liked to have lingered there. But the chamber was occupied by Gammage's people, one of whom Liliha had persuaded to allow Furtig to sample the machine, and they were plainly impatient to get along with their work. Perhaps they had allowed such an interruption at all only because Furtig had been sent by Gammage.

For Furtig was not finding the warriors here friendly. They did not show the wary suspicion of strange tribesmen. No, this was more the impatience of an Elder with a youngling—a none-too-bright youngling. Furtig found that attitude hard for his pride to swallow.

Most of these workers displayed the same bodily differences—the slender hands, the lessening of body fur—as Liliha. But there were a few among them not different, save in coloring, from himself, and they were as impatient as their fellows.

Furtig tried to ignore the attitude of the workers, think only of what they were doing. But after a space, that, too, was sobering and disappointing. He, who was a trained warrior, a hunter of some note, an accepted defender of the caves (a status which had given him pride), was here a nothing. And the result of his tour with Liliha was a depression and the half-thought that he had much better return to his own kind.

Until they reached Foskatt. They stood in an outer room and looked through a wall (for it was the truth that here you could *see* through certain walls). Within was a pallet and on it lay the tribesman.

The lighting in the room differed from that where Furtig stood with Liliha. Also it rippled just as wind rippled field grass. Furtig could find no explanation of what he saw there. There was light, and it moved in waves washing back and forth across Foskatt.

The wounded warrior's eyes were closed. His chest rose and fell as if he slept, rested comfortably without pain or dreams. His wounded leg was no longer bloody, the fur matted with clots. A scar had begun to form over the slash.

Furtig, knowing how it might have gone had Foskatt lain so in the caves, how many died from lesser wounds in spite of the best tending their clanspeople could give them, drew a long breath. It was but one more of the wonders he had been shown, yet to him, because he could best appreciate the results, it was one of the most awesome.

"This can be done for the coughing sickness?" he asked. He had set his two hands flat on the surface of that see-through wall, pushed so close even his nose touched it.

"This can be done for any illness," Liliha told him, "as well as most hurts. There is only one it cannot cure so."

"That being?" A certain shading of her voice had made him turn his head to look at her. For the first time he could see uneasiness in her expression, the superiority gone.

"Gammage found a thing of the Demons. It spouts a mist—and when that meets flesh—" She shuddered. "It is the worst handwork of the Demons we have seen. There is no halting what happens to one unfortunate enough to be caught in the mist." She shivered again. "It is not even to be thought upon! Gammage had it destroyed!"

"Ah, and what do you think now of the lairs, Furtig?"

Gammage stood behind them. His sudden appearances—how did the Ancestor manage thus to arrive without warning?

"They are full of marvels."

"Marvels upon marvels," the Ancestor agreed. "And we have hardly touched the edge of what is stored here! Given time, just given time—" Once more he stared at the wall, as if his thoughts set a barrier between him and those he addressed.

"What I do not understand"—Furtig dared now to break in upon that withdrawal—"is why, when the Demons knew so much, they came to such an end."

Gammage looked at him, his gray frost-furred face alight.

"It was because they were greedy. They took and took, from the air, the earth, the water. And when they realized that they had taken too much and tried to return it, they were too late. Some went—we cannot yet read their records well enough to know how or where. They seem to have flown into the sky—"

"Like birds? But they were not winged, were they? Those I have seen represented . . ."

"Just so," Gammage agreed briskly. "But we have good evidence that they had some means of flight. So, a number of them flew away. Of those who were left— well, it seems that they worked very hard and fast to find some way of restoring the land. One of their attempted remedies became instead their doom. We have found two records of that.

"What developed was an illness like our coughing sickness. Some it killed at once. Others—it altered their minds so they became like those Barkers who foam at the mouth and tear madly at their own kin. But with all it had one sure effect: They bore no more younglings.

"Also—" Gammage hesitated as if what he would say now was an important thing, a wise utterance of an Elder. "This sickness had another effect. For it made us, the People, the Barkers, the Tusked Ones, even the Rattons, what we are.

"This is the thing we have learned, Furtig. We were once like the rabbits, the deer, the wild cattle we hunt for food. But we had some contact with the Demons. There is good evidence that some of us lived with them here in the lairs, and that"—his voice grew deeper, closer to a warrior's growl—"that they used *us* to try out their discoveries, so we were their servants to be used, killed, hurt, or maimed at their will.

"But it was because of this that we grew in our minds—as the Demons dwindled and died. For they forced on us their fatal sickness, trying to discover some cure. But us it did not slay nor render sterile. Instead, though our females had fewer younglings, those younglings were different, abler in ways.

"And the Demons, learning too late that they had set those they considered lowly servants on a trail which would lead those servants to walk as their equals, tried then to hunt them down and slay them, since they wished not that we should live when they died. But many escaped from the lairs, and those were our forefathers, and those of the Barkers, and the Tusked Ones.

"The Rattons went underground, and because they were much smaller, even than they are today, they could hide where the Demons could not find them. And they lived in the dark, waiting, breeding their warriors.

"The hunting of our people by the Demons was a time of great pain and terror and darkness. And it set in us a fear of the lairs, so great a fear that it kept our people away, even when the last Demon met death. That was a disservice to us, for it cost us time. And even now, when I send to the tribes and tell them of the wonders waiting them here, few conquer their fears and come."

"But if we learn the Demon's knowledge," asked Furtig slowly, "will not all their evil learning perhaps be mixed with the good, so that in the end we will go the same way?"

"Can we ever forget what happened to them? Look about you, Furtig. Is there forgetting here? No, we can accept the good, remembering always that we must not say 'I am mightier than the world which holds me, it is mine to be used as *I* please!' "

What Gammage said was exciting. But, Furtig wondered, would it awake the same excitement in, say, such an Elder as Fal-Kan? The People of the caves, of the western tribe, were well content with life as it was. They had their customs, and a warrior did this or that, spoke thus, even as his father before him. A female became a Chooser and set up her own household, even as her mother. Ask them to break such patterns and be as these of Gammage's clan, who paid more attention to learning the ways of Demons than to custom? He could foresee a greater difficulty than Gammage could imagine in that. Look at what the Elders now said of the Ancestor, in spite of his years of free giving, because he had tried to breach custom in a few of their ways.

6

While he was with Gammage, listening to the Ancestor, inwardly marveling at the fact that it was because of the will and curiosity of this single member of his own cave that the lairs had been invaded, that its secrets were being pried open, Furtig could believe that this Elder was right. Nothing mattered save that they learn, and learn in a race against time with some invisible enemy who might at any moment arrive to do battle. And that the only weapons which would adequately protect them were those they still sought in that time race.

However, Furtig's own part was not only insignificant but humiliating. For he, a seasoned warrior, must return to the status of youngling, studying with those half his age, even less. For learning here did not go by seasons reckoned from one's birth, but rather by the speed with which one absorbed lessons in the instruction rooms.

He wore that ill-fitting headgear until his head

ached. So equipped, he watched pictures flit across the wall, listened to that gabble of voice wherein about every third word had no meaning for a hunter-warrior. And those in the room sharing these periods of instruction were all so *young!*

The air of superiority worn by the lair people chilled him, seemed to erect an unscalable barrier. The adults Furtig dealt with were curt, always hurried. If they had any leisure, they spent it in some section to which he had not been invited. None were interested in Furtig as an individual, but merely as another mind to be pushed and pulled through learning.

His resentment grew, coloring what he learned. Though at times there were things so interesting he forgot his frustrations and became genuinely enthralled. He was especially fascinated with the series dealing with the latter days of the Demons—though why they had wished to leave such a sorry record, save as a warning, he could not understand.

He learned to hate as he had never hated the Barkers, though his detestation of the Rattons approached it, when he saw those sections dealing with the hunting down of his own people after they had not only proven to be able to withstand the disease wiping out the Demons, but had benefited in some ways from it. The ferocity of the Demons was a red madness, and Furtig, watching them, broke into growls, lashed his tail, and twice struck out at the pictured Demons with his war claws. He came to himself to see the younglings cowering away from him, staring as if the horrible madness of the Demons had spread to him. But he was not ashamed of his response. It was so that any warrior would face the enemy.

During this time he saw nothing of Liliha. And only once or twice did Gammage make one of his sudden appearances, ask a little vaguely if all were well, and go again.

Furtig longed to ask questions, but there was no one who showed enough awareness of his presence to allow him to do so. What did they all do? Had anything at all been discovered to hold off any Demons who might return? What and what and what—and sometimes who and who and who? Only there was no one he could approach.

Not until one day when he returned to his own chamber, that in which he had first awakened and which apparently had been given to him (the lairs were so large there was no end to the rooms to be used), and found Foskatt sitting on his bed.

It was like meeting a cave brother—so Furtig thought of the other now.

"You are healed?" He really did not need to ask that. There was only the faintest trace of a scar seam, hardly to be seen now, where mangled flesh had once oozed blood.

"Well healed." Foskatt's upper lip wrinkled in a wide grin. "Tell me, brother, how did you get me here? They say that we were found at the door of a rise shaft. But I know from my own hunting in the ways below that we were far from that when we had our last speech together. And what became of that Ku-La, who was with us in the stinking Ratton pen?"

Furtig explained the break-through of the rumbler. Foskatt nodded impatiently. "That I know. But how did you control it? I must have gone into darkness then."

"I did as you did, used my tongue in the cube," Furtig replied. "We put you on the top of the rumbler and it carried us—but the stranger you name Ku-La would not come. He went on his own. And since the Rattons were everywhere"—Furtig gave a tail flick—"I do not believe he made it."

"A pity. He would have been a useful contact with a new tribe. But if you used the caller—how did you? Touch starts the servants, yes, but you would not know the proper touch for a command."

"I put in my tongue and it started," Furtig repeated. "I gave no command—"

"But what did you *think* when you did that?" Foskatt persisted.

"Of Gammage and the need for reaching him."

"Just so!" Foskatt got to his feet and began to stride up and down. "It is as I suspected—one touches, but it is not the touch alone as they have said, the pressure once, twice, and all the rest they would have us learn. It is the thought which directs those! For you have proved that. You knew no touch pattern, you merely thought of where you would like to be—and it traveled for you!"

"Until it died," commented Furtig, "which it did."

"But if it died, how then did you have any guide through the ways?" Foskatt halted, stared at Furtig.

"I—" Furtig tried to find the proper words. "I tried hunting search—"

"The person tie!" Foskatt's eyes grew even wider. "But you did not know Gammage, had no tie with him."

"None except that I am of his blood kin in direct descent," Furtig agreed. "I do not know how I was able to do this thing, but I did. Had I not, neither one of us would be standing here now." He added to his tale the finding of the moving table, their arrival at the shaft, rising to the right level via that.

"Has Gammage heard this?" demanded Foskatt when he had done.

"No one has asked how we got here. They probably think you played guide." For the first time Furtig realized this. He had been overwhelmed by the wonders of the lairs, yet no one had asked him questions in return.

"But he must be told! Only a few of us can so depend upon hunting search." Foskatt's moving tail betrayed his excitement. "And never have I heard of a case wherein it could be used if the two involved were not close. This may mean that there are other changes in us, ones which are important." He started for the door as if to hunt immediately for Gammage. Furtig moved to intercept him.

"Not yet. Not until we are sure."

"Why not? Gammage must hear, must test—"

"No!" That was almost a warning growl. "In this place I am a youngling, fit only for lessoning with those still warm from their mothers' nests. If I claim some talent I do not have, then I shall be rated even less. And that I will not have!"

"So once did I believe also," Foskatt answered. "But all that matters is learning something to add to the knowledge of all."

Now it was Furtig's turn to stare, for it seemed Foskatt meant that. Of course a warrior stood ready to defend his home cave. But, except when pressed by battle, a warrior was concerned not with others but with himself, his pride. And to keep that pride, those who lost at the Trials wandered. If he had not done so himself, he would have been less than an untried youngling in the eyes of his own clan. Yet now Foskatt calmly said that he must risk the jeers of strangers for no good reason—for to Furtig the reason he offered was far from good.

"Do you think I was welcomed here, by any but Gammage?" Foskatt asked then. "To stand as a warrior in the lairs one must have something to give which others recognize as worthy of notice. And since the In-born have always had the advantage, that is difficult. It is a Trial in another fashion from our own."

"How did you then impress them with your worth?"

"By doing what I was doing when the Rattons took me. It would seem that the gain of one kind of knowledge is sometimes balanced by the loss of another. How learned you the hunting lands of the caves, brother?"

"By running them, putting them in my mind so I could find them day or night."

"Yes, we have a place here"—Foskatt tapped his forehead with one stub finger—"to store that knowledge. Having once traveled a path we do not mistake it again. But the In-born, they do not possess so exact a sense of direction. If they go exploring they must mark that trail so that they will know it again. And with the Rattons invading, that is the last thing we want, trails to direct the enemy into our territory.

Therefore we who have not lost that inner sense of homing, we do the scouting. Look you, Furtig, do you not see that you have something more of benefit even than that which is common to all of us? If we can find out how you are able to fix upon one you have never seen, use him as a guide, then we shall be even more free to explore."

"Free to face Rattons? You can trace them by the stink alone."

"Rattans, no. Any one of us could spy upon Rattons. Nor does that duty need us going on two feet or four, or will soon. For the In-born have recently found another device of the Demons which moves through the air—though it has no wings. As it moves so it gathers pictures of what lies beneath it and sends those back to be viewed at a distance—"

"If Gammage has such a thing, why did he not use it to see you taken by the Rattons and come to your aid?" Furtig interrupted. He had seen many marvels here, but the idea of a flying picture taker— Only, Foskatt was not making up a tale for younglings; it was plain he meant every word.

"For two reasons. First it has not been tested to the full. Second, it is again as with the other servants; these spy boxes fly only for a short space. Then they ground and there is nothing to be done to get them aloft again. Either the Demons had some way of infusing life into them at intervals, or they have grown too old to be trusted.

"But what I went to find was knowledge. You have seen the disks of tape which are fed into the learning machines. It is from these that Gammage and others have learned all they know about the machines and secrets of the Demons.

"However these disks are not stored in one place. We have found them here, there, in many places. Though why the Demons scattered them about so is a mystery. Gammage has a theory that all of one kind of learning was kept together, then the kinds separate. A little time ago he found what may be a guide to locate several different stores, but that was guessing. Much we learn here must be connected by guessing. Even when we hear the Demons' words, we know only perhaps half of them. Others, even though many times repeated, we are not sure of. When we can add a new word, be sure of its meaning, it is a time of joy.

"It has long been Gammage's hope that if we uncover all the tapes, use them together, we can learn enough to run all the servants of the Demons without the failures that now make them unreliable. And with such servants, is there any limit to what we may do?"

"Some, perhaps," Furtig said. "Did the Demons not think that once also? And they were limited in the end. Or so it seems."

"Yes, there is that danger. Still—what if the Demons return, and we are again their playthings—as we were before? Do you wish that, brother?"

"Playthings?"

"So they have not shown you that tape yet?" Foskatt's tail twitched. "Yes, brother, that we were—playthings of the Demons. Before the time when they began to use us in other ways—to learn from our torments of body what some of their discoveries would do to living creatures. Do you wish those days to return?"

"But this feeling Gammage has, that they will return—why is he so sure?"

"At the centermost point in the lairs there is a device we cannot begin to understand. But it is sending forth a call. This goes to the skies. We have tried to destroy it, but it is safeguarded too well to let us near. And it has been going so since the last Demon died.

"We have discovered the records of those Demons who took to flight when the last days came. If they escaped the disease which finished their tribe here, then that device may call them back."

So serious was Foskatt's tone that Furtig's ears flattened a little to his skull, his spine fur ridged. As Gammage had the power to enthrall when one listened to him, so did Foskatt now impress his companion with his conviction of this truth.

"But Gammage believes that if he has the Demons' own knowledge he can withstand them?"

"It will be a better chance for us. Which would you choose to be in battle, a warrior with claws or without? For weapons support one at such times. Thus we seek all these stores of disks to learn and learn. It may be even the next one we find which will teach us how to keep the servants running. But, as I said, Gammage thought he had heard such a store place described, and I went to seek it. The Rattons took me. They work with traps, brother, most cunningly. Since it was not known they were in that part of the lairs, I was taken. Nor can I hold my head high, for I was thinking more of what I hunted than the territory I moved through. So I suffered from my own carelessness, and would have paid full price if you had not come."

"But you would go again?"

"I will go again when I am needed. Now do you see, Furtig, what we have to offer here? We can be the seekers, using all the craft of the caves. And if it happens that you have something to better that seeking—"

Furtig remained unconvinced. "Not until I have proven it for myself," he repeated stubbornly.

"Prove it then!" Foskatt retorted.

"How can I? If I trail through Gammage again," Furtig pointed out, "then I am doing no more than our people have always been able to do."

"Not all our people. You know that well. It is a talent which varies."

"But it is not uncommon. I could fasten on you, on Gammage—and it would not be extraordinary. You found my sensing strange because I used the Ancestor when I had never seen him."

Foskatt limped a little as he strode back and forth, as if his wound plagued him somewhat. Now he sat down on the bed place.

"Let me tell Gammage, or better still, tell him yourself. Then perhaps he can see a way to test this—"

"I will think about it." Furtig held stubbornly to his own will. He was interested by all Foskatt had told him, impressed by the other's belief in the Ancestor and what he was doing here. But he wanted a chance to prove to himself that he need not fear the scorn of the In-born before making a bold claim.

"Did you know really what you sought when you fell into the Ratton trap?"

"A secret place holding learning tapes—but this, Gammage thought, was larger than most by the reference to it which he had discovered. He wanted to find more dealing with the skyward-call. We had avoided that section, for twice we lost warriors to the protective devices of the Demons. Only at this new hint of the store place Gammage asked for volunteers, and I said I would go. For we of the caves have keener senses to detect what may lie in wait in places of danger. I was passing through what we thought a safe section when I was entrapped."

Foskatt seemed convinced that the cave-born had certain advantages over the In-born. Or did he cling to that thought because he, too, smarted from the superior airs of the In-born? Was he convinced, or had he convinced himself? It did not matter; Furtig was not going to put himself on trial until he could prove that he had something to offer. Though it seemed that Foskatt's story contained a clue as to how he might do so.

"How close were you to this place you hunted when the Rattons took you?"

"Some distance. I was taking a circle trail because I was not sure of Demon traps. Part of the first ways fell in with a loud noise when I tried to reach the signal."

"Closing off that section of the passage?"

"No, only the main trail. Look—"

From his belt pouch Foskatt brought out a slender stick. Its point, drawn along the floor, left a black line easy to see. With quick marks and explanations, he began to show Furtig the sweep of the underground ways. Though Furtig had never seen such a way of displaying a trail before, he grasped the advantages of this and commented on them.

"But this writing stick is nothing! Wait until you see—no, better—come and see!"

He put the stick away, scrambled up, and made for the door. Furtig, drawn along by his enthusiasm, followed Foskatt to his quarters.

Those were indeed different from the bare room in which Furtig had made his home since coming to the lairs. Here were two tables, their tops well burdened by masses of things Furtig was unable to sort out in the single glance or two he had time for before Foskatt drew him to the bed place, pushed him down to sit, and caught up a small box.

This was about as large as his two fists set together, and he pointed it at the wall. As with learning devices there appeared a picture there, but this was a series of lines only. However, after a long moment of study Furtig began to recognize a resemblance between them and the ones Foskatt had drawn.

Foskatt wedged the box steady beside Furtig on the bed and then went to stand by the picture, thrusting his hand into it as he explained.

"We are here now!" An emphatic scrape of claw on the wall distorted the picture. Beginning so, he launched into a description of this corridor and that, up and down.

"If you have such as this," Furtig asked when he was done, "why do you need to search out these new trails in person?"

"Because these"—Foskatt came back and gave the box a tap and the picture disappeared—"are limited in what they show—each one portrays only a small section of the lairs. And if you cannot find the right box you have no guide."

"All this—" Furtig pointed to the mass of things on the tables. "What have you here?"

"Many things of worth for a scout. See, with this, one can carry food which is hot, and later open it and find the food still hot."

He turned a thick rod around in his hands. It split in two neatly.

"Food hot? But why should food be hot?"

"Wait and see!"

Foskatt put down the two pieces of rod and went to another box, much larger than that which had given the wall pictures. He took up a bowl in which Furtig could see a strip of meat, scooped the meat out, placed it within a mouth opening on the box, and snapped the opening shut.

Within seconds Furtig sniffed such an odor as he had never smelled before. It was enticing and his mouth watered. Before he knew it he had given one of the small mews a youngling utters when he sees a filled food bowl. And, startled, he was ashamed.

Foskatt might not have heard. He opened once more the mouth of the box. The meat he took out was now brown and the odor from it was such that Furtig had to force himself to sit quietly until his tribesman offered it to him. It tasted as it looked, different from any meat he had ever mouthed, but very good.

"It is cooked," Foskatt said. "The Demons did so to all their food. When it is so treated and put into carrying things such as these"—he picked up the rod again—"then it does not turn bad for a long time. One can carry it and find it as hot as when it came from the cooker. Then there is this—" He picked up a band which went around his middle like a belt. It had been rather clumsily altered to fit Foskatt, and at the front was a round thing which, at his touch, blazed with light.

"This can be worn in a dark place to make light."

There seemed to be no end to Foskatt's store of Demon-made treasures. There were slender, pointed rods one could use for a multitude of purposes. Something he called a knife—like a single straight claw mounted on a stick—which cut cleanly.

In fact Furtig was shown so many different devices so hurriedly that he lost count, and it all became just a whirling mass of strange but highly intriguing objects.

"Where got you all these?"

"When I go seeking new trails I bring back things small enough to carry. Sometimes I can see their use at once. Other times I turn them over to others for study. Now here—"

Another box. This time at his touch no picture appeared on the wall, but a portion of its lid rolled back and within—!

Furtig did not muffle his hiss of astonishment.

It was as if he were very tall, taller than the lairs, and stood looking down into a part of the country near the caves. Animals moved there, he recognized deer. But they were not moving as the wall pictures moved, rather as if they lived as very tiny creatures within the box. Furtig put out a finger—there was an invisible cover, he could not touch.

"They are—alive?" He could not believe that this was so. Yet the illusion of reality was so great he still had doubts that such a thing could be if it were *not* real.

"No, they do not live. And sometimes the picture changes and becomes— Watch!" Foskatt's explanation ended in a sudden exclamation.

The world within the box was hidden in a gathering fog. Then that cleared and — Furtig began to shout:

"The caves! There is Fal-Kan and San-Lo. It is the caves!"

7

When Furtig glanced around Foskatt was not watching him, but staring at the cave scene as if he, too, found it astounding. Then Foskatt's hand shot out, his fingers tightened about Furtig's arm.

"Think," was his order. "Think of some particular place—or person—and look at this while you do so!"

Just what he meant Furtig could not understand. But when he heard the urgent tone in the other's voice he did not mistake its importance. Obediently he looked at the box—though what he should "think" about momentarily baffled him.

The scene of the tiny world was again obscured with the fog, the caves hidden. Then—just why he did not know—a mind picture of Eu-La as she had watched him leave on this venture came to him from memory.

Mist cleared, revealing a small rise north of the caves. But that was not quite the scene he remembered. Somehow small differences were vivid: more leaves had drifted from the trees, a patch of silver frost was on the grasses.

Then a figure climbed to stand, facing him. Eu-La, but not as he had seen her last. Again certain subtle differences marked the passage of time. Furtig had a jog of guilty memory when he thought of how she had asked him to speak for her to the Ancestor and of how, until now, he had forgotten. He must do that for her as soon as possible.

She shaded her eyes with her hands as if she stood in the full glare of the sun. No, this was no memory picture which Furtig was in some manner projecting into the box. It was independent of any memory of his.

"Who is she?" Foskatt demanded.

"Eu-La, who is of the Ancestor's cave kin. She is daughter to the sister of my mother, but much younger than I. At the next Trial of Skill she may go forth to another cave. Alone among the People she wished me well when I came to Gammage."

Mist once again, hiding Eu-La. When it faded, there was nothing inside, only empty dark. Furtig turned almost savagely upon his companion. He felt now as if he had been made the butt of some game in which he did not know the rules and so appeared stupid.

"What is this thing? Why does it make me see Eu-La and the caves when we are far off?"

Again Foskatt paced up and down, his tail swinging, his whole attitude that of a warrior disturbed in his mind.

"You have again proved, brother, that you have something new to our knowledge, though these lairs are full of things always new to us. That box has shown many pictures from time to time. At other times it is dark and empty as you now see it. I have looked upon the caves through it, seen distant kin of mine as I remember them. Only now you were able to summon, yes, summon, one person and see her perhaps as she lives and moves at this very hour! This is perhaps allied to that talent which guided you to the Ancestor. Do you understand? If we can use these" —he gestured to the box—"and see by only thinking of a person or thing we would look upon—"

He paused, his eyes agleam, and Furtig thought that now he was caught by a new idea.

"Listen, brother—look now at this and think of learning disks!"

Furtig thought of such disks as he had seen fed into the learning machines.

Straightaway a small picture, though dim, blurred, and fuzzed, came into view. There was the learning room in which Furtig had spent such weary hours. Two of the younglings were wearing the head bands, and Liliha tended the machine into which the disks were fed.

They saw the room for only a moment or two. Then it blurred and was gone. Nor could Furtig bring it back.

He said as much. But Foskatt did not appear too disappointed.

"It does not matter. Perhaps you are not so familiar with the disks. But what *does* matter is that you could do this. Do you not see? If we can learn your secret, such boxes as these will keep us in contact with one another though we are apart. What would scouts not do to have such devices!"

What it would mean as an aid in hunting was immediately plain. If the caves could be so equipped, one would never have to fear a surprise attack from a Barker. Scouts in the field could send in early alarms. Or perhaps the boxes could even be hidden and watched from the caves without the need to use scouts! Furtig's thoughts leaped from one possibility to the next, and his excitement grew.

"It may be that only you have such a talent, brother," Foskatt said, interrupting Furtig's line of thought. "Unless this is a thing which can be learned. But the Ancestor *must* know of it—come!"

Seizing the box, Foskatt herded his companion out of the chamber. They tramped along corridors Furtig remembered from his first tour, coming to one of those shafts where air could so remarkably carry one up or down. Liliha had earlier admitted that the People had never been able to discover what particular device of the Demons governed this. But their workings had been discovered by Gammage on his first penetration of the lairs when he had fallen into one. And they were now accepted by his clan as matter-of-factly as the cave people would accept a trail.

So borne aloft, they went past three more levels, emerging in a place which startled Furtig, though with all he had seen in the past few days his ability to be surprised should by now have been dulled. They appeared now to be standing on a ledge with one side open to the sky. There was such a sensation of height as to make Furtig crowd back against the stone wall, avoiding that open space.

"There is a wall there, though it cannot be seen." Foskatt must have sensed his unease. "See here, brother." He walked calmly to the far edge, raised one hand, and rapped against an unseen surface.

As Furtig observed more closely, he sighted here and there smears on that transparent covering. More than a little abashed at his display of timidity, he made himself join Foskatt and look out, fighting the strong feeling that he was standing on the edge of a drop.

They were far above the ground level here. A strong morning sun, which awoke points of glitter from the sides of many of the upward-shooting towers, beamed warmly at them. Furtig stared in wonder. From the ground level he had marveled at the height of the lairs. But from this vantage point he could see even more. He had had little idea of the extent of the buildings before. They seemed to go on and on forever. Even in the far distance there was a hint of more. Had the Demons covered most of this part of the world with their buildings?

"Come—later you can climb higher if you wish, see more. But now is the time to tell Gammage this new thing."

Foskatt set off at a bold stride. In spite of his knowledge of the invisible wall, Furtig kept a path closer to the building. They rounded a curve. From this angle he could see a green shading which could only be trees at a distance. It was as if in that direction the lairs narrowed and one could sight open country beyond.

The corridor ended in a bridge connecting two of the towers. Foskatt trotted out on this as one who has made the journey many times. Furtig, in spite of his discomfort, paced close behind, keeping his attention focussed strictly on the path ahead, glancing neither right nor left.

He had always thought that heights did not bother him—nor had they in the cave world. But this was not that natural world, and now, his body tense, he hurried until he was almost treading on his companion's heels in his eagerness to get to the solid security of the building ahead.

This time their way was not invisibly walled; instead they were in the lair chambers. Here the walls were lighted with a brilliance that ran in swirls and loops, patterns which Furtig found he did not care to examine too closely.

Also, here the floor was soft under his feet, being covered with a material which yielded to pressure when he stepped. Without being asked, Foskatt offered explanations as they went.

"This is the manner of all those rooms where the Demons once lived. They have many unusual things —springs of hot and cold water which flow at the touch. Sounds—listen, now!"

But he need not have given that order. Furtig was already listening to a sound, or a series of sounds, such as he had never heard before. They certainly came from no living creature, but apparently from the air about them. Low sounds, lulling in a way. At the moment he could not have said whether he liked what he heard or not; he only listened and wondered.

"What makes it?" he asked at last.

"We do not know. It does not come regularly. Sometimes we walk into a room and sounds begin, stopping when we leave. Sometimes they start with the coming of dark, just as certain lights come on then. There is so much we do not know! It would—will—take the lifetimes of five times five of such long-living Ancestors as Gammage to learn only a few of the mysteries."

"But Gammage does not believe we will have such time undisturbed?"

"He is increasingly fearful of the Demons' return. Though just why he fears this so strongly he has not told us. If there were more of us— You see, brother, Gammage believes one thing. When our people fled from the lairs and the torments of the Demons, they were not all alike. Oh, I do not mean different in color and length of fur, shape of head—the usual ways one differs even from a litter brother. No, we differed inside. Some were closer to the old Ancestors who were born for generations here in the lairs, whom the Demons controlled and used as they pleased.

"But others had the change working more strongly in them. And so their children, and children's children differed also. Though all the People grew in knowledge and were different from their older kin, still they were so in varying degrees.

"Gammage himself differed greatly, so greatly he was almost cast out as a youngling from the caves—until he proved his worth. But he believed early that there was a way to learn more and that that lay hidden in the very place of horrors his people shunned. So he came back. And to him from time to time came those who also had seeking minds, who were restless, unhappy for one reason or another in the life of the outer tribes. It was this very restlessness that he put to service here. And those who settled, took mates, who absorbed more and more of what the lairs had to offer, and produced the In-born, still more changed. It is Gammage's belief that no warrior is drawn to the lairs unless he has that within him which reaches for what is hidden here.

"It is his hope, his need, to bring all the People here, to make open to all the ways of learning, of healing"—Foskatt's hand went to the wound seal on his leg—"so that we can be as much masters here and elsewhere in this land as the Demons were. But mainly so that we can stand firm and safe when the Demons return, and not be hunted for their pleasure. For that was how they served our Ancestors."

As he talked they went from the chamber with the twisting lights on the walls through a series of further rooms. These were furnished with more than just beds and tables. There were hangings on the walls with pictures on them, many seats, and even large pads, as if someone had heaped up five or six thicknesses of bed pallets to make soft puffs. And crowded in among these were a great medley of things—boxes, containers, other objects Furtig did not know.

It reminded him of the crowded state of Foskatt's quarters. Here, too, there had been an ingathering of things found throughout the lairs.

Among these moved several of the In-born, though none of them paid any attention to the two newcomers threading a path here. These workers were females. Some sat on the chairs or puffs intent on bits and pieces laid out on low tables before them. Others stood over devices which purred or clinked or made outlandish noises.

"All small strange devices are brought here," Foskatt needlessly informed him. "First Gammage and his Elders, those who have worked the longest and know best the dangers which might exist, inspect them. In the early days there were accidents. Dolar has no hand on one wrist because of an incautious examination of a new find. So each is tested. When they are sure that it is not dangerous, it is given to those who try to unravel its secrets. For these gathered here have the best hands for that."

Furtig saw what his companion meant. The fingers of those at work here were indeed as unlike his own stubby ones as Liliha's—longer, less clumsy in movement.

It was Liliha herself who stood in the doorway of the third room. She folded, with quick, graceful turns of hands and wrists, a long strip of material which seemed bulky until she dealt with it firmly. Then it made a neat and surprisingly small pack.

To Furtig's surprise she gave them the customary greeting of the cave people:

"Fair morning and smooth trail, warriors."

"And a fair morning to you, One-Who-Chooses," he replied.

"One-Who-Chooses," she repeated. "Yes, of that custom I have heard, warrior. Though we do not altogether follow it here. If you seek the Ancestor, he is within. A new find, Foskatt?" She looked to the box.

"No. Just perhaps a new use for an old one. You see, Liliha, even we who are not seekers-in-depth may make discoveries also."

Did Foskatt then sound defensive, as if he had a need to outdo the In-born in some way? If he did, Furtig could well understand that emotion.

"All knowledge is three times welcome," was Liliha's answer. Once more she was industriously flipping the fabric into those smooth, much deflated folds.

Gammage was not alone in that last chamber. He was seated on one of the wide seats of the Demons', all of which were raised just the wrong distance from the floor to be comfortable for one of the People, unless the feet were drawn up.

Beside him on the same seat was a powerfully built warrior with a notched ear and a long scar on his jaw. His one hand rested on his knee, and he gestured with his other arm as he talked. There was no fur-backed hand on that arm; instead, it ended in a ball of metal equipped with claws, and a cuff which was lashed to his own flesh and bone. This must be Dolar, Furtig reasoned.

The other there, a Chooser, was plainly of the In-born, just as Dolar was of the out-country. Her fur was silky black, and around her neck was a chain of bright stones. She wore bands of a like nature about her wrists.

Both she and the battered warrior showed no welcome to those who entered. But Gammage gave a purring call:

"What have you, Foskatt? It seems that you come in haste with something new."

"It is one of the see boxes," the female broke in. "Of these we have plenty—amusements for younglings."

To Furtig's secret satisfaction, Foskatt caught her

up quickly. "Not used as this brother can use it!"

"How?" Gammage squirmed off his seat and came to them. "How do you use it?"

Between them Furtig and Foskatt explained. Then Furtig demonstrated. He produced two pictures, the first of the caves, the second of Eu-La.

In that small, vivid scene she was busied with a number of strips cut from hide. These she twisted and turned in a fashion which seemed to Furtig useless. And it was apparent she was frustrated at not achieving what she attempted. But Gammage uttered an exclamation.

"Lohanna, see what this young female does!"

At his call the In-born looked. After a long moment of close attention she turned on Furtig almost accusingly.

"Who is this youngling?" she demanded, as if Furtig were attempting to conceal a matter of importance. He remembered his promise to Eu-La—this was the time to carry it out. And he freed the bag from his belt.

"She is Eu-La of Gammage's cave. This she made and asked me to show to Gammage."

The Ancestor took the bag, turned it about as if it were indeed some treasure newly discovered, then passed it to Lohanna. She studied it with the same attention and then said to Gammage:

"She is one we should have with us, Elder. Though she is not of the In-born, yet see what she has wrought. And what does she there?" She gestured to the picture. "She rediscovers by herself one of the secrets of the Demons—doing it clumsily, but from her own mind! The old strain is not finished in the Out-World!"

"So it seems. And we shall try to bring her, Lohanna. Now—" Gammage looked to Furtig. "So you can make the picture become what you wish— How?"

"I do not know how. I think—and there is the picture of the one I think of. Not as I remember them last, but perhaps as they are at present. But how can I be sure? I do not know it for the truth!" He was not going to claim any talent which could later be proven false. In spite of Foskatt's enthusiasm, Furtig was stubbornly determined to walk cautiously before the In-born.

"Tell him how you were led through the lairs—"

Reluctantly Furtig added that piece of information.

"Not so strange." For the first time the metal-handed Elder commented. "We have long known that certain of us can be so guided—"

"But the point Foskatt would make," Gammage said, "is not that Furtig was guided, but that he used it with one he did not know, had had no contact with before. So it would seem his use of that talent is also different. If such a change breeds true, we can hope for much in the future. Yes, Furtig, our brother here has been right to urge you to tell us this. Now, what else can you see—perhaps here in the lair?"

Furtig took the box. The picture of Eu-La had vanished in the fog. Should he try to see an unpeopled place—or one with people? He tried to fasten on the prison room in which he had found Foskatt, but the box remained dark.

"It will not show me a place without people," he reported.

Gammage did not seem in the least disappointed. "Then your ability must tie with a living thing. Well, can you think of a person in the lairs—"

Furtig chewed his lower lip and thought. Then an idea flashed into his mind. It would be the highest test of his ability. He summoned to mind the picture of the second Ratton guard he had seen before the prisoners' cell.

To his surprise and delight the fog gathered. The picture which emerged was blurred, but not so much that he could not distinguish part of it. And small sounds from two of those with him indicated that they saw also.

There was the Ratton. But he lay on the floor of the guard room. A piece of rubble, probably dislodged by the battering of the servant, pinned his leg to the floor. However, he still lived, for reddish eyes glinted and Furtig saw his mouth open as if he called for some help that would never come. Perhaps his fellows had left him to die because he was now useless.

"The Ratton guard!" Foskatt cried out. "Him I have seen! And that place—"

The blurring was complete, the scene vanished.

"That was one of the guards who held me!"

"So it would seem you can pick up other than our own people!" Gammage was excited. "Yes, these boxes, if others can learn to use them so, will become far more than just something to amuse younglings. Lohanna, would it not be well to check immediately on all those who have used them idly to see whether they were thinking of anything when they did so, or if they had any control over their viewing? If they can control it—or only a small number can control it—"

"Scouts," the warrior broke in. "Send scouts and turn this on them—you could have instant warning of what they viewed. We could prepare for attacks in good time."

He raised his false hand and used its harsh talon tips to scratch his chin.

Lohanna was already at the door. "You shall have the answer as soon as possible, Elder," she assured Gammage.

"Lohanna knows very much about the learning machines," the Ancestor told Furtig. "I only wish we had more of the ancient records—"

Foskatt stirred. But Gammage was continuing: "Do not take those words of mine as a complaint of your failure to find such records. We had no idea the Rattons had invaded that section of the lairs in force. It is a great danger that they have. We dare not underestimate them in any way. They breed in greater numbers than we do. Though the same illness which changed us in the beginning also cut the numbers of our litters, the Ratton females have many offspring in a single season.

"And among the Rattons are those whose cunning has greatly advanced, so that they have their own seekers of Demon knowledge. Being small, they can slink along ways we cannot follow. It would be very difficult to seal off any part of the lairs so that they could not find their way in. Also, they have their traps.

"We have certain Demon weapons. But, like the servants, those are uncertain as to performance and to depend upon them in time of need and then have them fail—" He shook his head. "But still, the records we have found reference to—they must lie in the very territory the Rattons have invaded. Should they find them first—and I am firm in the conviction that they have among them those who are able to put Demon learning to use—then we may be in a very dangerous position. Time—we have so little time!"

8

There is only one thing to do," Foskatt said slowly. "I shall try again. Though this time, being warned, I do not think I shall be entrapped." There was dour determination in his voice.

Gammage shook his head. "Remember, younger brother, you are but fresh out of the place of healing. Your wound may seem closed, but if you were put to some severe test this might not hold. Do you not remember what happened under similiar circumstances to Tor-To?"

For a moment Furtig thought Foskatt would protest. Then his tribesman gave a sigh. "But who then can go? And if the Rattons have taken over that part of the lairs, will we ever be able to reach the records if we wait longer?"

"He is right," the deeper half-growl of Dolar rumbled. "Were I but able—" His speech became a full growl, and he brought his metal hand down upon the edge of a table with such force that the claws left deep indentations in its surface.

"Dolar, my close-brother, were you able, yes. But this needs youth and quickness of body such as we have both long since lost."

To his inner astonishment, some other seemed to take over Furtig's voice then, for he heard himself saying:

"I am warrior trained and skilled, Elder. Also I have the homing sense which before led me through unknown ways. Let me know just what to search for and—"

"No!" Gammage was emphatic. "We must have you here, to work with the box, to learn how you are able to do this. Can you not see that is of the greatest importance?"

"More," Dolar asked, "than saving records from the Rattons? We have but six now of the warrior Out-World breed, and the other four are abroad on missions to contact tribes. If Foskatt cannot go, dare we send an In-born? They cannot learn the ways without many journeys under guidance. Those we cannot give them. But now this matter of boxes—let Foskatt and this young warrior try between them such sendings. If they find they can use it as a scout might, then there may be a way out of this difficulty."

His sensible suggestion carried, and so for the rest of that day and part of the night, taking only short rests and eating the trail rations they carried with them, the two played a hunt and search game through the echoing corridors of the above-ground lairs. When Furtig set off to wander, Foskatt sought him with the box. At first they were defeated over and over again, Foskatt seemingly unable to pick up any clear picture. Though once or twice the mist formed, enough to encourage Foskatt to keep on trying.

Just as they were ready to surrender to disappointment, Furtig, returning to the point where he had left his partner, discovered Foskatt wildly elated.

"You stood in a room where there were shining strips on the walls!" he cried out hoarsely. "And then you went and put your hands against one of the strips. On its surface was a second you who also put forth his hand to meet you palm to palm!"

"That is right." Furtig slumped against the wall. "That is what I did just before I started back. Then it works for you, too!"

When they returned with the news of this small success, they were greeted with a disturbing report from another scout. He had tried to reach one of the tribes of the People reputed to have hunting grounds to the north, only to be cut off by a pack of Barkers who, it appeared, were settling in.

Gammage paced up and down as if his thoughts would not let him sit still. His tail switched and his ears were a little flattened. Had not Furtig known that in the lairs Trials were forbidden, he would have believed the Ancestor was preparing to offer challenge.

"In the records there is proof that the Barkers were, even more than we, the slaves of the Demons, licking the ground before their feet—which the People, owned though they were, never did! I had hoped — But that is another matter. If the Barkers now ingather about the lairs, can we believe that is a sign pointing to Demon return? Perhaps the Demons have in some secret manner signalled the Barkers to them.

117

Though if the Barkers remembered the Demon end here as well as we do, they would not be so quick to answer such a call."

"The Barkers," offered Dolar, "are rovers, not liking settled lairs. Other times they have come near, but they never stayed for any length of time."

"Hunting parties, yes," Gammage agreed. "But this time they bring their females and young. Ask of Fy-Yan, who has been three suns watching them. We must have knowledge—"

"Which perhaps we can gain for you, Ancestor," Foskatt said. "We can use the box. I have seen Furtig afar in it."

Gammage turned with the quick grace of one seasons younger. His yellow eyes glowed.

"Sooo—" In his mouth the word became a hiss, almost akin to the warning one uttered when entering a hunting country. "Let us lay hands upon those records and perhaps we can hold the lairs. Even if the Barkers continue to be our enemies."

"Continue?" Dolar clicked his claws. "Think you it can be otherwise? Do you also fear that they might swear truce with Rattons?"

"Not impossible. In times of war it is best never to say in advance this can be, that not. Be prepared for any danger. And I say to all of you, though perhaps I have said it so many times before that the words will have no effect, with Rattons one cannot be sure of anything! Remember that well, Furtig, if and when you go into ways where they can be found."

Furtig thought he needed no warning. His hatred for the creatures, together with his earlier brush with them, had been enough to arouse all his caution. No warrior ever trusted anyone or anything, save his own clan brothers and the lair which gave him shelter.

He listened, impatiently but curbing the outward show of that, to all the information and instructions which those who had explored the ways could provide. Foskatt gave him directions—vague enough—as to what he sought. He was to watch for certain marks on walls—which might or might not be there—and would have the use of a secondary guide.

This was a cube similar to that with which Foskatt had summoned the rumbler. But its buzzing had another use. They had discovered a season back that this sound was emitted when the cube was brought near Demons' record disks.

With this instrument, and trail supplies, Furtig at last descended to the lower runways of the lairs. As yet they had no knowledge as to how far the Rattons had penetrated, though they had stationed scout-guards at important checkpoints to warn of any spill-over into their home territory. Metal servants of the Demons could also be used for this service and Furtig passed some of these on the way.

At last he slid into the dark of those tunnels, which could be runways for either the People or their enemies. There were doors here, but he wasted no time in exploring. This was not the area of the reputed cache. He moved noiselessly along, depending upon both ear and nose for warnings. The smell of Ratton he would never forget, and that warning the enemy could not conceal.

As a hunter he knew that many of the wild creatures had senses of smell far superior to his own. The Barkers did. But his hearing and his sight, which was hardly limited by the dim grayness of these ways, were his own weapons.

There was not complete darkness here. At long intervals small vertical bars were set in the walls to emit a dull light. Whether those had once been brighter and had dimmed through the years was not known. It was enough that the light aided the sight of the People.

Furtig had eaten, drunk, and slept before he had set out on this quest. At his belt a packet of food was balanced by a container of water. They did not expect him to be away too long, but he was prepared for possible delays.

Under his feet dust formed a soft carpet, but he trod so lightly that little of it was disturbed. His one hand was never far from the butt of a new weapon Dolor had given him out of their small store. The difficulty was that it was too big to handle with ease, having been fashioned to fit a hand much larger than his own. In order to use it at all (one leveled the barrel and pressed a firing button on the butt), Furtig had to discard his familiar and useful claws.

But having seen it demonstrated, Furtig was certain that the results might well outweigh those disadvantages. For when the button was pressed a vivid crackle of white (as if the Demons had indeed tamed lightning and compressed it into this weapon) shot forth like a knife of light. What that touched ceased to exist at all! It was indeed a fearsome thing. But, like all the Demon treasures, it was erratic. Explorers had found many of these, yet only a small number worked. It was if they had been drained of life during the long time they had lain unused.

Furtig turned from the main passage into a narrower one and began to count the dim lights in the wall. At the fourth he stopped to look down. There was a grating such as had given him entrance to free the prisoners—that was Foskatt's first guidepost.

Kneeling, Furtig slipped on his claws. With their added strength he was able to hook into the grating, work it out of place. Foskatt had warned him how sound carried and he was sure it had been his own handling of that grating which had alerted the Rattons, so Furtig moved very slowly.

As he worked he thought about Foskatt, hoping that their practice had proven the truth, that the other was now picking up the picture of where he was. Having held that concentration on his part as long as he could, Furtig found the grating loose, laid it on the floor, and ran his hand into the lightless space beyond.

It was large enough for him to crawl into, but Furtig hesitated. If the Rattons were suspicious, they might well have rigged another trap. Yet this was the only known way in since the fall of roof and walls had closed off the corridor passages ahead.

Carefully Furtig lifted the grating, fitted it back into place. He had made his decision. To follow exactly in Foskatt's path was folly. During his time of instruction in the lairs he had been shown various types of Ratton traps. Some of them were practically undetectable. Therefore he must find another way in. Or Foskatt must be able to suggest a possible other trail, knowing the ways of the lairs.

Furtig squatted on his heels and once more concentrated on a mental picture, this time not of what he was doing, for Foskatt's pickup, but of Foskatt himself.

The picture was vivid in his mind. Furtig closed his eyes—now, he might be looking directly into the other's face. He shaped his need for further information. This was something entirely new he was trying. Could he communicate this way—even with Foskatt's see box as an aid?

Ways—

Furtig could not be sure of that. *Was* he receiving a message from the other, or was it only that he wanted an answer so badly that his mind deceived him?

"On–right–down—"

Furtig opened his eyes. He was certain *that* was not his own thought. On–right–down— On along the passage, right—down— Well, it was either believe that to be a message or try a passage which could be a trap. And of the two alternatives, he would rather believe that he had received a message.

So he left the grating that had been Foskatt's entrance and padded on. The passage ran straight, with no breaks except a few doors. Then Furtig could see a wall at the end—a dead end with no turn right or left, only a last door to his right.

Furtig turned in there. The room was bare of any furnishing. The only break in its walls was the door through which he had entered. There were two floor gratings; a distinct current of air flowed from one of those. Furtig went to his knees to better sniff at it.

No Ratton stench, nothing but the acrid odor common to all these levels. There was a good chance that he had bypassed the dangerous territory. At least he must now chance this or fail without even trying.

The grating resisted his efforts to free it. Furtig had to use force with his claws to lever it out. When he lowered it to the floor and swept his hands within, he discovered that this was even more spacious than the area beneath the first grating.

He crouched for a long moment before he entered, once more making a picture that Foskatt might or might not be able to pick up. Then he took from his belt one of the tools Gammage had provided. It was no longer than the palm of his hand when he pulled it from the loop, but when he pressed it here and there it unfolded longer and longer, until he held a slender pole twice his own height in length. This detect was his only protection against traps, and he must use it with all the skill he could.

Resolutely he crawled into the duct. The interior was large enough for him to go on hands and knees, but it was too dark for his sight to aid. Instead he must depend on that thin rod as he edged slowly forward, sweeping it back and forth, up and down, to test for any obstruction. Explorers had used these successfully to set off traps in confined spaces. But they had failed, too. And at that moment such failures were to be remembered vividly.

Suddenly the point of the device struck against solid surface ahead. A crosswise sweep, a second vertical one met opposition all the way— There was a wall ahead, yet air continued to flow—

Side walls? Furtig tapped right and left: only solid surface. Which left only up or down—and down had been Foskatt's message. Furtig slid the detect along the flooring of the duct. There was an opening. By careful tapping he measured it to be a wide one. He edged closer, hanging his head over the rim, trying to discover the length of the drop, what might be below.

He folded the detect, put on his claws, and swung over. There were places in the walls to set claw tips so that he did not slide down too fast. But it was a chancy trip, and he had no idea how long that descent lasted. It seemed to his aching arms, his tense body, far too long. Then he came, not to the end, but to another cross passage leading in the right direction.

Thankfully Furtig pulled into that and lay panting, his whole body sweating and weak. It was not until some small measure of strength returned that he pulled out the detect rod, stretched it again to explore by touch.

The new passage was smaller than the one from which he had come. It was necessary to wriggle forward on his belly. But it pointed in the right direction, there was no smell of Ratton, and he had no excuse not to try it.

It was prod, slide, prod, a very slow advance. But his detect found no more barriers. Now there was even a faint glimmer of light to be sighted ahead. It was so welcome, Furtig hurried more than he had dared since he had entered the ducts.

Soon he peered through what could only be a grating. But, like that of the Ratton prison, this was set not at floor level but near the ceiling, so that he had to squeeze close to it in order to get even a limited view of the floor.

He was just in time to witness action. Rattons! Even before he saw them, their foul smell arose. Furtig froze, afraid of making some sound. But with that stench came the smell of blood and that of his own People. His stiff whiskers bristled.

He could hear sounds almost directly below his perch, but the angle was such that he could not view what was happening. There was a low moan of pain, a vicious chittering in the Ratton tongue. Then a body rolled out far enough for him to see it.

Though the fur of the prisoner was matted with blood, he was able to recognize Ku-La. So the stranger had not made his escape after all! He was not only back in Ratton claws but had suffered their cruel usage. That he still lived was no mercy. And his end would mean only one thing, food for the Rattons.

Plastered against the grating, Furtig listened, as if he could do that not only with his ears but with his whole body. He could hear small scuffling noises, a few chitterings. Then those grew fainter, stopped. He was certain after a long wait that the Rattons had gone, leaving no guard here.

Ku-La's own actions proved that. He was striving to raise his battered head from the floor, making efforts which brought cries of pain out of him, to somehow reach his bonds with his teeth. But the Rattons were no fools; he had been well and skillfully tied. His struggles did not last long. With a last moan he went limp as if even that small effort had finished him.

Ku-La was not of Furtig's clan, and one did not champion strangers. But—common blood—he was of the People. And his fate might be Foskatt's, or Furtig's.

Furtig started to move away from the grating, but he discovered that something would not let him go in comparative safety, leaving Ku-La to Ratton-delivered death. He edged back and began to feel about the edge of the grating. At first he thought that too tightly set, that fate had decided for him, giving him no choice.

Then there was a click which startled Furtig into instant immobility. After listening, and hearing nothing to suggest the enemy had returned, he began once more that patient prying and pulling.

To work the grating loose in those confined quarters was difficult, but Furtig managed it. Once more he had recourse to his belt and the various tools and aids he carried. Wound there was a length of cord, seemingly too thin and fine to support even a youngling. But this was another of the Demons' wonders, for it could take greater weights than Furtig.

He used the grating to anchor one end. Then, as he had used vines in the trees, he swung out and down. Furtig hit the floor in a half crouch, ready to take on any Ratton. But the door was closed; there were none there.

Sighing with relief, he moved to the captive in a single leap. Ku-La stared up at him in wide-eyed amazement but made no sound. Nor did he attempt to move as Furtig slashed through his bonds. The extent of the other's injuries made Furtig sick, and he was not sure he could save him. If Ku-La was unable to follow him into the duct, perhaps it would be his choice to ask for a throat slash and go out as a warrior should, rather than linger in the enemies' hold.

Furtig extended his hand that the other might see his claws and understand the choice it was his to make. Ku-La's blue eyes regarded those claws. Then he moved, slowly, painfully, levering himself up, looking not to the promise of a clean and speedy death, but to the cord dangling beyond. He had made his choice, and Furtig was forced to accept it.

For a moment he was bitterly resentful. Why did he have to turn aside from a vital mission to aid this warrior who was not of his clan, to whom he owed no duty at all? He did not understand the impulse that had brought him to Ku-La's aid, he only mistrusted it and the difficulties into which it had plunged him.

Ku-La could not get to his feet, but he crawled for the end of the cord with such determined purpose that Furtig hurried to help. How he could get the almost helpless warrior aloft he had no idea. And he was driven by the fear that at any moment the Rattons might return. In the end he managed by looping the cord about Ku-La, then returning aloft to pull with all the strength he could summon.

Had the distance been greater, Furtig could not have done it. But somehow he had the energy left to bring that dangling body within reaching distance of the opening. Then Ku-La himself, with what effort Furtig could imagine, raised one arm to the edge and drew himself within.

Wasting no time in trying to tend the other's hurts, Furtig hurried to reset the grating. Only when he had done that did he squirm beside Ku-La, unhook his water container, and let the other drink—which he did in a way that suggested that his thirst had been almost as great a torment as his wounds.

"Where now?" Ku-La's whisper was very weak.

Well might he ask that! Furtig's impatience flared again. In this tight duct he could only tug the other on. He was sure Ku-La could not climb up the vent down which he had come. It could well be that he should leave the other here, momentarily out of harm, and go on his own mission. As he was considering that, the same idea must have come to Ku-La, for he said: "They will seek—"

Naturally they would. And they would not be long in finding the grating. It would take them some effort to reach the opening, but Furtig could not gain much satisfaction from that. He set to work to see if he could wedge the grating more securely. He broke off a length of his detect and rammed it well into place. They would have some trouble breaking that.

"We can only go on," he said at last. But how far— and to where? The pace Ku-La could keep—His concern over the other had indeed put him in awkward straits; it might even lead to disaster.

Perhaps Ku-La could help. Let them get away from the grating, and he could ask the other what he knew of this section of the lairs.

"Can you crawl?"

"While there is breath in me," replied the other. There was that in his tone akin to some blood-oath promise. Furtig believed he meant it.

He put out his hand, caught the other's right arm, and hooked Ku-La's fingers into his own belt.

"Hang on then and let us go!"

9

They lay together in the small space the meeting of three ducts provided. Furtig could hear Ku-La's harsh gasping and knew, without need for confirmation, that Ku-La had come to the end of his strength. Yet he himself found that he could not just crawl on and leave the other to die in this hole. That drag upon him produced a dull anger in him.

It was Ku-La who spoke first, his voice a thread of sound which Furtig had to listen to well to hear at all.

"No–farther—"

So he was accepting defeat. Furtig should now feel relief. It was as if Ku-La had accepted the inevitable, laid his throat open to the mercy claws. But he spoke again, and this time he asked a question which surprised Furtig, for he believed Ku-La sunk in his own misery.

"What seek you?"

"Knowledge." Furtig answered with the truth. "The hidden knowledge of the Demons."

"So–also—" came the whisper. "I–found–before–I–was–taken—"

Furtig, startled, rolled over, trying to see the other in the dark. Only Gammage's clan combed the lairs for knowledge. Yet this stranger spoke with certainty.

"Records?" Furtig demanded. He could accept that Ku-La prowled perhaps hunting a superior weapon. But certainly he could know nothing of the tapes Gammage wanted.

"Demon knowledge." Ku-La's whisper was a little stronger, as if the necessity for communication actually produced strength to aid him. "They kept records–in–rolls–of–tape. Our people know this. You put them in—" His whisper died away.

But Gammage and his people were the only ones who had learned that, who studied such. Yet Ku-La spoke as one who had used such tapes. Furtig had to know more. Putting out a hand, he touched the other's shoulder, only to feel Ku-La wince with a gasp of pain.

"How do you know this?" Furtig demanded sharply.

"—live in lairs—to the east–lairs very large. We–hunt knowledge—"

Another clan such as Gammage's, busy at the same task on the far side of the lairs? But it was not possible. As Ku-La had said, the lairs were large. But that they had not had contact—that hinted that Ku-La's people may have been hiding with no good intent. Had he brought out of the Rattons' claws one who was as much an enemy as a Barker or one of the evil-smelling runners in dark ways?

"Came–from a smaller lair–found knowledge there which brought us hunting here—" Ku-La continued that thread of tortured sound, bending his strength to an explanation. "We have old story–lived–with–Demons until they died–then learned—"

Could it be that elsewhere the Last Days had been different? That dying Demons had not turned upon Ku-La's tribe as they had so mercilessly here? Furtig decided that such history was possible. And if that were so, surely Ku-La's people had a head start on Demon discoveries. Yet they had come here seeking knowledge—which made Gammage's need doubly important.

Ku-La said he had found what he sought just before the Rattons had taken him! Which meant that a cache was either in Ratton territory or close enough for them to patrol there. Was that cache the one Foskatt had been aiming for?

"Where is this place of tapes?"

"There is a hall where stand many of those things like the one which broke down the wall." Ku-La's voice was steadier, even a little stronger, as if fixing his mind upon his search had drawn him a little out of his present misery. "On the wall facing the door of that—there is a space there as if one had set his hand into it. Into that you must put a light—Then it opens—" His whisper ended with a sigh. Though Furtig shook the other's shoulder there was no flinching or answer.

Was Ku-La dead? Furtig fumbled for the other's head, held his fingers over the half-open mouth. No, there was breath coming. But he did not believe he could get any more directions. This chamber—where would he find it? He had better advance in the general direction suggested by Foskatt. But in any case he could linger here no longer.

Furtig dropped his head on his crooked arm and thought of the face of Foskatt. Then in his mind he retraced his passage along the ducts, concentrating hardest on the present point. He had no assurance his message was received, but it was the best he could do. Unlatching his container of water, he pushed it under one of Ku-La's limp hands. Then he scrambled into the duct at his right to continue his journey.

As he rounded a turn, he saw again the faint slits which could only be gratings. He hurried from one to the next. The chambers he saw were piled high with boxes and containers—as if they were part of a vast storehouse in which the Demons had laid up treasures. Furtig had no idea of their contents. It would take seasons and seasons—even if Gammage realized his impossible dream and united the many tribes of the People—to explore this place.

So much of what had already been discovered was not understood, for all the prying and study of those best qualified among the In-born. If they were given time and peace—what could they learn?

The sight of all that piled below had the effect on Furtig that a clean, newly made track might have on a hunter. His fingers twitched with the desire to swing down, to claw open this or that shadowed container. But this was not what he had been sent to find. He forced himself past those tantalizing displays.

With a shock he realized that the last grating gave him a new view. He pushed close to the grill to assess what he saw. Machines—lines of those strange willing-unwilling servants lined up. And a single door at floor level. Ku-La's tale—had he found by chance the very storage place the other sought? But this could not be Foskatt's cache, unless the vague description he had caught varied in details.

In the dim light Furtig could not see any such space in the wall as Ku-La had described. He used his nose as well as his eyes and ears. The usual smell of these burrows—no taint of Ratton. If this was the chamber of Ku-La's story, there was no enemy guard. Dared he pass up the chance to prove or disprove what the stranger scout had said?

If Ku-La's people had had a longer association with the Demons, a knowledge exceeding the hard-won bits and scraps Gammage had unearthed, than any cache the other had come to find might well be superior to that listed for Furtig. He must put it to the proof!

Once more he loosened a grating, used his cord to drop to the floor below. But before he sought the end of the room, he went to the door. That barrier was shut and he wished to barricade it—but saw nothing large enough to use. He could only hope that the Rattons might betray their arrival by the noise of their coming, their rank scent.

Furtig hurried to the wall Ku-La had spoken of. And he was really not surprised to find just such a depression as had been described. It was high up; Furtig had to scratch above eye level to fit his hand into it.

What had Ku-La said—light— What light? Furtig leaned against the wall to consider the problem. Light —the Demon weapon spat lightning— He had nothing else, and he was firmly determined to force this door if he could.

Furtig drew the weapon. Dolar had drilled him in the charge of force it would spit. The wave of fire which answered was governed by the turning of a small bar on the butt. He could set that as low as it would go—

Having done so, Furtig put the mouth of the barrel to the depression. More than a little nervous to be using forces he did not understand, he pressed the firing button.

There was an answering glow reflected back from the cup. Then, slowly, with a dull rasping sound, as if something which had been a long time sealed was being forced, the wall split open. It did not crumble as had the wall in that other chamber when the rumbler had battered it, but parted evenly, as if slashed carefully by claw tip. Furtig uttered a small purr of triumph.

But he had prudence enough not to enter a place with a door that might close and entrap him. His inbred caution warred with curiosity, and caution won to make him take what precautions he could.

Though the door remained open, Furtig turned to the machines in rows behind him. The one which had rescued them had traveled easily enough. Even if none of these were alive, could one not be pushed forward? He darted down the nearest line, trying to find one small enough to be managed. And finally, though there did not seem to be much choice as to size, he singled one out and began to pull and shove.

Then he became aware of the device that Gammage had given him, that which must locate the tapes. It was buzzing, loudly enough to sound beyond the pouch where he carried it.

134

Heartened by that, he redoubled his efforts and his choice moved, rolling with greater ease once he got it started, trundling forward to the door. There Furtig maneuvered it into position across the threshold so the opposed leaves, if attempt to close those did, would be held apart by its bulk. Only when it was set in place did he scramble over it.

There was a light bar within on the ceiling, so he could see before him a narrow aisle of drawered containers such as were always used for tape storage. Hooking his fingers in the pull of the nearest, he gave it a jerk. The drawer rolled open to display boxes of record tapes. Furtig was amazed by the number. If each of these—he glanced down the double row of containers—held as many as this one drawer, this was just such a storehouse as Gammage had long hoped to find.

Furtig slipped along the aisle, opening one drawer after another. But before he reached the end of that short line, he could see that the racks within were more and more sparsely filled. And the last section of drawers on the very end were entirely empty. Even so —this was a find to rejoice over.

Transportation— Furtig leaned against the far wall, looked back to the wedged door. That was a new problem. He had brought a bag, now tightly rolled in his belt, which would hold three or four double handfuls of tape cases. But how could he know which in this storehouse of wealth were those that mattered the most? There was nothing to do but make a clean sweep, transport everything here, at least into a hiding place of his own choice—which could mean somewhere along the ducts—until it could be carried back to Gammage.

Furtig went into action, filling the bag, climbing into the duct to dump its contents, returning to fill and climb again. He was beginning to tire. His effort at dragging Ku-La along the duct told when added to this. But he kept to his task, making sure he left nothing behind in any drawer he emptied.

It took ten trips, and at the end he was shaking with fatigue. By rights he should move that machine back, try to reseal the door, cover his tracks so that no prowling Ratton could be guided to the treasure trove he had to cache in the duct. But he simply could not summon the strength to accomplish all that. Instead he swung up for the last time, lay panting there until he could bring into his heavy, aching arms energy enough to reset the grill.

About him lay the tape cases in a drift which rattled and rolled as he moved. And he knew that he dared not leave them so near the spot where he had found them. So he began once more, this time not only filling his bag but pushing before him an armload of loose tapes, taking what he could back along the duct.

When he reached the meeting of the ways where he had left Ku-La, he heard a stirring.

"You–have–found—" Ku-La's whisper was stronger, or did Furtig only imagine that because he hoped it was so?

"Yes. But I must bring these here." Flinging out his arm, Furtig sent the cases spinning, hastily emptied his bag. He wasted no more breath on explanation but set to retrace his way.

How many such trips he made he did not know. Furtig only understood that he could allow himself no long pause to rest for fear of not being able to start again. But in the end he lay beside Ku-La with the tide of cases piled up like a wall about them.

Something pushed against his forearm persistently. He roused enough to shove it away, to discover that it was the water container he had left with Ku-La. Furtig pulled it to him, opened it, and allowed himself two reviving mouthfuls.

Revive him those did. But now hunger awakened in turn. He hunched up as well as he could in those cramped quarters to get at his supply pouch. In turn he was heartened when Ku-La accepted some of the dried meat he pressed into his hand. If the other could eat, perhaps he was not as badly off as Furtig had earlier feared. If Ku-La could move on, help himself somewhat, their return did not seem such an insurmountable problem as Furtig had thought it.

But he did not suggest that move as yet. Having eaten sparingly and drunk even more sparingly, Furtig settled himself full length, pushing aside the welter of tape cases to stretch out in what small measure of comfort he could achieve, and took the rest he knew he could no longer do without.

How long he dozed he did not know. But he awoke, aroused by a clicking near to hand. His body tensed, his hand crept to the butt of the Demon weapon. The tapes!

"You wake?" Ku-La spoke. "I count our find—"

Furtig realized that the other must be piling the cases into some sort of order. For when he put out his hand he discovered that those he had shoved aside were gone. But—"our find"? Did Ku-La think to claim that which Furtig by his own efforts had brought out of danger? When Furtig had succeeded where the other had failed?

Save that this was no time for quarreling. Neither one would have any chance to claim anything if they did not get out of here. He was sure, in spite of the partial recovery Ku-La appeared to have made, that the other could not retrace Furtig's way in. Which meant either that Furtig must leave him here—with the majority of the tapes—or find another way out for them both.

They lay in this wider space, the junction of three ducts. Two would lead them nowhere they could go, which left the third. It was the left-hand way, which might or might not carry them deeper into Ratton territory. He said as much.

"Your way in—" began Ku-La.

"There would be a hard climb back. It was difficult to descend and I had use of both hands."

"While those gray stinkers have left me the good of only one!" Ku-La interrupted. "But *you* can return—"

"With a chance that the Rattons have already marked the route?" Furtig countered. "I cannot carry you—or more than a few of the tapes. Should I leave all easy prey for them?"

"The tapes being the more important. Is that not so, warrior?" Ku-La asked quietly. "Tell me, why did you risk so much to free me from the Rattons? You could not have known then that I had information about the tapes. And I am no clansman or litter brother of yours; we have shared no hunting trail.

This is not the custom of your tribe, any more than it is of mine, or so I would guess."

Furtig told him the truth. "I do not know, save I could not leave any of the People, clansman or stranger, to the Rattons. Or perhaps I have listened to the Ancestor—"

"Ah, yes, your Ancestor. I have heard of his strange thoughts—that all the People, clan upon clan, must draw together in a long truce. One of his messengers spoke so to our Elders. But we could not see the wisdom in that—not then."

"There has been a change in your thinking?" Furtig was interested. Did Gammage indeed have a strong enough message to convert those with whom he had no kin tie? When his own clan would not listen to him?

"In *my* thinking, though I am no Elder. You did not leave me to die under Ratton fangs. Though earlier I left you and your kin brother so. And you took the knowledge I had given you and returned with what you found. Yes, one begins to see the worth in your Ancestor's suggestion. Together we have done something that neither might have succeeded in alone."

"Save that we have not yet succeeded," Furtig pointed out. "Nor shall we until we are safely back in that portion of the lairs held by the People. And with what we have found. Now we must do just that."

In the end Furtig made a blind selection from the tapes, knotting as many as he could into the bag. The rest he stacked around the duct walls. This hollow of a three-way meeting was as good a place as any to store them. Having done this, he tried his powers of concentration for the last time, tried to contact Foskatt.

There was no way of knowing whether he got through. In fact the farther he was in space and time from his contact, the more he doubted the worth of their communication. With Ku-La he ate and drank again. There was very little water left now—he was not sure it would last long enough to carry them both to some source for more. But he would not worry about that until it became a matter of real concern. Rather he must keep his mind on what lay directly before him.

Again crawling with Ku-La's one hand hooked into his belt, Furtig worked into the left-hand passage. If they moved now behind the walls of separate rooms there was no way of telling it, for there were no gratings. And distance in the dark and under such circumstances was as hard to measure as time. The duct ran straight, with no turns or side cuttings. Furtig could not help but believe they must be heading back toward the lairs used by his own kind.

He tried to tap that directional sense which had guided him so surely before. But whether he had exhausted his talent, if he had any special talent in message sending, he did not know. One thing only was certain: He had no strong urge in any direction and could only crawl unguided through the dark.

Far ahead there was a glimmer of light. Another grating? He did not greatly care, he merely wanted to reach it, the need for light as much an ache within him as hunger or thirst. As he advanced, Furtig was sure it was stronger than the weak glimmers of the other gratings.

They reached the opening, which seemed, to eyes accustomed to the black of the ducts, a blaze of light. It was a grating, but one giving on the open, even though they must be many levels into the earth. Rain was falling without, and the dampness blew through the grating to bead their fur.

Here a well had been cored through the lairs, large enough so that with the haze of the rain they could hardly see the far side. What they could make out of the walls showed them smooth, unbroken by more than gratings. Only in one place the smooth wall was blackened, broken with a hold of jagged edges.

Furtig thought of lightning and how it could rend even rocks if it struck true. Also of the lightning of the Demon weapon. Perhaps that could not have caused that hole. But suppose the Demons had similar but greater weapons, ones of such force as to knock holes through stone walls? Like giant rumblers? The old legends of how the Demons had turned upon each other in the end, rending, killing—this might mark such a battle.

On the other hand, that hole could well give them entrance into the very parts of the lairs they wanted to gain. Furtig was heartily tired of crawling through the ducts. There was something about being pent in these narrow spaces which seemed to darken his mind so that he could not think clearly any more. He wanted out, and the fresh air beyond was a restorative moving him to action.

"But this place I know!" Ku-La cried. "I have seen it—not from here, but from above—" He crowded against Furtig, pushing the other away from the grating, trying to turn his head at some impossible angle

141

to see straight up. "No, I cannot mark it from here. But there are places above from which one can see into this hole."

Furtig was not sure he wanted Ku-La to recognize their whereabouts. It would have been far better had they found a place *he* knew. But he did not say that. Instead he pushed Ku-La away in turn to see more clearly; he wanted another look at the wall break. Yes, it was not too far above the floor of the well. He was sure they could reach it. And he set to work on the grating.

As he levered and pulled, he made his suggestion about going through the break.

"A good door for us," Ku-La agreed.

The grating loosened, and he wriggled through into the open. He was glad for once to have the rain wet his fur, though normally that would have been a discomfort he would have tried to avoid. He dropped easily, and water splashed about his feet. That gathered and ran in thin streams to drain through openings in the base of the walls.

Furtig signalled for Ku-La, turning his head from side to side watchfully. Above, as the other had said, there were rows of windows. And he could see, higher still, one of those bridges crossing from the wall against which he stood to a point directly opposite. Or had once crossed, for only two thirds of it were still in existence, and those were anchored to the buildings. The middle of the span was gone.

There were no signs of life. Rain deadened scent. However, they would have to take their chances. Furtig tugged the cord which he had made fast above for the second time. Ku-La descended by its aid, the rain washing the crust of dried blood from his matted fur as he came.

Those windows bothered Furtig. He had the feeling which was so often with him in the lairs, that he was being watched. And he hated to be in the open even for so short a time. But Ku-La could not make that crossing in a couple of leaps. He hobbled, and Furtig had to set hand under his shoulder to support him or he would not have been able to make the journey at all. It seemed long, far too long, before they reached the break and somehow scrambled up and into that hole.

10

Ayana lay pent in the web, staring up at the small visa-screen on the cabin bulkhead. So she had lain through many practice landings. But this was different—this was real, not in a mock-up of the ship while safely based on Elhorn II, where one always knew it was a game, even if every pressure and possible danger would be enacted during that training.

Now that difference was a cold lump within her, a lump which had grown with every moment of time since they had snapped out of hyper to enter this system. Were the old calculations really to be trusted? Was this the home planet from which her species had lifted into space at the beginning of man's climb to the stars?

When one watched the histro-tapes, listened to the various pieced-together records, one could believe. But to actually take off into the unknown and seek that which had become a legend—

Yet she had been wildly excited when her name had

appeared with the chosen. She had gone through all the months of testing, training, of mental conditioning, in order to lie here and watch a strange solar system spread on the visa-screen in a cramped cabin— know that they would flame down, if all went well, on a world which had not been visited for centuries of planet time.

She saw the shift in the protect web hung above hers. Tan must be restlessly trying to change position again, though the webs gave little room for such play. Even their rigorous training had not schooled that restlessness out of Tan. From childhood he had always been of the explorer breed, needing to see what lay beyond, but never satisfied with the beyond when he reached it, already looking once more to the horizon. That was what had made life with Tan exciting— on Elhorn; what had drawn her after him into the project. But what can be a virtue can also be a danger. She knew of old that Tan must sometimes be curbed, by someone close enough for him to respond to.

Ayana studied the bulging webbing—Tan safe, but for how long? His nature had been channeled, he had been educated as a First-in Scout. Once they had landed, he would take off in the flitter—unless there were direct orders against that. Now Ayana hoped that there would be. She could not understand the deepening depression which gathered as a fog about her. It had begun as they had come out of hyper, growing as she watched the visa-screen. As if those winking points of light which were the world awaiting them marked instead the fingers of a great dark hand stretching forth to gather them in. Ayana shivered.

Imagination, that was her weak point, as she had been told in the final sifting when she had almost been turned down for the crew. It was only because she was an apt balance for Tan, she sometimes thought unhappily, that she had been selected at all.

"Well—there they are!" There was no note of depression in Tan's voice. "So far the route equations have proved out."

Why could she not share his triumph? For it was a triumph. They had had so little to guide them in this search. The First Ship people had deliberately destroyed their past. A search of more than a hundred years had produced only a few points of reference, which the computer had woven into the information for this voyage.

Five hundred planet years had passed since the First Ships—there had been two—had landed on Elhorn. What mystery had made those in them deliberately destroy not only all references to the world from which they had lifted but some of the instruments to make those ships spaceworthy? The colonists had suffered a slow decline into a primitive existence, which they had actually welcomed, resisting with vigorous fanaticism any attempt by the next generation to discover what lay behind their migration.

There were two—three such stagnated generations. Then, with all those of the first generation gone, their stifling influence removed, again inquiry. Explorers had found a closed compartment in one ship with its learning tapes intact; though those were spotty, sometimes seemingly censored.

After that came rebuilding, rediscovery, the need to know now almost an inborn trait of the following gen-

erations. There had been a search lasting close to a hundred years, until at least nearly all the resources of Elhorn had been turned to that quest alone. Not without opposition. There had been those in each generation who had insisted that their ancestors must have had good reason to suppress the past, that to seek the source of their kind was to court new disaster. And those had been gaining followers, too. They might have prevented the present voyage had it not been for the Cloud.

Ayana's face suddenly mirrored years of parched living when she thought of the Cloud. It had been such a little thing in the beginning. Scientists had wished to get at the rare ores their detectors had located on the impenetrable South Island of Iskar, where volcanic action produced unpredictable outbursts of lethal gases. From the old records, they had created robos like those the First Ship people had used, and these had been dropped on Iskar to do the mining. But the gases apparently had eaten away the delicate robo "brains," in spite of all attempts to shield those against infiltration. Then the scientists had turned to chemical countermeasures. To their own undoing. For the equipment the "dying" robos had installed in the mines had malfunctioned. And the result was the birth and continuing growth of the Cloud.

That did not rise far in the air; it crept, horribly, with a slow relentlessness which made it seem a sentient thing and not just a mass of vapor. So it covered Iskar, where there was little to die, but later it had headed out over the sea.

The water itself had been poisoned by the passing

touch of that loathsome mist. Sea life died, but died fleeing. And those refugees contaminated others well beyond. Those died also, though more slowly.

At last those who had resisted the hunt for the home world capitulated. With their limited knowledge, lacking as it was in those portions the First Ship people had destroyed, they could not deal with the monster from Iskar. And they must either find a way to strike it a death blow, or else transport all their people elsewhere.

Even as the Pathfinder had lifted, the rest of the labor force (which now meant all the able-bodied dwellers on Elhorn) had been at work rehabilitating the two colony ships. Whether those could ever be put in condition to take to space again no man knew. The Pathfinder had been constructed from a smaller scout which had been in company with the colony ships.

There were only four of them on board the Pathfinder, each a specialist in his or her field, and able to double in another. Ayana was both medic and historian; Tan, a scout and defense man; Jacel, the captain, was their com expert and navigator; Massa, the pilot and techneer. Four against the whole solar system from which the First Ships had fled in such fear that they had destroyed all references to their past.

Had there been a Cloud on the ancestral planet, too? Of worse still (if there could be worse), had men hunted other men to the death? For that, too, had happened in the past, the tapes revealed. At least on Elhorn, they had not resorted to arms to settle differences in belief.

The closer the Pathfinder came to their goal, the more Ayana feared what they might find.

For days of ship's time their flight within the ancestral solar system continued. By common consent they chose their target—the third planet from the sun. From the computer reports, that seemed to be the planet best suited to support life as they knew it.

All this time Jacel tried to raise some response to their ship's broadcast, but none came. That silence was sinister. Yet the mere lack of a reply signal could not turn them back now. So they went into a braking orbit about the world.

That it was not bare of life was apparent. Or at least it had not lacked intelligent life at one time. Vast splotches of cities spread far over the land masses. They could be picked up by viewers in daylight, and their glow at night (though sections were onimously dark) provided beacons. Still there was no answer to their signals.

"This I do not understand." Jacel sat before his instruments, but his voice came to Ayana and Tan through the cabin com. "There is evidence of a high civilization. Yet not only do they not answer our signals, but there is no communication on the planet either."

"But those lights—in the night!" Massa half protested.

Ayana wanted to echo her. It was better to see those lights flashing out as day turned to night below, than to remark upon the glow which did not appear— the scars of darkness. Yet one looked more and more for those.

"Have you thought," Tan asked, "that the lights may be automatic, that they come on because of the dark, and not because anyone presses a button or

pulls a switch? And that where they are now dark some installation has failed?"

He put openly what was in all their minds. And that was the best explanation. But Ayana did not like to hear it. If they now raced through the skies above the dead world with only that vast sprawl of structures its abiding monument for a vanished people, then what had killed them, or driven them into space? And did that menace still lurk below?

Ayana wanted to turn her head, not watch the visascreen. But that she could not do. It had a horrible fascination which held her in thrall.

"Without a signal we cannot find a landing site—" Jacel paused. "Wait! I am picking up something—a signal of sorts!"

They were once more in a day zone. Ayana could mark the shape of an ocean below. The land masses on this world was more or less evenly divided, two in each hemisphere. And they were over one such mass as Jacel reported his signal.

"Fading—it is very weak." His voice sounded exasperated. "I shall try to tune it in again—"

"A message?" Tan asked. "Challenging who we are and what we are doing in their skies?" He spoke as if he expected that hostile reaction. But why? Unless the memory of the fears of the First Ship people touched him, even as it had her, Ayana thought.

But if that were so, if they were to be greeted as enemies—how could they hope to land? Better by far to abort— Though she was sure Tan would never consent to that.

Jacel, using the ship's resources, had another answer. The signal, he was certain, was mechanically

*beamed and carried no message. And as such it could
have only one purpose—to guide in some visitor from
space.*

*Hearing that, they made their decision, though not
without reservations on Ayana's part, to use the
beacon as a guide. As Massa pointed out, they could
not continue in orbit indefinitely and they had no
other lead. But they prepared for a rough landing.
The computer gave no answers, only continued to gulp
in all the information their instruments supplied.*

*With every protect device alerted, Ayana lay in her
bunk. She shut her eyes, and would not look at the
screen, glad in a cowardly fashion that it was not her
duty to be in the control cabin, where she would have
to watch.*

*The usual discomforts of landing shut out every-
thing beyond the range of her own body, and she
tensed and then relaxed. She had done this many
times in practice, yet the truth differed so much from
the simulation. A second or so later she blacked out.*

*As one waking out of a nightmare she regained con-
sciousness. Then duty made its demands, and she
fumbled with the webbing cocooning her body. It was
only when she wriggled out of that protection that the
silence of the ship impressed itself upon her; all the
throbbing life in it was gone. They must be down, for
the engines were shut off.*

*Not only down, but they had made a good landing,
for the cabin was level. They must have ridden in the
deter rockets well. So Jacel had been right to trust
the beam.*

Ayana stood up and felt the grip of gravity. She

took a step or two, feeling oddly uncertain at first, holding to a bunk support, looking at Tan.

He lay inert, a thin trickle of blood oozing from one corner of his mouth. But even as she raised her hand to him, he opened his eyes, those wide gray eyes, and they focussed on her.

"We made it!" He must have taken in at once the silence of the cabin, the fact that it was in correct position for a good landing. His hands sped to unhook his webbing.

"You are all right—?"

"Never better! We made it!" And the way he repeated that gave her a clue to his thoughts. Perhaps for all his outward show of confidence, Tan had had doubts, strong doubts after all.

He was out of the cabin ahead of her, already climbing for the control cabin before she could follow. Voices from there announced that the two responsible for what Ayana privately believed to be a miracle— their safe landing—were already rejoicing over that.

The scene outside as shown on the visa-vision quieted them. They had indeed landed in what must have once been a spaceport, for the scars of old deter and rise rocket fire were plain to be marked as the picture slowly changed. However, there were buildings also, towering bulks such as they had never seen on Elhorn.

To their sight, though those buildings stood at a distance, there were no signs of erosion or the passing of time. But neither were there any signs of life. And Jacel, monitoring his com, shook his head.

"Nothing. No broadcast except the signal which brought us in. And it is set—"

Set by whom, why? The questions in Ayana's mind must be shared by her crew mates. If they had landed on a silent and deserted world—what had rendered it so?

Massa was consulting other instruments. "Air— nothing wrong with that. We can breathe it. The gravity is a point or two less than we have known. Otherwise, this is enough like Elhorn to suit us."

"Like Elhorn? With all that to explore!" Tan waved a hand at the screen where more and more of the huge building complex showed as the pickup slowly turned. This must be a city, Ayana decided. Though it pointed higher into the sky with its towers and blocks than any city did—or should.

To look at it aroused a queer repugnance in her, a feeling of reluctance to approach it. As if it were some crouching animal ready to pounce, perhaps actually ingest what came too near. She wanted none of those walls and towers. Yet on the screen the constantly moving scene proved that their landing site seemed to be completely surrounded by those buildings.

She could see no green of vegetation. No growth had seemingly dared to invade this place of stone. Nor was there any other ship berthed here.

"I think," Jacel said as he leaned back in his seat, "this place is deserted—"

"Don't be too sure of that!" Tan retorted. "We could be watched right now. They might well have some reason to want us to believe no one is here. Just because you flashed out the old code, or what we believe is the old code, does not mean that they could understand it. How long has it been since the First Ships lifted? We have been on Elhorn five hundred

planet years, but we have no idea how long was their voyage out, or ours back. A lot can change even in a single generation."

He pointed out the obvious, but Ayana wished he would not. With every word he spoke those distant windows seemed more and more like cold eyes spying on them. And in all that mass of buildings there could be many hiding places for those who had no wish to be found.

"We cannot just stay here in the ship," Jacel said. "Either we explore here—or we lift, try for a landing somewhere else."

Ayana saw her head shake mirrored by the others. Now that they were down, the best thing to do was abide by their choice—explore.

Fiercely she fought her fears under control. Even if the people were dead there would be records. And those records could hold some secret which might halt the Cloud or otherwise aid those who had struggled to send them here. They had a duty that was not to be balked by shadows and uneasy fears. Some rebel emotion, though, replied to that argument; this fear she felt was not small, and she must work hard to subdue it.

They ran out the ramp. Tan opened the arms locker, and they all wore blasters at their belts as they went out. Massa remained on guard at the hatch, ready to activate the alarms at any sign of danger. There was a wind, but the sun was warm. Ayana could detect no odor in the breeze against her face. It was like any wind, and this might be a fall morning on her own home world.

"A long time—" Jacel had trotted over to the

nearest burn scar, was down on one knee by that scorched fringe. "This was done a long time ago." He held a radiation detect, and its answering bleat was low.

Tan stood with his hands on his hips, turning slowly as if he himself was a visa-recorder. "They were builders!" And there was excitement in his voice as he added: "What a world to claim! An empty world waiting for us!"

"Do not be too sure." Jacel joined him. "I have a feeling—" He laughed as one startled and a little dismayed by his own thoughts. "I feel we are being watched."

Tan's answering laugh had none of the other's apologetic undertones. He threw out his arms wide and high. "Ghosts—shadows—let them watch us if they will. I say mankind has come again to claim his home! And—let us get busy out there"—he waved to the buildings—"and find out what awaits us."

But training remained to tame his exuberance a little. He did not indeed urge them to instant invasion of the watching, waiting city (if city it was). He was content to wait for their agreement that that must be done. Instead he got busy in the storage compartments, transporting to the open the parts of the flitter which must be assembled for a flight of discovery.

It was well into late afternoon by the signs before the framework of the small flyer was together. Tan was still working on it when Jacel appeared, stringing behind him a length of cord, while stacked in his arms were small boxes. Tan, perched on the nose of the flyer, hailed him.

"What are you doing?"

"*Seeing that we—or the flitter—have no unheralded visitors. Nights can be dark.*" Jacel set down his load. Without being asked, Ayana came to help him place the detects, string cord between them to complete a circle about the flitter.

This was one of the best warning devices they carried. Nothing could cross that circle of cord once it was set, for it created a repelling field of force. Not only that, but any attempt to approach would ring alarms in the ship.

"A trap for ghosts," Tan said. But he did not protest as Jacel carefully triggered each box.

Tan finished and left the flitter, and Jacel made the final setting. They were safe within the ship once the ramp was in. For there was no possible way of attacking those holed up in a spacer; the ship was a fort in itself.

However, Tan seemed reluctant to follow the others up the ramp, to seal up for the night. He turned to look at the towers.

"Tomorrow!" He made a promise of that one word, spoken loud enough for Ayana to hear. Though whether he meant it for her or only himself she did not try to learn.

Tomorrow, yes—there would be no holding Tan back then. He would circle out, looping wider and wider with every turn, relaying back all the information the instruments on the flitter could pick up. Then they would learn whether the city was truly dead or not, for among those devices was one which registered the presence of life force. They were not altogether helpless—

Now why had she thought that? As if they were in-

deed under siege and had only the worst to fear? Ayana ran her tongue across her lips. She had been passed as emotionally stable, enough so (and the tests had been as severe as those preparing them could devise) to be selected for the voyage. But the minute she had entered this solar system, it was as if she had been attacked by forces which tampered with her emotions, threatened that stability in ways she could not understand. She was a medic—a trained scientist—yet she feared windows! Now she once more fought those fears—pushed them back—strove to conquer them.

They ate, of ship's rations which tonight seemed even less satisfying and tasteless. Would they find fruit, or perhaps other food they could stomach here? She would be a party on the second or third trip—to be sure no ghost of disease lingered. She would have to go muffled and clumsy in a protect suit, but that she had practiced on Elhorn.

"Tan—Ayana!" Massa's voice over the com and the excitement in it made Ayana reach for the blaster on her discarded belt. "Look at the screen!"

Windows were alight! The dark ringing the ship was not complete. Apparently Massa had set the pickup on the move again to give them the changing view. There was one lighted tower and then another. Not all were alight. Ayana managed to be objective after her first startled reaction. There were blocks of lights, then again scattered single ones. Some buildings were altogether dark. Such uneven lighting hinted of inhabitants. There were people there—there had to be!

"Tan—do you see?" Ayana's question was a kind

of plea against his plans for tomorrow. He must not take off alone, cross that grim, watching place, in the light flitter. That had a shield, of course, every protect device they could give it. But above that giant, and she was sure hostile, pile—

Those lights, surely Tan would accept them as evidence of life. They could lift ship, find one of those all-dark cities they had marked from space. That was only sensible. But she knew she would not have a chance to argue that when Tan answered:

"Doesn't mean a thing! Do not worry, Big Eyes. Those are probably automatic and some circuits have long gone. Anyway, I have the force shield."

Even his use of the private name he had for her (which she cherished because of the sweet intimacy it stood for)—even that hurt. It was as if he deliberately used it to scoff at her concern. Ayana closed her eyes to those lights, tried to find sleep and perhaps dream of the safety of Elhorn before this wild venture became her life.

11

The sudden clamor outside this new corridor was one
Furtig had heard before, which set fur erect along his
spine, flattened his ears to his skull, parted his lips to
hiss. He caught an echo of that hiss from Ku-La. Yet
in a second or two both realized that this was not the
hunting cry of a Barker pack.

No, it held pain and fear rather than the hot
triumph of the hunter upon his quarry. Furtig, belly
down on the floor of the corridor, wriggled forward to
peer through the transparent outer wall.

There was the Barker, threshing wildly about, one
foot—no, a foot and a hand caught in something. He
was in such a frenzy that he snapped with his well-
fanged jaws, striving to cut what held him. Then his
head was caught! His flailing body fell, or was jerked,
to the ground. Seconds later he was so trapped in the
substance which had entangled him that he could not
move save in spasmodic jerks, each of which worsened
his plight. His baying came in muffled snorts.

They came running from concealment where even Furtig's sharp sight had not detected them. Rattons —a gray-brown wave of them. They piled on the Barker, seeming to have no fear of what had felled him, and began to drag the captive away.

Toward this building! Furtig hissed again. He had not smelled Ratton, seen Ratton, heard Ratton, since they had come through that break in the wall into these corridors. But if the Rattons were towing their catch into this structure, it was time to be gone.

He crept back to Ku-La, reporting what he had witnessed.

"A stick-in trap. They coat the ground with something you cannot see or scent, but it entangles you speedily," the other said.

"Yet they went to the Barker, handled him without getting stuck—"

"True. We do not know how they are able to do that. Perhaps they put something on themselves to repel the trap. We only know—to our sorrow—how it works on us!"

"A Barker in the lairs—" Furtig picked up the bag of tapes, was ready to help Ku-La on. "A scout?"

"Perhaps. Or they may also seek knowledge." Ku-La gave an involuntary cry as he pulled himself up. He was limping very badly, keeping going by will alone, Furtig knew.

His admiration for the other's determination and fight against pain had grown. No longer did he wonder why he had endangered his mission to rescue Ku-La; he accepted him as a comrade like Foskatt.

"If they bring the Barker here," he began warningly. It seemed cruel to keep urging Ku-La on, but Furtig had lately picked up the homing signal in his mind, knew their goal, and also that they dared waste no time in these dangerous corridors.

"True. Though Rattons seem to have little liking for going aloft," Ku-La commented, drawing small breaths between words. "They keep mainly to the lower ways."

They rounded a curve in the wall. Furtig stayed close to the inner wall; that long expanse of almost invisible surface on the outer made him uneasy. Today that feeling was worse as the wind and rain beat hard in gusts which vibrated in the walls about them.

But—as they rounded that curve, looked out upon a new expanse of open, Furtig came to a halt— Light —a moving light!

It rose from the ground, soaring high as if a flying thing carried a huge hand lamp. Now it danced back and forth erratically in the sky, swooping out and away. And through the curtain of the rain Furtig could not follow it far.

Ku-La made a sharp sound. "A sky-ship—a sky-ship of the Demons!"

Furtig did not want to accept that. In fact at that moment he discovered he had never really believed in Demon return. But there was such conviction in Ku-La's identification that belief was now forced on him.

The return of the Demons! Even in the caves of the People such a foreboding had been used as a horrible warning for the young. But as one grew older, one no longer could be frightened so. Only enough remained of the early chill of such tales to make one's blood run faster at such a time as this.

One ship—a scout? Just as the People sent one

warrior, two, three, ahead to test the strength of the enemy, the lay of the land, how it might be used for offense or defense before a clan moved into hunt?

Such a scout could be cut off. And, with small clans, the loss of a warrior was warning enough. They fell back, sought another trail. No tribe was large enough to take the loss of seasoned warriors as less than a major calamity.

Only, in the old tales the Demons had been countless. Cutting off a single scout would not discourage a migrating tribe with many warriors. Gammage might have an answer; he was the only one among the People now who would.

"We must hurry—" Furtig said, though he still watched for that light marking the Demon ship.

Furtig leaped back toward the inner wall. No light, yet something had almost brushed the rain-wet outer wall—something far larger than any flying thing he had ever seen. Luckily there were no wall lights here, nothing except the wan daylight. Perhaps they were lucky, and the flying thing in its swift passage had not seen them. For Furtig had the dire feeling that it might possess the power to smash through the transparent wall, scoop them out, were such action desired.

"Move!" He shoved Ku-La with his free hand. The other needed no urging; he was already hobbling at the best pace he had shown during their long, painful journey. As if the sight of that Demon thing had spurred him to transcend the wounds he bore.

They reached a second curve in the corridor, and this time Furtig gave a sigh of relief. For that transparent wall which made him feel so vulnerable vanished, there were solid barriers on either side.

That relief was very short, for they came soon to one of those bridges in the air. Furtig crouched, peering into the outer storm, his hands cupped over his eyes. What made his disappointment the greater was that they were now close to their goal. For he recognized the tower at the other end of the bridge as the building in which he and Foskatt had tested the communication box. They need only cross this span and they would be in their, or Furtig's, home territory.

Only, to cross, they must go along that narrow and slippery way, under not only the beating of the wind and rain, but perhaps also the threat of the flying thing. He thought he could do it—the People were surefooted. But Ku-La—

The other might be reading his thought. "What lies there?" His throaty voice was near a growl.

"The lair where my people hold."

"Safety of a kind then. Well, we can do no less than try to reach it."

"You are willing to try?" Surely the other could see his danger. But if he chose to go, then Furtig would do what he could to aid him.

He pulled out that cord which had served them so well, was preparing to loop them together belt to belt. But the other pushed his hands aside.

"No! I shall take the way four-footed. And do not link us—better one fall than both, the second without cause."

"Go you first then," Furtig replied. He did not know what he might be able to do if the other, unlinked, did slip. But he felt that if he could keep Ku-La before his eyes during that crossing he might be able to help in some fashion. And four-footed was surely the best way for them both.

Not only would it make them more sure-footed, but it would also make them less distinguishable to the flying thing. If they were unlucky enough to have that return.

The rain hit them like a blow, and Ku-La moved under its pounding very slowly. While Furtig wanted nothing so much as to be free to leap over that creeping shape before him and run with all possible speed to the promised safety of the far doorway. Yet he crawled behind Ku-La, the bag of record tapes slung about him, the water soaking his fur and trickling from his whiskers. He did not even raise his head far enough to see the doorway; rather he concentrated on Ku-La.

Twice the other halted, went flat as if his last strength had oozed away with the water pouring on him. But each time, just as Furtig reached forth a hand to try to rouse him, he levered up to struggle on.

They had passed the halfway point, though neither of them was aware of that in the agony of that slow advance, when the sound came. It was warning enough to flatten them both to the bridge, striving to give no sign of life as the thing drew closer.

It did not scream as one of the preying flying things, nor give voice in any way Furtig recognized. This sound was a continuous *beat-beat*. First to the left as if it hung in open space viewing them, then overhead. Furtig's nerve almost crumbled then. He could somehow see in his mind giant claws reaching out—coming closer—ready to sink into his body, bear him away.

So intent was he on that fearful mental picture that he was not even aware that the *beat-beat* was growing fainter, not until it had vanished. He lay on the bridge, unharmed, able to move. And the thing was gone! Had—had it taken Ku-La then, without his knowing it in the depths of his fear?

But when Furtig raised his head the other was there, stirring to life, creeping—

If they had time now before the thing returned—! For somehow Furtig could not believe that it was going to let them go so easily. There was a menace in it which he had sensed. And that sense he trusted, for it was one of the built-in protections of his kind and had saved lives many times over. The flying thing was to be feared, perhaps as much, if not more, than anything he had ever in his life faced before.

Tan ran a finger approvingly along the edge of the recorder. Got a good taping there. Tan's luck again. He smiled. Tan's luck was something which once or twice had made a real impression on the trainees back on Elhorn. He had managed so many times, usually through no reason he was aware of, to be at just the right place at the right moment, or to make the right move, even when he had no idea whether it was right or wrong.

So—with all those faint life-readings he had picked up in this pile but nothing in the open where he could get a visual record, it was his luck to catch that thing or things (in that poor visibility they had looked like blobs as far as he was concerned)—right out in the open. They might have posed to order so he could get a good tape.

Blobs—certainly they did not look like men. He had sighted them edging out on the bridge and they had wriggled along there, almost as if they were crossing on their bellies. Nothing about them to suggest they were of his species at all. Tan tried to picture men crawling on hands and knees. Would the blobs resemble those? Could be. Except they were smaller than men—children?

But what would children be doing out alone in such a storm as this, crawling from one building to the next? No, easier to believe that they were something else, not human at all.

Tan was no longer smiling. After all, they had never discovered what had sent the First Ship people to Elhorn. It had been a very strong motive, not only to force them to take the perilous trip across space, but to leave them so intent thereafter on suppressing all they could of the world of their origin and the reason for colonizing another.

Tan had picked up some dim life-readings here, but not, oddly enough, in the buildings which had shown the greatest wealth of lights at night. No—they were widely scattered. And the readings varied. Enough that Ayana ought to be able to make something out of the variance. Such would not show up so plainly just because the pickup carried over unequal distances. It was more as if the life forms themselves varied. At least he had a reading and a picture of the blobs to turn in and that would give them a beginning reference.

And—there was not a single one of these life-

readings which touched the proper coordinate for man on the measuring scale. That was what had made him buzz lower and lower, hang between the towers in a reckless fashion, trying to pick up as many registrations on the tapes as he could.

Men had built this place. Tan knew enough from his race's own fragmented records to recognize the form of architecture of his ancestors. But if there were no readings for "man" here—what did live within these walls?

The enemy of which they had no records? Only surmises presented by their imaginations? If the former, then the enemy was those blobs, and the quicker they were identified the better. Tan turned the flitter, swept out and away from the structures, heading for the ship with the small scraps of knowledge his first scouting flight had gained.

There was no *beat-beat* now—none at all. Ku-La scrambled ahead with a burst of speed Furtig hoped would not hurl him off that narrow way. But—in the doorway ahead was movement!

Rattons? Barkers? Furtig had the Demon weapon. The past hours had conditioned him to expect the worst, even in the People's lairs. Then he made out a furred head— They were coming forward to aid Ku-La—his own kind at last!

Gammage was at ease on the wide bed place. His tail curled across his thighs, and only the tip of it, twitching now and then, betrayed his excitement at Furtig's report.

The tapes had been carried off by the In-born

trained to evaluate them. And a picked group, led by Foskatt, had set out to salvage the rest of Furtig's haul from where he had left it in the ducts.

Ku-La was in the room of healing, and Furtig was finding it difficult to keep his eyes open, his mind alert to answer the Ancestor's questions. But he discovered to his amazement that Gammage was not startled by the flying thing.

That a Demon sky-ship had landed was already known to the lair People. Its coming had been foretold by certain watchers who were not of flesh and blood, but servants of metal. When those gave the alert, the People had first been baffled, then made guesses as to the cause for alarm. And, hiding out, scouts had witnessed the actual landing of the ship.

Every device which could be put to defense or used to gain knowledge of the invaders had been trained on that ship. Without, it was hoped, having yet aroused the suspicions of the old masters of the lairs.

"They are indeed Demons," Gammage said. "Drink this, clan son, it will warm you. It is made of leaves and is refreshing to our spirits."

He waited while Furtig sipped from the bowl Liliha brought him. She did not leave, but settled on the other end of Gammage's divan as one who had a rightful part in this conference. Furtig was aware she watched him unblinkingly. He wondered if she did so to weigh within her own mind the truth of his tale.

The odor of the hot liquid was enticing, so much so that just to sniff its vapor raised his spirits, gave him courage, and renewed his energy. The taste was as good as the scent. The feeling of warmth that spread through him made him even more drowsy than he had been. But two full swallows were all that he took, holding the cup from him lest his pleasure in its contents cloak his mind to what must be firmly faced.

"We viewed them through those glasses which bring the far close," Gammage continued. "They brought many things from their ship and put together a flying thing. By that time it was night, and they went again into the ship and closed it, as if they believed they might be in danger. Four of them only, though there may be more inside we did not see.

"With the morning, in spite of the storm, out came forth and entered the flying thing. He raised it into the air and flew back and forth, in and out, among the buildings. He did not try to land, but hovered above. As if the Demon sought something. But we cannot guess what he sought, nor the manner of his seeking. With Demons—who can know?"

"He found us on the bridge," Furtig returned. "But he did not attack, only stayed above us for a space and then flew away."

"Returning," Liliha said, "to the ship. It could be that when he hung above you he marked who—or what —you were."

Gammage chewed reflectively on a claw tip. "What you found, with the aid of Ku-La, is a treasure of knowledge. But whether we shall be given time to use it is another matter. If these Demons plan to reclaim the lairs I am not sure we can defeat their purpose."

"You can withdraw—to the caves—as our forefathers did when the Demons hunted them before," Furtig suggested.

"That is the last resort. The lairs are very large and, as you proved, clan son, there are ways we smaller people can travel in secret. The Demons cannot force their greater bodies into such passages."

"Perhaps we shall be both Demon-hunted and Ratton-attacked in the end." Furtig saw the gloomiest of futures.

"There are also the Barkers—" Gammage chewed again on his claw.

For the moment Furtig was content enough to sit and let his fur dry in the warmth of the chamber, sniff at the odor of his good drink, and now and then sip it. But he longed for sleep; even if the Demons were to tramp these corridors soon, a warrior had to sleep.

He fought his eyes' closing by drinking the last of the liquid. Gammage spoke again:

"The Barkers are not ones to take kindly to the trapping of their scout. Unlike our people, they are happiest in the pack rubbing shoulders to the next. And they will move as a pack to avenge their kind."

What the Ancestor said was no more than all knew. You killed or took a Barker prisoner, and you had to face his fellows in force. It was one of the things that made the Barkers so feared.

"They hunt by scent." Still the Ancestor recited common knowledge. "Therefore they will trail in here, and find the trap of the Rattons. The Rattons will take to inner ways, and in doing so, they may escape the Barkers. But—if the Barkers invade they can well pick up our scent—

"Ku-La, when he is healed, will go to his people and invite them to join us. As he has told me, those know about the Demons, and the lairs—of how we must labor to save what we have learned. If we take to the wilds, it will need many backs and hands to help carry what we must. Therefore, as Ku-La goes to his tribe, so must you and Foskatt go to the caves. There you must tell them of the coming evil and that they must send their warriors—or bring hither all the People—"

"Do you think they will listen to me, Ancestor? I am not an Elder, I am one who failed in the Trials, and went forth from the caves. Will they heed my words? You know our clans and that they are slow to believe in new things."

"You speak as a youngling, clan son. From here you will carry certain things to impress the Elders. And you do not go alone—"

"Yes, Foskatt, too." But privately Furtig thought Foskatt, for all his longer time in the lairs, would have little more weight than he had himself.

Gammage had been a long time away from the caves, he had forgotten the hold of custom on those living there.

"Besides Foskatt," Gammage said, "Liliha goes, also, by her own choice. And she, as well as you, shall take weapons such as those of the caves have no knowledge of. These are gifts, and you shall promise more if your people come to us.

"This," he continued, "will be easily done—"

Furtig did not agree with that statement in the least, but he had no chance to protest, as the Ancestor swept on—

"The Barker must be found. If he still lives, he must be freed and returned to his People. That will give us for the first time a small chance of holding a truce talk with them. Otherwise they will storm into the lairs, perhaps causing a disaster at the time when we must unite against Demons, not war among ourselves. Now we have a common cause with even Barkers."

So they were back to Gammage's wish, that all the peoples, even those hereditary enemies, make a common cause against the greater menace. Listening to him, sometimes one could almost believe that would work. But perhaps he would even suggest sending a truce flag to the Rattons—!

Apparently Gammage was not prepared to go that far. He was nodding a little, his tail tip beating back and forth.

"To the Barkers we shall suggest a truce. The Rattons—no—we cannot deal with them in any way! They are as accursed as the Demons and always have been. We must warn whom we can to stand together. Liliha, see to the clan son. I think he sleeps now, even though his eyes are open!"

Furtig heard that as a distant murmur. There was a touch on his arm. Somehow he blundered to his feet and wavered off, that light touch steering him this way and that, until he had come to his own bed place and stretched out there.

Demon—Ratton—Barker—sleep won out over all.

12

"*Animals!*" But even as Ayana spoke she knew that was not true. Yes, those bodies were furred. And they had tails. But neither could it be denied that they wore belts around their waists, and attached to the belt of one was a laser! The thing was armed with a weapon much like the most potent in the ship's locker.

She studied the scene on the record reader into which Tan had fed his tape. The light was admittedly poor, but the longer she looked the more new details she could see. Animal, no, but neither was it like her norm for "man."

However, it had a haunting familiarity. And it carried a lumpy burden—the rear one of the two, that is—on its back. Animals were used so. What of the gorks on Elhorn—ungainly, half-feathered, half-scaled, of avian descent but lacking their ancestors' wings? For an instant or two she remembered gorks with a homesick nostalgia.

No, the bundle did not mean that the creatures on

the bridge were servants of men—not as the gorks served. Not when one of them also wore a laser. Still —she was teased by a wisp of memory.

"Animal—you are sure?" Jacel roused her from that search.

"No, it is armed and wearing the belt—how can we be sure?"

"It is matched with this life-reading." Massa consulted the dial. "And there are similar life-readings here, here, and here." The computer had produced a sketch map earlier and Massa's pointer tapped that. "Now here, and here are two other readings of a different type, one differing from the other—three kinds in all." She made checks now on the map surface with yellow for the first, red for the second, blue for the last.

Yellow marked the building toward which the two on the bridge headed, red lay behind them.

"Those blue—they are near the outer rim." Tan surveyed the results with satisfaction. He had brought back enough to keep the computer busy. Catching those two in the open had been the crowning bit of luck—Tan's luck.

"The creature to the fore,"—Ayana moved closer, "it has been hurt." Her medic-trained eyes were not deceived by the effects of rain and wet fur. Was she watching part of a drama such as one had on a story tape—perhaps the rescue of a wounded comrade from the enemy?

"Fighting?" Tan sounded excited. "Two species at war?"

She looked up from the screen, startled by that note in his voice. His eyes were shining. It took a cer-

tain temperament to produce a scout. Tan had tested high in all the attributes the commanders believed necessary. But there had followed rigid training. And the Tan who had survived that training, winning over all others to gain his place with this crew, was not exactly the same Tan to whom she had been drawn.

Ayana knew that her own place in the ship depended not only on her ability to do her own job, but also on the fact that she was a complement to Tan, supplying what he lacked. It was the same with Jacel and Massa. They had to complement one another or they would not have been put together to form a crew, necessarily living closely during the voyage; their personalities were so related as to assure the least possible friction.

But now there was something in Tan Ayana shrank from, refused to face. The Tan who had come out of the grueling training had a hardness which she secretly feared. He could look upon that wounded body dragging painfully along, and what he thought of was the struggle which had caused those hurts. It was as if he actually wanted to watch such a battle. And that Tan—no, she would not believe that that Tan was the ruler of the mind and body she loved.

"But there is not"—Massa, frowning, paid no attention to Tan's comment "a single life-reading for our own kind! Yet this is a city built by man. We have landed on a site such as our fathers made on Elhorn, save that they did not ring it about there with a city—a city so vast that Tan's record"—she shook her head—"is more than we expected—"

"Expected?" Tan challenged that. "We can expect anything here! This is the world which sent the First

Ships into space, where secrets, all the secrets we need, lie waiting!"

"And from which," Jacel pointed out dryly, "our own kind seems to have gone. We had better keep that in mind when we go prying about for secrets, lest some of those we find are other than we care to own or discover. Do not forget that this city has inhabitants—such as these—" He pointed to the reader. "And do not forget either, Tan, that those men of mighty secrets, our parents of the First Ships, fled in such fear that they tried to keep hidden the very existence of this world."

Tan looked impatient. "We have protection that those animals do not know of—"

"Animals who carry lasers?" Jacel was not to be shaken. "And if this is indeed a storehouse of waiting secrets, perhaps some of them are already in the paws—or hands—of those who intend to keep them. We walk softly, slowly, and with all care now. Or it may be, in spite of caution, we cease to walk at all."

He did not put any undue emphasis on those words. Yet they carried the force of an order. Ayana hoped that the conditioning they had all accepted—that the will of Jacel was to hold in any final decision—would continue to control Tan. Let him work off his restlessness, his energy, in his sky exploration of the city.

It would seem that her hopes held the next day. The storm died before midnight, and sunrise brought a fair day. The light caught the windows in the buildings, some of which did not seem windows at all but clear bands running in levels around the towers. And those blazed as the sun struck them fairly.

Tan took off in the flitter, this time to trace the

outer boundaries of the city. Again he carried equipment to feed back to their computer all the data he gained. The others did not lift ramp at once, but set out sensors to pick up any approach at ground level. Jacel supervised that, being very careful about the linkage. When he had finished he stood up.

"Nothing can pass that. A blade of grass blown by the wind would cause an alarm," he said with conviction.

Ayana had climbed part way up the ramp. She shaded her eyes against the steadily warming blaze of the sun, tried to view the flitter. But Tan must have streaked straight away, wasting no time hovering as he had yesterday.

That furred creature, the hurt one—it must have long since reached the tower. She wished she could remember why it seemed so familiar. The records of the First Ships, because of that destruction, often withheld just the details one needed most.

Oddly enough it came to her back in her own cabin, and from the strangest source. She had been led by that feeling of nostalgia to open her small packet of allowed personal items. They were, perhaps to a stranger, a queer collection. There was a flower preserved between two inch-wide squares of permaplast, its violet-blue as richly vivid as it had been when she had encased it. And a water-worn pebble that came from the stream outside her home at Veeve Station. She had kept it because the crystalline half was so oddly joined to the black stone. And then there was Putti—

Ayana stared now at Putti wide-eyed. There had always been Puttis—round and soft, made for chil-

dren. They were traditional and common. She had kept hers because it was the last thing her mother had made before she died of the one illness on Elhorn they had found no remedy for. Puttis were four-legged and tailed. Their heads were round, with shining eyes made of buttons or beads, upstanding pointed ears, whiskers above the small mouth. Puttis were loved, played with, adored in the child world; their origin was those brought by children on the First Ships.

She had seen one of those original Puttis, also preserved in permaplast. And that one had been covered with fur.

Putti! She could not be right, to compare the soft toy with that muscular furred creature on the bridge. But Putti could have been made by someone trying to represent just such a creature in softer materials than flesh, blood, and bone. She was about to start up, to hunt Jacel and Massa with news of her discovery, when second thoughts argued against that. The resemblance, now that she studied Putti closely, grew less and less. She might make the connection in her own mind, but that was not proof. Putti, a toy—and a weapon-bearing primitive (if not an animal) skulking through buildings long deserted by her kind— No, it was foolish to expect the others to accept that suspicion.

Furtig held the platter of meat on his knee and tried to show proper manners by not stuffing his mouth or chewing too loudly. He was hungry, but there was Liliha, smoothing her tail as she rested on a thick cushion, now and then fastidiously flicking some small suggestion of dust from her fur. He could hear, just, her very muted throat purr, as if she were lost in some pleasant dream. But he did not doubt she was aware of every move he made. So he curbed his appetite and tried to copy the restraint of the In-born.

"The flyer"—she broke her self-absorption—"is in the air again. It does not hang above us but has headed toward the west. Dolar and two scouts saw it rise. There was a Demon in it."

"It is not like the servants here then, able to go on its own?" Furtig wanted to keep her talking. Just to have Liliha sitting there while he ate, relaxed in the thought that he had won to safety through such adventures as most warriors never dreamed of, and that he had rested well and was ready to follow the outer trails again, was pleasing.

"So it would seem. They made it of pieces they brought in the sky-ship."

Furtig marveled at her patience. He should have remembered that; Gammage had spoken of it the night before. But at that time Furtig had not been thinking too clearly. Now he glanced up hastily, but Liliha was not eyeing him with scorn.

"If they made it," she continued, "then within these lairs may lie that which can also be used for the same purpose. Gammage has set those who watched the making into search for such."

Privately Furtig did not doubt that, given the time and the means, the Ancestor and his followers would be able to duplicate the flyer. But then to find someone to fly in it—that was a different matter. Though he could imagine Gammage ready to make the attempt if offered the chance. He, himself, preferred to do his traveling—and any fighting—on the solid and dependable ground. But there were advantages to such craft. They could take a scout higher than any spy tree. Just as the Demon was now viewing the lairs from above.

On the other hand, unless the Demon had some un-heard-of way of looking through solid roofs and walls, he would see only the lairs and not what or who moved in them under cover. Only in the open country could such servants be used to advantage.

Furtig swallowed the last mouthful of meat. Now he raised the bowl and lapped as mannerly as he could at the residue of good juices gathered in the bottom. The lair people lived well. They had fish, found in small inner lakes (made it would seem for no other purpose than to hold them in readiness to be eaten). And there were other places where birds and rabbits were preserved in runs, fed and kept safe until they were needed.

The cave people might well think of that. Suppose they kept alive some of the creatures they hunted or netted, fed them in pens. Then when game became scarce and the weather ill for hunters, there would be food at hand. Yes, there were more things than Demon knowledge to be learned here in the lairs.

He ran his tongue along the bowl rim to gather up the last drop, then licked upper and lower lips clean.

"What of the Barker?" he asked.

He still believed that Gammage's plan of trying to make truce with Barkers would not work. But he was also wary of guessing the outcome of any of the An-cestor's plans. He had witnessed too much of what had been accomplished here for that.

"Dolar has sent a party with two of the rumblers. The Rattons fear those greatly, for they run forward, crunching all in their path, and cannot be turned aside in any way the Rattons have yet discovered. With those to break a path for our warriors we hope to free the Barker. In the meantime—Foskatt has found the other tapes, and they are being brought back. Ku-La is out of the healing place. Soon he will go to talk to his people."

"As I must to the Elders of the caves." Furtig stood up. He was no longer tired, nor was his fur matted by crawling through the dust of the ducts and then through the pelting of the storm. It was sleek and smooth. He fastened on his belt neatly, seeing that in the newly improvised loop there was still the lightning-bolt weapon of the Demons. Apparently that was yet his.

Such a weapon would impress the Elders. If he remembered rightly Gammage's words during that last meeting, he would be given other weapons to influence their decision. The sooner he took the trail to that purpose then, the better. He said so as he finished checking his belt.

"Well enough," Liliha agreed. Her guidance would take them through the lairs to the best point from which to strike out for the caves.

Furtig had slept a long time, almost a full day. It was close on evening and shadows were painting larger and larger pools for concealment as, at last, the three of them threaded a way through silent corridors, past echoing rooms which might not have known life and use since the Demons died or fled. As a guide Liliha went first, wearing a pack between her slim shoulders and around her waist the same belt of tools and weapons as the warriors wore. Then came Furtig and Foskatt, ready to play rear guard if needed.

They must move their swiftest while under the protection of the lair roofs, Furtig thought. For he did not forget the flyer. Why the Demon had not killed them on the bridge was a mystery to him. And he did not want death to strike out of the sky now. It was difficult enough to fight at ground level.

If Demons could see in the dark, then even the coming of night would not aid them. To the end of the lairs they could keep under cover, descending to the underground ways when there was need. But Furtig did not forget that wide expanse of open between the lairs and the beginning of the growth that provided normal cover for his kind. He hoped the night would be cloudy when they reached that point.

Liliha brought them to a window from which they could see that open space. They were at the edge of the lairs. Furtig's sense of direction was in operation. They were to the north of that place where he had crossed before, but not too much so.

He studied the strip narrowly. His own fur was dark, not far different in shade from the withered grass. And Foskatt had the same natural adaptation to the country. It was different for Liliha. Not only was her fur lighter, but it was so thin a coating of fluff that she might well be sighted from above.

"Look you, woods warriors," she said as he commented on that. She slipped off her pack and shook out something she had taken from it. Now she held not a small square but a mass of something—

Furtig shook his head and tried to concentrate on

what she held. But it was no use—his keen sight failed him. He could *not* look at it directly! To do so made him queasy. He wanted to strike out, tear that disturbing substance from her.

But she was winding it about her. And where that stuff covered her body, he could no longer look. Finally only her head remained free of the distortion.

"Another Demon secret, and one but lately discovered. Gammage has but two of these, cut from a single one. When I wear this no one can look at me. Unless he wishes to have his eyes turn this way, that way, and his head whirl about. Now, do not worry about me, look to yourselves, warriors, and cross quickly. The flyer makes itself known by noise. If you hear it coming, take what cover the land offers.

"I shall meet you where the trees grow. Good traveling to you."

Furtig could not look at her at all now. She had pulled a flap of the distorting stuff up over her head and become hidden. He had to turn away and knew she slipped out the window only by the faint sounds made by her going.

"The Demons," remarked Foskatt, "seem to have an answer for any problem. Let us hope that such answers can, in turn, be used against them. She is well gone. It is indeed a kind of hiding I am glad we do not have to deal with often. To the trail then, clan brother!"

The window was wide enough to let them slip through together. Furtig crouched on the ground almost happily. It was good to feel fresh soil and not pavement, the ways of the Demons. He did not look ahead yet, having no wish to see some eye-twisting shimmer in the moonlight covering Liliha's going. His hunter's training took over, and he fell back into the patterns he had learned as a youngling.

It was difficult to keep on listening for the beat in the sky, the possible return of the flyer. Once within the screen of the brush beyond the open, Furtig rose to his full height and gave a purring sigh of relief.

"For so far," Foskatt echoed his feeling, "we have done well. But—"

Furtig swung around. He had picked up a scent that was not Liliha's. No, this was strong and rank. He was downwind of a Tusker, probably more than one. And that surprised him, for Tuskers had no interest in the lairs, very little curiosity about their past, and were seldom to be found hereabouts.

There was still a truce between the People and the Tuskers. And they shared the same territories, since the Tuskers fed upon roots and vegetation. Though the Tuskers were meat, they had no appeal for the People, they were far too formidable to be prey.

Furtig could hear now that low grunting which was Tusker speech. None of the People could imitate it, any more than Tusker throat and tongue could shape the proper words of a warrior. But they understood sign language and could answer it.

A warning? Did the Tuskers know of the flyer? It might be well to suggest that they keep under cover. Furtig uttered a low wailing cry to announce his coming. And without waiting to see if Foskatt followed, swung into the heavy, disagreeable scent which would lead him to the grubbing ones.

When he reached them, they were in battle formation, their big heads, weighed down by the great curved tusks which named them, low to the ground. The old warriors stood still, watching with their small red eyes. One or two of the younger ones on the back fringes of the party pawed the soil, kicking it up in warning.

They were not a full family party as Furtig had expected. There were no females or younglings behind that outer defense of one great Elder and such of his male offspring as had not yet gone to start their own families. Furtig knew that Elder—the seam of an old scar across his nose marked him. Unlike the People the Tuskers had kept to four feet, never learning to walk on two. Also they used no weapons except those nature provided. But mind to mind they were no less than warriors of the caves or the lairs.

Furtig saw that they were deeply angered and would have to be approached with care. For the temper of such as Broken Nose was uncertain when he was in such a mood. Furtig advanced no closer, but sat down, curling his tail over his feet in a peace sign.

The younger Tuskers snorted. One pawed again, wrinkling lips to show fangs. Furtig paid them no attention. It was Broken Nose who ruled here. Having waited for a small time to show that he had not only come in peace but for good reason, he held out his hands and began to try to tell the complicated story of the Demons' landing, of the flyer, in a series of signs.

One of the younglings grunted and his neighbor shouldered him roughly into silence. Encouraged, Furtig ran through his signs slowly, began to tell the same tale again. This was no exchange of general news about the countryside; he must improvise signs to explain things totally new to both their peoples.

And having told it twice, he could only wait to see if he had been clever enough to get his message into a form Broken Nose could understand. For a very long moment he waited and his heart sank. The boar made no move. It could be Furtig had failed. He was about to begin again when Broken Nose grunted.

One of the younger of his band moved forward a little. He squatted clumsily on his haunches, balancing so he could raise one hoofed foot from the ground to gesture or use to draw in the leaf mold.

It was a complicated business that exchange of information. But at last Furtig thought he had the story, and his fur stiffened and he hissed.

The Tuskers had witnessed the landing of the Demon ship, though its final settling to the ground had been hidden by the lairs. The unusual flashing of fire had alarmed Broken Nose. He was old and wily enough to know that suspicion and safety went hand in hand. So he had sent his females and younglings into what he believed good hiding in a rock-walled place where there was but one entrance, which would be well defended by two nonbreeding females, both formidable opponents. Then he, with his warriors, had set out to discover the meaning of the strange fire.

Having prowled along the edge of the flat lands beyond the lairs, they had decided there was no danger and had withdrawn. But they had been starting out of their stronghold among the rocks only this afternoon when the flyer had appeared.

There was a sudden giddiness, a strange feeling in their heads. Even Broken Nose had fallen as one gored. From the belly of the flyer had come what the Tusker could only describe as a long root. This had somehow caught up two of the smallest younglings, jerked them aloft. Then the flyer had gone away.

It was Broken Nose's firm intention to track down the attacker and wreak full vengeance—though he was clever enough not to charge in, but to scout the enemy position first. And the fact that he had seen the flyer disappear into the lairs had shaken him. For that was country he did not know, and many dangers might lurk there.

13

"Hunters—at least of Tuskers—" Foskatt spoke for the first time.

The soft growl in Furtig's throat grew louder. Not that he had any kin ties with the young of the Tuskers. But if today it had been those of Broken Nose who disappeared into the flyer, tomorrow that might appear at the caves and lift some youngling Furtig knew.

That there was any hope of freeing the captives he doubted. And Furtig thought the old Tusker knew that, knew also that his proposed expedition against the lairs would be hopeless.

Alone, yes. But what if Gammage's urging could not only bring in the People, but the Tuskers as well? Furtig rubbed his hands across his furred chest, tried to think out telling signs for communication.

Furtig was startled by a sharp grunt from one of the young Tuskers. A moment later the familiar scent of Liliha filled his nostrils. She came to sit down beside him, no longer muffled in that distorting material. And her coming gave him an idea of how to approach the Tusker Elder.

Swiftly he began to sign, trying to put all the meaning he could into that flexing of fingers, waving of hands, drawing on the ground. The moon was full tonight, and this small clearing was well lighted.

The Tuskers appeared to follow the explanation that this female was one who lived in the lairs, one who sought the secrets of the Demons in order to defeat them with their own weapons. Having finished, Furtig spoke to Liliha without turning his head:

"Show them something to prove the powers of the lairs."

There on the ground where he had drawn suddenly shone a round of yellow light. The Tuskers grunted. Furtig could hear the youngsters stamp nervously, though Broken Nose betrayed no sign of surprise. As Elder he must so assert his superiority.

"This"—Furtig moved his hands into that light— "is one of the secrets of the lairs. We have others, many others. So that this time the Demons will not find us defenseless. There is one ship of them only, and we have counted but four Demons."

"Scouts may run before the tribe," pawed out the young boar. "There may be many more coming."

"True. But now we are warned. There are many hiding places in the lairs." Furtig was getting a little excited. It might be he was going to win allies for Gammage even before he reached the caves and had to face the skepticism of his own Elders.

"And no dangers?"

"There are Rattons there, on the lower levels."

This time Broken Nose himself grunted. Rattons could be understood better than Demons. If the Tuskers had not seen Rattons, they had heard of them and their devilish traps. Then Foskatt spoke softly:

"We have little time to argue with the Tuskers. This is a matter of our own people."

He was right. They had delivered a warning to the Tuskers, who must now make their own decision to flee beyond the range of the flyer or to stand and fight. Furtig began the last signs—

"We go to our people. But watch for the flyer—stay under cover."

Again Broken Nose grunted. This was an order to his own followers, for they turned and trotted into the bushes, only the old boar and his interpreter lingering. The latter signed:

"We stay to watch."

Furtig was glad of their choice. Those eyes in the huge tusked head, swung low before him, seemed small. But he knew their keen vision. There was no more deadly foe to be faced than this clan when its anger was roused and it prepared for battle. There could be no strangers leaving the lairs along here that the Tuskers would not mark. And, Furtig thought, even armed though they might be with strange weapons, if the Demons came on foot, they had better come warily. For all their bulk and seeming clumsiness, the Tuskers were able to lurk undetected in hiding. They had vanquished Barkers many times in red defeat, using the wind itself to mask their scent.

Ayana gazed at the plate before her. The meat's rich

juices formed a natural gravy. The others were eating eagerly, with the greed of those who have been on E rations for a long time. The meat had tested harmless, resembling the best one could find on Elhorn. Why then did it nauseate her to look at it? She lifted a piece to her lips, found she could not bite into it. Why?

"A whole herd," Tan said between mouthfuls. "We shall have food in plenty close to hand."

Ayana continued to look at the meat. It was well cooked, and, while it had been cooking, the savor had made her mouth water. She had hardly been able to wait, any more than the others, until it was ready. She had been as eager as they to taste the first real food they had seen since they lifted.

"Luck, pure luck," Tan continued, "running into these on my first cast into the open country. They have not been hunted for a long time. Easy enough to pick up a couple."

Ayana stood up. She had been fighting the thought valiantly with all her strength of will. But it broke now through her defense, and she could not control her words.

"How do we know that—this is an animal?"

She was a fool, of course. But there were those furred things on the bridge. Without the trappings, the weapon, they might be called animals. Yet she was sure they were not. These things they had cooked had not had the same appearance, that was true. But they knew too little, far too little of this world. She could not stomach meat which might be—be the flesh of intelligent beings. There, she had faced the thought which had struggled darkly in her mind. With a little

194

cry she clapped her hands over her mouth, pushed past Jacel, and hurried, not only from the cabin but down through the ship until she reached the ramp hatch.

But that was closed; they were sealed in. And it seemed to her that she must have fresh air, that the fumes of the cooked meat, which she had thought so appetizing earlier, were now a sickening vapor.

Ayana battered at the hatch fastening, the door rolled open, and she could fill her lungs with the air of night. Then hands fell in a harsh, punishing grip on her shoulders, jerking her back into the ship's shell.

"What are you trying to do? Set yourself up as a perfect target for anything out there?" Tan was angry. She had heard that note in his voice only a few times in her life.

He pushed her to one side forcibly, turned to reseal the hatch. Ayana rubbed her arm, blinking fiercely. Tan was not going to see betraying tears in her eyes.

When he had the seal tight, he swung around, his eyes hot and hard, watching her.

"Now—what did you mean by that scene?" he demanded as if there had never been, or could be, any good feeling between them.

And his hostility awakened her own spirit.

"Just what I said. We know too little of the situation here. You thought of those beings on the recorder tape as animals. But they are not, and deep in your mind, you know that. Now—you bring others back— for food!" Her revulsion returned. She had to cover her mouth for a moment. "We do not know what they are!"

"You need a mind-clear treatment!" His anger was

chilling, no longer hot and impulsive but worse. He was entering one of those remote moods when he froze anyone who tried to communicate. "You saw what I brought back. It was all animal. Perhaps"—he came a little closer, stood looking down at her with that cold menace—"perhaps you do need a mind-clear. You did not test out as entirely level-stable—"

"How do you know that?" Ayana demanded.

Tan laughed, but there was no lightness of spirit in that sound.

"I had my ways of learning what I needed to know. It is always well to be aware of the weaknesses of one's fellows. Yes, I know your L report, my dear Ayana. And do you believe that I cannot put that knowledge to the best use?"

He caught her shoulders again and shook her, as if to impress her with his strength of both body and will. It was as if that ruthless handling shook from her mind a shield she had clung to for years. Tan was—Tan was— She stared at him, beaten for the moment, not by his will, but by her own realization of what Tan really was.

"We will have no more stupid imaginings." He did not wait for her to answer; perhaps he believed she was fully cowed. "Eat or not—if you wish to starve that is your decision. But you will keep your mouth shut on such ideas!"

Jacel, Massa, were not fools, nor, Ayana believed, could they be dominated by Tan. If what she had said made them consider— But for the present, until she had time to think, she must let him believe that he had won. Though he appeared to have no suspicion that he had not. There was confidence in the way he pulled her around, shoved her at the ladder, with the unspoken but implied order to go aloft.

The worst was that Ayana must continue to share their small cabin. The horror that grew in her was even greater than the desolation she had known moments earlier. Tan would enforce such a relationship, she knew. There was only one escape. She was the medic—and the cramped medic-lab cabin was hers alone. She could shelter there until she had time to think things out.

She climbed, her thoughts racing. If Tan believed he had broken any resistance in her— One level more —the medic cabin. She had hardly believed she could escape him so easily. But she made a quick dash, thumb-locked the door behind her. She fully expected him to bat out his rage against its surface. But there was only utter and complete silence.

Ayana backed away until she came up against the patient's bunk. She faced the door, taut, listening. When there came no assault, she relaxed on the edge of the bunk.

The palms of her hands were sweating, she felt weak, sick. The confrontation of the past few moments had frightened her as she had never been frightened before in her life. Tan knew her L report. He could turn that to his own advantage. Every weakness, every way of reaching her had been charted on that! He could use such knowledge to influence the others to distrust her. Her outburst at the table had given him a base on which to build false claims. She had played directly into his hands— She was—

Ayana began to fight back. He had thrown her so far off base that he had gained the advantage for a

197

while. It was time she forgot what had happened and began to consider the immediate present. She had been warned; perhaps Tan had made his first mistake in revealing that he thought he could dominate her.

Think, use her brain; she had a good one, L report or not. Ayana had a good and useful mind. Now was the time to put it to work, not allow herself to become enmeshed by emotion, let alone fear, the most weakening of all.

She must not depend on either Jacel or Massa, but stand alone. For if Tan could prove to be an entirely different person from the one she thought she knew, loved, then whom could she trust? Herself—and her skills. Ayana began to look about the cabin and what it contained. Herself and her skills—perhaps she would find that enough

Though she did not rise, her head was up, her shoulders no longer hunched as if she expected at any moment to feel the sting of a lash laid across them. She was Ayana and she fought to remain that—herself, not something owned by Tan!

Bright as the moon had been in the clearing, it was no guide to paths under the growth cover. But Furtig slipped along easily, treading the way in memory as well as if he walked one of the well-paved ways of the Demons. These were hunting lands where those of the caves often came.

The night had voices, birds whose hunting also depended upon the cover of the dark hours, insects, smaller life, which stilled instantly as the scent of the travelers reached them.

Furtig breathed deeply, planted each foot with pleasure in the fact that it met soil and not the hard surface of a corridor. He was of the caves after all. And with every whisper of sound, the rich scents the wind brought him, he rejoiced.

Liliha, for all her In-born life, did not lag, but with gliding grace matched the pace the two warriors set. Perhaps she looked from right to left and back again more often than they, for to her this was all new. But she appeared to find more interest than cause for alarm in what lay about.

They halted at a spring Furtig remembered well, drank their fill, ate of the supplies they had carried with them from the lairs. But always they listened, not for the usual night sounds, but for the beat of the Demon flyer within weapon reach overhead.

"If there are only four of them," Furtig said, "then they can be defeated. Even if they are scouts—if they did not return, their clan would take warning."

"It depends," Foskatt pointed out, "on why they scout. If it is merely to seek new ground, and they do not return, yes, perhaps that would be the end for their kin."

"We cannot," Liliha said with the assurance of the In-born, to whom the study of Demons was a way of life, "judge anything that the Demons do by what we would do in their place. They do not think as we."

"If they think straightly at all," Foskatt growled. "Remember the old tales—in the final days after the Demons had loosed their own doom, they were so twisted in their ways that they hunted and preyed upon each other, dealing death to their kin as well as to our kind in turn. And it would seem that they have begun such ways once more. At least they have taken the Tusker younglings without cause—for one purpose—"

"Again you are not sure," Liliha countered. "It may be they have taken the younglings to study them, to see what manner of people are now in possession of the world they ruled so evilly in the old days."

"I do not think so," Furtig said. He was unable to prove that Foskatt was right in his reading of the Demons' motives. But somehow he was as sure of it as if he had indeed witnessed the outcome of the stealing of Broken Nose's young.

"Why did they not capture Ku-La and me in the same fashion?" he continued. Ever since he had heard of that seizure from the air which the flyer had practiced, this had puzzled him. It would have been very easy to capture the two of them from that open bridge. Of course, had the Demon tried it, Furtig had held the lightning weapon. Was that why they had escaped? Had the Demon seen and recognized from aloft the lightning thrower? If so—then Gammage's plan to arm as many of the People as they could had great merit.

It was as if Liliha now read his thoughts. "You were a warrior, armed—not a helpless and frightened youngling. It may be that the Demon wanted no trouble with captives so he chose the least dangerous that could be found. How much farther are these caves of yours?" she ended briskly.

"If we do not have to turn from the straight trail, we shall be there shortly after sunrise."

They kept on under trees, using brush as a canopy where trees thinned or failed. They crossed any open space with a rush, always listening for ominous sounds from the air. Dawn found them working their way into the higher lands of the caves. Furtig heard the yowl of the first sentry, alerting the next. That cry would pass from one to the other until it reached the ears of the Elders. He did not know if he had been recognized for himself, or merely as one of the People.

But the fact that the three came openly was in their favor. Sentries and guards would loosely encircle them as they went but would not try to stop them. However, as the three breasted the next-to-the-last slope before they reached the cliff of the caves, they were fronted by one who rose out of the dried grass to await them. Her gray fur was silken, shining in the sun. And though she was small, she held herself proudly erect.

"Eu-La!" The sight of her brought back the warm memory of how she had sent him forth on this venture armed not only with the fighting claws she had found, but also with her belief in him.

"Cave brother," she said gravely, as gravely as one who had mothered younglings, so dignified was she. But her eyes slid from him to Liliha and her lips parted on a hiss.

"You bring a strange Chooser—!" She spat the words as if they were an ill saying.

"Not so!" He should have known. Just as a warrior would flatten ears and twitch tail at the sight of a non-kinsman, so would female meet strange female. "This is Liliha, an In-born of the lairs. She has not

201

chosen, nor will she, save among her own kin—that is lair law."

Eu-La was openly suspicious, but she looked again to Liliha, studying her carefully.

"She is not like the cave Choosers. That is true."

"And it is also true, as your kinsman has said," Liliha uttered in the throaty, purring voice of friendship, "that I have not come to choose among you, but to speak of other things, things of danger, to your Elder Chooser."

She moved closer, and, as if Eu-La were suddenly convinced, they each extended a pink tongue, touched it to the cheek of the other, in the touch-of-friend.

"Open is the cave of Eu-La to Liliha of the lairs," Eu-La said. Then she looked to Foskatt, who had fallen a little behind. "But this is also a stranger."

"Not quite so, cave kin. I was once of the caves before I went seeking Gammage. I am Foskatt, but perhaps you have not heard my name, for I went forth seasons ago."

"Foskatt," Eu-La repeated. "Ah, you are of the cave of Kay-Lin. The Elder Chooser there has spoken your name."

He was startled. "And who is that Elder Chooser?"

"She is Fa-Ling."

"Fa-Ling! Who was litter sister of my mother! Then indeed I still have close kin in the caves!"

"But you, Furtig, have you learned all Gammage's secrets that you return?" There was a teasing purr in Eu-La's voice.

"Not all, sister. But a few—yes." His hand went to the lightning thrower at his belt. "But more than any talk of secrets, we bring news for the Elders."

"Two sets of Elders now," she told him. "There have been changes at the caves. The western People have come to join us. They have taken over the lower caves. A new tribe of Barkers moved into their lands and they lost five warriors and an Elder in battle. There is much fear now that the Barkers move against us next. And it is a large pack."

Furtig listened closely. Perhaps now the Elders might agree to Gammage's plan. If they believed that they could not hold the caves, even uniting two tribes, they might be pushed into trekking to the lairs.

Save—the Demons and what had happened to the younglings of the Tuskers. Perhaps one could suggest that the cave clans take to flight, yes. But away from both Barkers and lairs, not into the buildings where Rattons and Demons alike waited. Bad or good, Furtig could not judge. He could only deliver the message and warning he carried.

Resolutely Furtig continued on, Eu-La matching him step to step. Now and then she glanced at him measuringly, as if so trying to read his thoughts. But she asked no questions, seemed pleased enough that he had returned.

Her acceptance of Liliha had been quick. Furtig hoped that was a sign that the other females would do the same. If the In-born could continue to make it clear that she was no threat to their mate-choice, he did not see why they would be hostile. Compared to Eu-La—or Fas-Tan—her scantily furred body might not please, might seem to be ugly. Though being used now to the In-born Furtig did not consider it so. But he hoped, for the sake of their mission, that the others would.

If Liliha had any vanity she had not displayed it. And perhaps now she was quick enough to see that the uglier and stranger she made herself seem, the more acceptable she would be. Ugly, strange—the two things Liliha could never truly be!

Ayana moved in the medic cabin. Her body was stiff; she had held herself so tense, her muscles had cramped. At least she had a plan, but its success depended upon a great many factors. And most of those could only be resolved by time. She had no idea how long she had crouched here, considering what Tan might do, and then what she could do to oppose him.

Yes, time and patience. She must hold on to patience as if it were a safety line. Yet patience had never been a strong part of her.

She rubbed her hands down her cheeks; her face was cold, she shivered slightly. Nervous chill. Suddenly she wished for a mirror, to look into it and see the new Ayana, how much she had been changed by this time of facing black truths and learning that she might live and die by uncertain choices. Just as Tan would never again look to her as when he wore that mask he must always have assumed before her.

As she arose she swayed, clutched for a hand-hold. Not only was she stiff, but movement brought vertigo, as if the whole world were unstable. But Ayana reached a cabinet in the wall, brought out a tube of tablets. One of those she held to dissolve under her tongue. She did not mind its bitter taste.

Now she worked swiftly, stripping the shelves of

*certain things, until a small pile of vials and tubes lay
on the bunk. Possession of those gave her weapons
and defenses. But she must find somewhere to conceal
them.*

14

"Thus it is." Furtig faced the Elders, and not only them but all those in the caves, who had crowded in crouching rows behind. He could read no emotion in their eyes, which, when the light of Gammage's lamp touched them, were like disks of glowing fires, orange, red, and green. At least the messengers had been given cave hospitality—not warned off.

Before him lay the weapons they had brought. And he had demonstrated each. There were two lightning throwers, another producing a thin stream which made ice congeal about the target, even though this was not the cold season.

The fourth, which Liliha had carried and which she alone knew how to operate, was the strangest of all. For a warrior might escape by luck or chance the other two. However, from this tube spun small threads at Liliha's twirling. Those floated as might a wind-borne spider's web. That web, once launched, was drawn instantly to the warrior at whom Liliha had aimed it, in this case Foskatt.

Once it had touched his shoulder, as if that touch was a signal, it straightaway wrapped itself about his body so he could not move. Nor could he break that hold, though the cords of the web were very fine and thin. Liliha had to cut it in two places, and then the whole thing withered and fell in small black particles to the ground.

The Elders, in spite of this display, kept impassive faces. But from the others came growls and small hisses of wonder and alarm that such things existed. Liliha was frank: these tanglers were few, some did not work at all. But the lairs held endless caches of other wonders.

"But you say"—it was Ha-Hang, one of the Elders of the western tribe, who spoke—"there are others in the lairs. You have spoken of Rattons in force, and Demons, at least as a scouting party. If the Demons have indeed returned, it is best to let them have the lairs. Those of our kind saved their lives before by taking to the wilds when the Demons hunted."

For the first time Foskatt spoke. "Only just, Elder. Remember the tales? It was only because the Demons sickened and died, fought among themselves, that our mother kin and a few mates escaped. It took many seasons thereafter of hiding and bearing litters, in which too many younglings died, before the clans could do more than run and hide.

"These Demons are neither sick nor fighting among themselves. If they come in strength, how long will it be before they hunt us again?"

Furtig did not wait for any to answer that question; he carried on the attack. "Also, Elders, in those days we had no Gammage, no seekers of Demon secrets, to aid us. Those who were our ancestors had no weapons and little knowledge. Compared to us they were as fangless, as clawless, as a newborn youngling. Perhaps these Demons are scouts, but among us how is the move to a new hunting ground made? We send scouts and if they return with ill news, or do not return, then what is the decision? We go not in that direction but seek another.

"These Demons' ancestors must have been those who fled the sickness and the fighting of their kind, even as we fled the lairs. Therefore their legends of the place are sinister; they will be ready to believe that evil awaits them here. And if their scouts do not return—"

It was the best argument he could offer, one which fit in with their own beliefs and customs.

"Demons and Rattons," Fal-Kan said. "And Gammage wishes all, strangers and caves alike, to gather to make war. Perhaps he also speaks of a truce with Barkers?" His voice was a growl, and he was echoed by those about him.

Liliha spoke, and, because she was a Chooser, even Fal-Kan dared not hiss her down. She held out her hand with its strangely long fingers, pointed to where the Elder Chooser of Fal-Kan's cave sat on a cushion of grass and feathers, holding the newest youngling to her furry breast.

"Do you wish the little one to become Demon meat?"

Now the growl arose sharply, ears flattened, and tails lashed. Some of the youngest warriors rose, their claws ready for battle.

"The Tuskers believed they were safe. Would any

of you dare to take a Tusker youngling from his mother's side?"

That picture startled them into silence. All knew there was no fiercer fighter in the whole wilds than the Tusker female when her young was threatened.

"Yet," Liliha continued, "a Demon flying through the air did so. Can you now say that you will be safe in the wilds when this Demon can fly at will, attack from above, perhaps kill with such weapons as these?" She gestured to the display. "In the lairs we have hidden ways to travel, so small the Demons cannot enter. Our only chance is to turn on them, while they are still so few, the very deaths they used in the old days to destroy our kind.

"You war with the Barkers, but not the Tuskers— why is that so?"

It was not an Elder who answered when she paused but Furtig, hoping to impress at least the younger warriors of that company—those not so set in the ways of doing as always.

"Why do we fight the Barkers? Because we are both eaters of meat and there is a limit to hunting lands. The Tuskers we do not fight because they eat what is of no use to us. But there is food in the lairs, much of it, and no need for hunting. And if you saw before you a Barker and a Demon and had a single chance to kill—which would you choose? That is what Gammage now says—that between Barkers and Demons he chooses the Demons as the greater enemy. As for the Rattons, yes, they are a spreading evil within the lairs, and one must be on constant guard against them.

"But also they promise an even worse fate if they

are not put down. For Gammage has proof they seek out the secrets of the Demons also. Do you want Rattons perhaps riding sky things and capturing warriors, and Choosers, and younglings with such as these?"

With his foot he edged forward the tangler so that they could understand his meaning. This time the growl of protest was louder. War with the Barkers was open and fierce, yet there was a grudging respect for the enemy on both sides. The Rattons were different; the very thought of them brought a disgusting taste to the mouth. There were far off, strange legends of individual Barkers and People living together when they were both Demon slaves in the lairs. But Rattons had always been prey.

Ha-Hang spoke first. "You say Barkers are less dangerous than Demons. We have lost warriors to Barkers, none to Demons. And what is a Tusker youngling to us?"

He had a gap on one side of his jaw where he had lost a fighting fang, and both ears were notched with old bite scars. It was plain he was a fighting Elder rather than a planning one.

"Truth spoken!" applauded Fal-Kan.

They were losing, Furtig knew. And perhaps the Elders were right to be cautious. He himself, until he had heard the Tuskers' story of the flyer, had been of two minds about the matter. But those moments when he had lain on the bridge with the Demon hovering over him had given him such a deepset fear of the flyers that he wished he could make it plain to these here what an attack from the air might mean.

Yes, they could hide in the caves. But what if the

Demon took up patrol so they could not come forth again? What if the flyer swept low along the very edge of the cliffs, attacking the cave mouths? Furtig had a hearty respect now for Gammage's warnings against Demon knowledge. One could expect them to do anything!

"This affair concerns not only the caves and their defense," the Chooser of Fal-Kan's cave, she who was of the Ancestor's blood, said throatily. "It also concerns our young. And this matter of the Tuskers' young whose mothers could not defend—"

"We live in the caves, the Tuskers in the open," growled Fal-Kan. And his warriors added a rumble of approval.

"Younglings cannot live in caves all their lives," the Chooser continued. "I would listen to this Chooser from the lairs; let her tell us of the younglings there and how they are cared for. What knowledge have they gained beside that of knowing better how to fight, which is always the first thought in the mind of any warrior?" Fal-Kan dared not protest now, nor interrupt.

So Liliha spoke, not of battles or the need for fighting, but of life within the lairs as the Choosers would see it. She spoke much about the ways of healing which had been discovered, how Choosers about to bear young went to places of healing, and how thereafter the young were perfect in form and quick and bright of mind. She spoke of new foods which ensured even in the times of poor hunting that there would be no hunger, and told of the many things a Chooser might do to make her own life of greater ease and interest.

Some of what she said Furtig had seen with his own eyes, but much of it was as a Chooser would explain it to a Chooser, and this talk in a mixed assembly was new. At first the Elders stirred, perhaps affronted by the breaking of custom, yet not able to deny it when the Choosers themselves, who were even sterner guardians of custom, accepted it. Then Furtig could see even the males were listening with full interest.

She talked well, did Liliha. Foremost in the line of Those-Who-Would-Come-to-Choose sat Eu-La, her eyes fast on the almost hairless face of the female from the lairs. Furtig looked from his clanswoman to Liliha and back again. Then he caught a glimpse of Foskatt.

Perhaps the other had heard Liliha's information many times over, for there was an abstraction about him. He was leaning forward a little, staring at—Eu-La! And there was a bemusement on his face which Furtig knew for what it was. Just so had he seen the Unchosen look at Fas-Tan when she passed with a slow swing of her tail, her eyes beyond them as if, as males yet Unchosen, they had no place in her life.

Eu-La—but she was hardly more than a youngling! A season at least before she would stand with the Choosers. Startled, Furtig studied her. She was no longer a youngling. He had seen that when she had met them outside the caves, but it had not really impressed him.

Eu-La a Chooser? There was a small rumble of growl deep in his throat as he thought of her perhaps in the open with a Demon flyer above. Furtig's fingers stretched and crooked involuntarily, as if he wore his fighting claws.

213

But he had no time to consider such things now, for Liliha had finished and the Elder of the Choosers spoke:

"There is much to be thought on, kin sisters. Not yet, Elders, warriors, Unchosen, are the cave people ready to say that this or that will be done."

Never in his life had Furtig heard a Chooser speak so before. But perhaps the Elders had, for not one of them protested her decision. And the gathering broke up, the Choosers threading into the caves, Liliha following the Chooser who had spoken.

Furtig and Foskatt gathered the sample weapons into their carrying bag again. The warriors padded out into the dark, making no sound as they moved. And the guardian of the lamp had come to stand beside it as if impatient for Furtig and Foskatt to follow.

"What do you think?" Furtig asked in a whisper. "Has Liliha made the right impression?"

"Ask me not the way of a female mind," returned Foskatt. He was tightening the cords about the bundle. "But it is true that when it comes to the general safety and good of younglings it is the Choosers who decide. And if they believe that the lairs promise more than the caves, then these people will go to Gammage."

Had Tan thought about the advantage this cabin gave her? Ayana sat up on the bunk in the medic-lab. She had no idea how long she had been asleep, but she awoke with a mind free of that fear and despair which had held her. Was it the fact that she had been selected, even conditioned, to be the other half of Tan that had made her so helpless?

But, if they had selected, conditioned her so, that preparation had not endured. She would think for herself, be herself—and not Tan's mate, Tan's other part, from now on.

Looking back at the years on Elhorn, even the days of the voyage, Ayana could not understand the person she had been. It was as if she had slept and was now awake. And Tan—certainly Tan had changed too! It could not be only the alteration in herself which had caused the break between them.

She had known him to be impatient of restraint, curious to the point of recklessness. But now all his faults were intensified; never before had he been ruthless or cruel. It was as if this world, the long-sought home of their kind, had acted on him—on her—

And if that was so—what of Jacel, Massa? Were they, too, other people? If they were now four others, their old, carefully cultivated close relationship broken, how could they work as a unit, do their duty here?

Ayana looked at the small kit she had put together before she had slept, and she shivered. What had been in her mind to seek out those particular drugs and want to hide them—or USE them? She had been more emotionally disturbed than she could believe possible, in spite of all her training.

If she, a medic, one supposedly dedicated to the service of life, could, in some wild moment of terror, contemplate such an array of armament, what would the others do? She might do well now to destroy all which lay there, so that if such wild thoughts came to mind again there would be nothing—

Save that which lay there could help as well as harm. The drugs were specially selected for this voyage and they could not be replaced. No, not destruction; however—concealment.

No one knew this cabin, its fittings, better than she did herself. Ayana began a careful search for a hiding place, finding it at last, and strapping the packet on the underside of the bunk.

That done, Ayana faced her ordeal. She must leave the safety of this cabin, go out into the ship. Somehow she must be able to pass off what had happened as a temporary emotional storm, and present to all eyes, including Tan's, the appearance of firm self-control.

As she forced herself to her own cabin, she met no one. There was no sound in the ship. Twice she paused to listen. Without the vibration, the life which had coursed through its walls while they were spaced, this whole complex of cabins had a curious hollow and empty feeling.

It—it was as if she were encased in a dead thing! Ayana caught her lip between her teeth, bit upon it hard that that small pain might be a warning. Emotions rising, fear— What was wrong with her?

She would have no armor against Tan's charges, against the others, until she could face this objectively. Was it herself—or this world? Was there something about this planet that upset her, forced her out of her pattern of living? It was better to believe that than to think that there was a flaw so deep in her that she was breaking because of it.

No one in the cabin. But Tan's protect suit was gone. He must have taken off again. And where—when—?

Ayana climbed to the control cabin. No one there—had they all gone and left her? Alone in a dead ship, on a world which their ancestors had fled after some disaster so great that it must be erased from all records?

She almost fell down the steps in her hurry to seek the cabin of Jacel and Massa. But now she smelled food—the mess cabin!

Massa sat there alone. Between her hands was a mug of hot nutrient. Of the two men there was no sign.

"Massa—"

She looked up and Ayana was startled out of asking the question she had ready. Massa was older than Ayana by a planet year or two. She had never been a talkative person, but there had been about her such an air of competence and serene certainty that her presence was soothing. Perhaps that was one of the factors the home authorities had considered when they made the final selection of the crew. She had always been detached, held people at arms-length. What she was in private to Jacel must have satisfied him. However, Ayana had held the other girl in awe, had not seen in her any ally against Tan.

But this was not Massa's usual serene and untroubled face. She looked as if she had not slept for a long time, and her eyes were red and swollen as if she had been crying. The way she stared back at Ayana—hostile!

That very hostility brought an end to the wall be-

tween them. Had Massa, also, discovered Jacel to be another person?

"Where is Tan—Jacel?" Ayana slipped by to the heating unit, poured herself a mug of nutrient, and seated herself to face Massa, determined now not to be driven off by a forbidding look. In fact, the signs of the disturbance in the other girl acted on her in an oddly calming way.

"You may well ask! Tan—he is like a wild man! What did you do to him?"

"What has Tan done?"

"He has persuaded Jacel to go in—on foot, not in the flyer. On foot! Into what may be a trap. He—he is unmotivated." She spat forth the worst she could find to say about a supposedly trained colleague.

"On foot!" Ayana nearly choked on the mouthful she had taken. Two men in that huge expanse of ruined buildings! They could easily be lost, trapped—

"On foot!" Massa repeated. "They have been gone"—she consulted the timekeeper on the cabin wall above them—"two complete dial circles."

"But the coms! Why are you not monitoring the coms?"

"The hook-up is in." Massa laid her hand on the wall com. "They have not reported for a half circle. I have the repeat demand on automatic. If they answer we can hear them at once."

"We can trace their way in then, through that." Ayana nodded to the com.

"Yes. But dare we try to use it so? I was trying to decide." Massa set her elbows on the table, leaned her head forward into her hands. "Trying to decide," she repeated dully. "If we leave the ship and go hunting and are caught by those creeping horrors—"

"Creeping horrors?"

"Tan went out early this morning. He returned with recordings. The picture was blurred, but it showed small life forms, in an open place between buildings. They signalled him with one of the old recognition codes—though it did not quite make sense by our records. There was no place near that point where he could land the flyer. That's why they went on foot. But I say that those things—they were not people!"

"But to go out like that, it is against everything we have been taught, against all the rules of safety."

Massa shrugged. "It seems that home rules do not apply any more as far as Tan is concerned. And—he came and talked at Jacel—not to him but at him! It was almost evil the way he worked on Jacel, made him believe he was not a real man unless he would go to meet those signalling things. They, neither one of them, would listen to me when I tried to urge some sense. It was as if they were different people from those I had always known. And sometimes, Ayana, I feel different, too. What is this world doing to us?"

There was nothing left of her serene confidence. Rather the eyes now looking into Ayana's were those of someone lost and wandering in a strange and frightening place. So—she was not alone! Massa felt it also, that this world was somehow altering them to fit a new pattern, one which was for the worse, compared to that they had known.

"If we only knew," Ayana said slowly, "the reason why the First Ship people left here. That reason—it *may be that we have to face it again now. And we have no defense, not even guesses. Was it invasion of furred creatures like those on the bridge, or like these others who now signal in our own old codes? Disease? It could be anything."*

"I only know that Jacel has changed, and Tan is a stranger, and I no longer understand myself at times. You are a trained medic, Ayana. Could this air here, which our ship's instruments tells us is good, be some kind of subtle poison? Or is it something from those rows of dead buildings, standing there like bones set on end to mark old graves which must not, for some terrible reason, be forgotten—something reaching out to send us mad?"

Her voice rose higher and higher, her hands began to twitch. Ayana put down her mug, caught those hands to hold them quiet.

"Massa! No, do not imagine things—"

"Why not? What have we left us but what we imagine? I did not imagine that Jacel has taken leave of his senses and gone out to hunt evil shadows in those buildings! He is gone, Tan is gone, and both for no sane reason. You cannot say I have imagined that!"

"No, you have not." By will Ayana kept her own voice level and steady. "But are you of any help now? What if—"

She had no time to see if that argument had any effect on Massa. For at that moment there was a clicking from the com, and they both looked to it, tense, reading in that rattle of sound the message.

"Need aid—Ayana—medic—"

"Jacel!" Massa jerked from Ayana's hold, was on her feet. "He is hurt."

"No. That was Jacel's sending. Did you not recognize it? And if he is sending, he cannot be the one in need." Clicks might not have any voice tone, but they had practiced so long together that they were able to distinguish the sender by rate of speed.

And it would only fit the pattern that Tan, driven by whatever beset him on this world, had gotten into difficulty—bad—or Jacel would not have sent for her.

"Keep on that direction beam." Now that she was being pressed into action, Ayana knew what to do. "We may need a beacon call back."

"I am going too—"

"No. They need a medic, and we must have someone in the ship. Your place is here, Massa."

For a long moment it looked as if she would argue that. Then her shoulders slumped, and Ayana knew she had won.

"I will take a belt com, go in on their out-wave. Set that for me, Massa, while I go to get a suit and my kit."

"And if this is somehow a trap?"

"We have to take that chance. I must go." Ayana faced the bare truth squarely.

15

It was mid-morning with no clouds or sign of storm. The sun was warm, too warm across the glare of fused scars where ships had taken off and landed—how long ago? Beyond, the gray-white cliffs of the buildings. Ayana wearing her protect suit, her belt heavy with explorer's devices and aids, the medic kit at her back, tramped on, the com beep at her belt as a compass.

As long as those she sought wore similar devices she would eventually find them. How long would that take? Her impulse was to run, her self-command kept her to a ground-covering stride which would not invite disaster. There had been no more messages. But she had left Massa at the com in the control cabin ready for any such call.

Massa would relay to her any message, but somehow she was sure that none would come.

Now she approached the buildings. Windows regarded her slyly. The sensation of being spied upon was like a crawling touch on her skin. She had to fight her fears to keep on in the direction the com marked for her.

Though at a distance the blocks of the buildings seemed to ring in solidly the open landing site, yet, as Ayana advanced, she saw that this was not true. There was a space at a side angle, where one could pass between two towers.

The opening was a narrow street at a sharp angle in relation to the port, so that when Ayana was only a step or so down it, she could no longer look back to the ship. But the com urged her ahead—this was the way.

There were drifts of sand and earth at the beginning of the street, but farther down, where the wind could not reach so readily, the pavement was bare. On both sides there were no windows or doors in the first stories of the buildings, leaving them blankly solid like the walls of a fortification. Though well above there were windows. It was not until Ayana reached the first crossway that there was a change. Here were doors, windows, at street level. The doors were closed and she tried none of them. Her beeping guide turned her into another cross street which headed yet farther into the city. They had believed that they had built cities on Elhorn during the last two hundred years. But what they had done there was the piling up of children's blocks compared to this! And what had brought it all to nothing?

There were no signs of such destruction as a natural catastrophe or war might have left. Just silence—but not emptiness! No, with every step she took, Ayana was aware of hidden life. She could not see it, nor hear it, and she did not have a persona detect *(that had gone with Tan), but she knew something was there. So her hand swung close to her stunner, and she looked continuously from side to side, sure that soon—from some doorway—*

Another crossway, again she was to go right according to the com. Something— Ayana stopped short, the stunner now drawn; something had scuttled away up ahead. She was sure imagination had not tricked her. She had actually seen that flicker of motion at a door. All her instincts warned her to retreat, but the beep of the com held steady. Somewhere ahead Jacel, or Tan, or both of them had their coms on call, and that would not happen unless need was greater than caution. She had no choice after all.

But Ayana kept to the middle of the street, well away from those buildings. The open would give her what small advantage there might be. Now she reached the doorway where she had seen the movement. The door there was open, but, as far as she could detect, nothing crouched within. She did not explore. But as she passed it, she went stiff and tense; to have that behind her was bad.

The second cross street brought her out into a place which was in direct contrast to the rest of the city. Here was a sprawl of growing things, a huge, autumn-killed tangle choked in a frame of corroded metal. Ayana, facing that mass, thought she could trace in some of the upright and horizontal crossbeams the frame of a building. But if it had ever been more than just the skeleton of such, the vines and other growth had taken over and destroyed all but the bones.

Much of the riotous vegetation was dry and dead. But from that black, withered mass new shoots rose.

Not of an honest rich green, but of a green that was oddly grayed, as if it were indeed only the ghost of the plants that had put forth new shoots and runners.

It was into the center of that sickly mass that the beep directed her. Though how she could enter such a tangle—

Ayana walked along the outer fringe of the growth, seeking by will, not by inclination, some possible opening. Shortly she came upon a path hacked, broken, burnt. Though why those she sought had forced their way into that unwholesome mass she could not guess.

What bothered her most was the sight of a couple of the ghost-gray vines, perhaps as thick as two fingers together, looped directly across the hacked way. They looked as if they had had days to reestablish themselves, although they could only have had hours.

Slipping her hands into the suit gloves, making sure her flesh was well covered. Ayana reached out and jerked at the stalks. They broke easily, showing hollow stems from which spurted thin streams of reddish liquid. But the noisome smell of rot made her gag.

Broken, the vines visibly shriveled, wilted back against the mass from which they had trailed. Ayana forced herself into the path.

Her boots sank a little at each step into a muck which gave off putrid puffs. Soon, unable to take that continued assault on her nostrils, she stopped to draw up her face mask. What this place had been she could not guess. But the eroded partitions showing here and there were pillars which must have once supported a roof.

The hacked way was several times barred by vines she had to snap. There was no difficulty doing that; they offered no resistance. Except that Ayana had such a horror of touching them, even with gloved hands, that she had to force herself to the act each time.

So she reached the center of this horror garden, if garden it had been. There was a wide, square opening in the ground. Oddly enough, none of the vegetation crowded near that hole, or door. For it was not a chance opening. Around it was a band of stone over which none of the vines hung.

The signal was—down! But how? Ayana shone her hand lamp into the hole. Flashing here and there showed her a room, or perhaps a section of corridor. And the floor was not too far below. If she hung by her hands, with her suit inflated for a landing, she could make it. Again it would seem she had no choice.

Ayana landed. When she got to her feet, swinging the lamp around, she saw that this was a small chamber with a door in only one wall—that way—

What had Tan—Jacel—been hunting which had brought them here? To her it had more and more the smell of a trap. But it had been Jacel who had beamed that help call, and he would not have urged either Massa or her into danger. Or, could one depend on Jacel's reactions any more?

In the underground ways the beep was even louder, more persistent than it had been above. By all indications she was close to what she sought. There was no turning back—

Ayana held the lamp in one hand, her stunner

*ready in the other as she went on. Then she stiffened,
stood very still, listening.*

*Sound ahead, but not a call of her kind, or the
tread of one walking in protect boots, but rather a
swishing noise. She longed to call out, to be reassured
by a human voice that one of those she hunted were
there. But fear kept her dumb. It needed all her will
power to force her ahead.*

*A crosswise passage— At her belt the beep was a
continuous note. She was close to its source. To her
right, along that sideway . . .*

"Ayana!"

*Jacel! Her lips, her mouth were so dried she could
not produce more than a hoarse croak in return. But
she began to run, turned right. And there was light
ahead.*

Furtig sat by the stream from the spring. The morning was going to be fair. He sniffed the air, good
smells. He had not realized how few good smells there
were in the lairs. Oh, there were those places where
things grew, but those seemed different, even if they
were plants. It was as if they had never been the same
as those of the wilds, or else that far back, like the
People, they had been somehow changed. He feasted
eye and nose now on what was familiar and right, and
had not been wrought upon by any Demon knowledge.

It was a promising morning—outwardly. But of
what it promised for his mission here there was no
hint. None of the Elders, or even the younger warriors, had spoken after the withdrawal of the Choos-

ers. Furtig thought that a bad sign. His people were normally curious. If they did not ask questions about the weapons or the lairs, such silence seemed hostile.

"A good day—" Foskatt came down the slope. He had spent the night in the outer part of the cave of his own family line. Now he squatted on his heels by the water, running the fingers of one hand back and forth across the scar of his healed wound as if that still itched a little.

"Any talk?" he asked.

"Not so. It was as if I had come from a hunt only, and an unsuccessful one at that," Furtig growled.

"With me the same. But do not forget that Liliha argued well for us. If she convinced the Choosers—"

Furtig gave a hiss of irritation, though he knew that Foskatt spoke the truth. It was the Choosers who ruled when it came to the point of safety for the full clan.

"*Ssss*—warriors who greet the dawn!" Both their heads turned swiftly.

Eu-La stood, her hands on her slender hips, her tail switching gently, evoking an answering whisper from the dry grasses it brushed. She was smaller than Liliha, but her body was well rounded. Yes, she was close to the season when it would be her turn to sit high on the Choosing ledge and watch warriors contend for her favor.

"We are not the only ones early astir," Furtig answered. "What brings the cave sister from her sleeping nest?"

"Dreams—dreams and wishes—" Suddenly she flung wide her arms, holding high her hands to the sky. "Long have I dreamed, and wished, and now it seems that I shall walk into the full of my dreams, have my wishes—"

"Those being?" Foskatt's question rumbled hoarsely.

"That I go to Gammage, that I learn more than can be learned in these caves—that I can use these, my hands, for greater things than I do here!" Now she held her hands before her face, flexing her fingers. These were not as long as Liliha's, but neither were they as closely stubbed as those of many of her sisters. "If the clans decide to go or not, still I travel with you, cave brother." She looked to Furtig. "I have spoken to Liliha and she has agreed. It is my right as much as any warrior's to go to Gammage!"

"True," Furtig had to agree. She was correct. If she longed for what the lairs had to offer, then she could profit by what she could learn there.

Perhaps this was another way out. Perhaps even if the Elders held back those of the clans who were bound by custom, there would be those, among the younger ones, who would go to Gammage and so swell even by a few the force within the lairs.

It was as if Eu-La could read his thought at that moment, for after she jumped lightly down beside them and leaned forward, about to lap daintily from the free-flowing water, she glanced up to add: "But I think that the Elders of the Choosers will have made up their minds soon. There was talk in the second cave last night. When it comes to the safety of younglings, then they listen well. And Liliha answered many more questions in the dark hours. Do not believe you have failed until you are told so."

She dabbled in the water, flicking droplets here and

there like a youngling playing. But Furtig, watching
her, was reminded again of Fas-Tan, who acted as one
alone even when she knew well that warriors watched
her longingly. Again he saw on Foskatt's face that
same intent look he had seen the night before.

For a moment a growl rumbled deep in Furtig's
throat. Eu-La, he had known Eu-La for a long time.
It was she who had encouraged him before he went to
Gammage. Eu-La was very precious. But if Eu-La
were at this moment a Chooser and looked at him,
Furtig, would he rejoice?

The turn of his thoughts surprised him almost as
much as Foskatt's reaction to Eu-La had done. Eu-La
choosing him? He liked her much, but not, he realized, as Foskatt did. He would fight for her in one
way, to protect her against harm. But he would not
strive to win her Choosing favor. That was not how he
thought of Eu-La.

When he thought of a Chooser— Sternly Furtig
tried to order those straying thoughts. There was no
more chance of that than there had been in the other
days of winning Fas-Tan's favor. Not all warriors won
even the passing interest of a Chooser. And they lived
and did as they had to—though many became far rev-
ers without clans.

He was lucky. Within the lairs there was much to
be done. If he could not equal the In-born with their
learning and their mastery of the Demon machines,
there was always exploring and fighting the Rattons.
Yes, he was lucky to have so much, and ought not,
even in his thoughts, reach for that which he could
never win. Foskatt—Eu-La—if it came to that it
might be very well.

But these were days to think not of Choosing and the beginnings of new clans and families, but of what was going to happen to those already in existence.

Eu-La proved right. In the end the Choosers' decision was that the move to the lairs was better than a life in the wilds, where younglings might be taken as had those of the Tuskers. Their answer to the threat of Rattons and Demons was that four Demons with their own weapons turned against them were not formidable. As for Rattons—from the earliest legends of the People such had been their natural prey. Therefore Gammage might expect these clans to come to him before the moon overhead vanished into the Nights of Dark.

But Eu-La wished to return with the messengers. So four rather than three set out again by night to return to the lairs.

There was no sign of the flyer, though they never felt safe from it. And when they met again the Tusker patrols, they learned it had not been seen.

The Tuskers had another message. One of their scouts had witnessed at the far end of their territory a strange thing. A truce flag had been set up. And, left by it with food and water to hand, a Barker who seemed to be recovering from ill treatment. Those who left him were a part of People from the lairs. He had been claimed by his own kind before nightfall, and the Barkers had not torn away the flag.

Rather they were now gathering, with more of their scouts arriving all the time. And there were signs they planned to camp nearby in the woods.

"So we freed that Barker from the Rattons," Furtig said. "But that may have been by far the easier part.

To get the People and the Barkers under a common truce flag is a thing unheard of."

"Yet," pointed out Liliha, "the Barkers did not tear down the flag. It still stands. Thus they have not yet refused to talk. They summon their own clans to speak together, even as we have gone to argue with those of the caves. But whether—"

"We cannot trust Barkers!" Furtig broke in. "Even if the Demons are all the legends say they were, we cannot trust Barkers."

"Barkers lived with the Demons," Eu-La said. "That is where they first learned evil ways." She was repeating the old legend of their own kind.

"But so did our people once," Liliha reminded her. "The First Ancestors fled from the lairs only when the Demons turned against them in their last madness and cruelty. But you are right in this—Gammage must have a powerful argument to make the Barkers listen. Saving one of them from the Rattons is not enough. But it is a beginning."

Furtig thought of the truce flag. Even though the Barkers had not thrown it contemptuously to earth, refusing contact, it would take great courage for any warrior of the People to go to it unarmed, trusting in the good will of his enemies. Who would Gammage choose—or who would volunteer to do that? And how would he who went know that it was the proper time? Would the Barkers advance a flag of their own in answer?

Furtig was suddenly more eager than ever to get back to the lairs, to know what had happened since they had left. Had the Demons been reinforced? But

233

a quick question to the Tuskers reassured them as to that—no second sky-ship had come down.

Broken Nose and his people would keep guard here, and, being informed of the coming of the cave clans, they would provide an alarm system to let those travel in such safety as could be devised.

Ahead lay the lairs and what might await them there. They slipped into the open with all the stealth and craft they possessed.

Ayana stripped off the sterile gloves, and crumpled them into a small ball, since they could not be used again. Jacel lay with beads of pain sweat still plain on his face. His eyes were closed, and she knew that the pain reliever had taken effect. Also the wound was not so bad as she had first feared. If they could now get him to the ship and under a renewer, in a day's time he would have no more to show for that gash than a well-closed seam.

But she was more than a little puzzled. There was a med-kit at Jacel's own belt. Tan wore another. And such a gash as this was easily handled by the materials they carried. Why had they sent out that panicked call for her?

She had asked no questions until now, being intent on the patient. Tan, standing against the wall, had volunteered nothing. Nor had Jacel. In fact he had appeared to be affected out of all proportion to the seriousness of the wound itself. Perhaps—Ayana glanced around the bare chamber—there had been some poisonous substance feared—but instant anti-spray would have handled such.

Now that she had time to think— Ayana did not look at Tan squarely, but as if she did not want him to see she noticed him. But Tan was not watching her; he was staring on through the other door in the room, seemingly so absorbed that he must see or hear something—or be waiting for something to happen.

"What is it?" Her words sounded too loud, even echoed a little.

Now he turned his head. And in his eyes Ayana saw that queer gleam which frightened her. She shivered. Cold as this place was, the protect suit should have kept her warm; but Tan now had the ability to chill her through when he looked like that.

"You will have another patient, a very important one. We have had wonderful luck, Ayana, we have made contact—"

"Contact with whom—or what?" she demanded when he paused.

"With those who live here. Do you know, Ayana, this is a storehouse of information. They have shown us tapes, machines— What we learned from the First Ships is nothing, nothing at all to what we can learn here! If we have time—"

"What do you mean?"

"Well, our friends are not the only ones trying to get this information. There are others—and they may be closer. There was a war here in the old days. And do you know what kind of a war?" He came away from the wall to stand over her.

Ayana rose quickly, not liking to have him towering above her so.

"A war between men and animals—animals, *mind* you! Things with fur and claws and fangs that dared

235

to think they were equal with man—dared!" He was breathing fast, his face flushed. "But there were others. Men in their last days here were few, they had to have friends, helpers—and they found them. Then, when man was gone those others were left, left to defend everything man had fought for, all the knowledge he had won through his own efforts, defended against the animals. They are still fighting that battle, but now it is our fight, too!

"They need you, Ayana. There is a place of medical information—think of it—a storage of all the wealth of knowledge of man's time on this world! They have been trying to hold that against the enemy. They need our help so badly. One of their leaders, a genius among them, one who has been able to untangle many of the old records, was badly injured in fighting the animals. He has been taken to this center, and now they need your aid.

"Think of it, Ayana—such devices of healing as were just hinted at in our records! You can see them, learn to use them—you can help this leader. It is such a chance as only luck could have given us."

He was in one of his exultant moods, but to a degree she had never seen before.

"Tan's luck—" she said before she thought.

He nodded vigorously. "Tan's luck! And it is going to help us—help us win a whole world for man again! But they're coming—listen!"

She could hear Jacel's heavy breathing, and then something else, a light pattering. There was a gleam of light beyond the door, and those Tan expected arrived. Ayana gasped and shrank back.

These were not the furred creatures of the bridge

which she had half expected, but something she instinctively found repulsive.

They scuttled on their hind feet, but they had naked tails at the ends of their spines. And they were small, the largest standing a little above her knee at its full height. Fur grew on them in ragged patches, with naked skin between. On some, the smaller, that fur was a dirty gray; on the two largest it was white. Their heads had the long, narrow muzzles of animals showing sharp teeth. Against the domes of their skulls their ears were pointed.

Ayana hated them on sight. She watched with frozen horror as Tan advanced to greet the tallest white-furred one, which seemed to be their leader, squatting down so that his head came closer to that of the creature.

Around its neck hung a small box. It reached with one paw—hand?—and touched that. Then it uttered a series of squeaks, but from the box came distorted but still recognizable words.

"Chief—waits—hurry—hurry—"

"She is here." Tan nodded toward Ayana. "She is ready."

"No!" Ayana cried. Not for all the knowledge, all the treasure of this world heaped up before her, would she go with these small horrors deeper into their burrows.

Tan, on his feet, came at her, and she could not get away. She could not even slip along the wall out of his reach.

"Little fool!" He caught her arm in so painful a grip that she gasped. "Do you go with them on your own two feet, or do I inject you with a sleep-shot and let

them carry you? No stupidity is going to wreck my plans now, do you understand?"

And she knew that he would do just that. If she went, perhaps with an outward show of willingness, she could at least see the road they took, might even be able to escape. If he drugged her and they took her—no, she had no choice.

"Try no tricks with them, they are not animals." Tan showed his teeth almost as if they were the fangs of the waiting squad. "Jacel discovered that. Now get going—"

He gave her a push, and she stumbled toward the door. Around her the creatures closed in.

16

Ayana stood looking about, first in bewilderment and then with a growing excitement which drew her attention from those chittering things which had brought her here—and even from Tan, who had followed behind and with whom she had not spoken since this nightmare began. For he had actually picked up and carried the chief horror—that half bald, half white-furred leader, exchanging speech with him. The girl had pushed ahead to avoid that monstrous companionship. For monstrous her emotions told her it was!

But this place! She had studied in detail every scrap of information having to do with medical knowledge that they had found in the looted tape banks of the First Ships. Ayana had had access in addition to all the combined learning, surmise, and speculation of those who had had more than a hundred years before her to study the same records.

So now she turned slowly about, surveying a vast and much better lighted chamber, cut by many parti-

tions rising to her shoulder height or beyond, into booths and cubicles. This was indeed a medical center such as her teachers had hardly dared dream existed on the parent world.

Some of the machines she recognized from old diagrams—diagnostic, operative, healing— For a moment, in her amazement and excitement, Ayana forgot her company and went forward confidently, pausing here and there before an installation she did know, passing for now those she could not understand. Why—with these—if they still worked—one could cure a nation!

Ayana put out her hand, ran finger tips along the outer transparent wall of a healing cell. If they worked! But how long had it been since they had been put to use? She might be able to work out the procedure for activating those she did know, always providing they were intact. But if their machinery was at fault, she had no way of knowing what a tech would do to put that right again.

She passed down one aisle between those partitions and came into an open space. There before her—

That table—the smell—the pools of—blood! Ayana recoiled as she faced it. Amid the sterile disuse of the rest of the place, this was like a blow in the face, to bring her to the realization of how she had come here. The tangle of blood-stained instruments thrown in an ugly pile on one end of the table hinted more of cruel butchery than of any desire to heal. What had they done here—these small monsters with whom Tan seemed to have made some evil pact?

"Well?" Tan's voice from behind made her start. "What do you think of this? Did I not tell you there was more to be found than you could guess? Now—

Oudu wants to know if you can use it to cure his chief."

She looked away from that blood-stained table with a shudder, tried to close her mind to it. And she was able to find voice enough to croak:

"Some of this was on the tapes. The rest"—Ayana shook her head—"is new. And we do not know whether the power works."

"Oudu will know." He looked at that thing he carried, as if, Ayana thought, it was human!

"Some work—" The dry rustle of the words overlay the shrill chittering as the box on the creature's chest translated. "There is material to try with—"

"Material?" Ayana could not force herself to look directly at Oudu, nor address it—him. "What does he mean?"

"I believe they have been experimenting for themselves. They have taken prisoners from time to time, the animals roaming in here. They use them, just as our ancestors used to do. That's why those were here in the first place—they were lab animals."

"We—we were helpers of the Great Ones!" came that other voice. "Workers here. The others, they were used to try the machines upon—as we do now. But many escaped, many lie in wait—kill—destroy. They destroy the records, the knowledge. Soon all will be gone if we do not stop them."

"See?" Tan demanded. "We have to stop such destruction—or we'll lose everything."

"Do not waste time!' Oudu cut in. "Shimog dies. Let this knowing female use her knowledge to make Shimog live again.'

Ayana swallowed. "I have to see—see—"

"Naturally. They have him down here." Tan passed that ghastly table as if it did not exist, and she followed, glad to leave it. But she knew now that she played a game, and it would not be Tan's. No alliance with these things—she could not do it. Not for all the knowledge here!

Not even, asked something within her, if it means the success or failure of your mission? The life or death of those on Elhorn? But Elhorn was far away, and here—here was now, before her. She could only follow Tan's lead for a time, waiting for a chance, a plan, to wrest herself free of this nightmare.

They came to a cubicle at the end of the line, and there was a gathering of the creatures, several on guard at the door, two by the cot within. Lying on the cot was one even larger than Oudu and even more scantily furred.

It—he—was swollen of paunch. And the skin, where it showed, was dark, scaled with sores. Breath came and went in slow, heavy panting, as if the effort to breathe was almost too great. Its attendants drew back as Ayana forced herself on her knees close to the creature.

She could not find any pity, even when the thing turned its head a fraction and looked at her. For the consciousness within those eyes was coldly evil. Ayana recognized intelligence of a type so alien to all she believed in that it was like meeting black and deadly hatred formed into a repulsive body.

There was no way of telling how or why Shimog suffered. She could only guess that it was from some disease. But that might be native to this planet, or to *the creature's own foul species. Certainly she had never seen such symptoms before.*

"What can you do?" Tan demanded impatiently.

What? She had no idea. Except one. She had seen something out there she had recognized—a renewal chamber. If this Shimog was in the least responsive to what would act for humans, that might be the best hope.

"The renewal chamber. If the installation works— that might help."

"A machine?" Oudu demanded. "You can run this machine?"

"I have seen directions for such," she answered, careful not to make any promises to these small devils. "I would have to try it, to make sure that it was running properly, before we used it on your chief."

"To do so then you must have an animal?" came the swift demand.

"But it will only work on one hurt—or ill."

"We have what is needed."

Oudu did not add to that, but he might have given some inaudible order, for most of those who had come with them scurried away.

Troubled, Ayana arose. "I must see the renewer—"

Free of that cubicle with its fetid odor, its aura of dark hate, she ran back to the glass-walled booth with the soft flooring. It was large enough to accommodate some twenty beings of Shimog's size, perhaps five humans.

She did not open the door, but went to the controls. Since she could not set for any particular disease, well, it would be full treatment. Yes, here were the symbols she had seen on the tapes. And a single

243

finger-press brought an answering spark of life—it worked! At least the power was still on. And—

Ayana whirled—those sounds!

Toward her—she wanted to be sick. Those they were dragging, crying, babbling. No—this was a deadly nightmare! Then her head rang as Tan slapped her hard across the face.

"Those are only animals, experimental animals, do you understand? Sure, the Rattons don't play pretty with their enemies but neither do the animals with Rattons!"

Ayana caught her tongue between her teeth, bit on it. Tan—was this Tan? Not her Tan but the one who had come alive since they had landed on this cursed world. For cursed it had to be!

The nightmare crew pulled, rolled those torn and mangled bodies into the renewal chamber, slammed the door.

"Get to it!" Tan's hands on her shoulders brought her about before the controls. "Prove it, one way or the other."

She could not think straight—but she must. Those poor wrecks, perhaps she could give them merciful unconsciousness, death. Ayana sent the machine into humming life. She did not look into the chamber as she jerked the lever up to full power, hoping that would kill mercifully, quickly. Now she was disciplining her thoughts into some kind of coherent order.

She would never join Tan in his alliance with these Rattons—not ever! There was a point past which no thought of gain could carry one. And Ayana was there. Therefore, if she was to get out of this venture

*alive, she would have to move before the Rattons real-
ized that she was not their ally.*

*Tan had taken her stunner, but she had something
else in her kit which could be a weapon. If she could
get that in hand—*

*"This will take time." She kept her voice level.
"And Shimog—a sedative might help."*

"Give it to him then."

*Still not looking into the chamber, Ayana went
back to the ailing leader. She brought out openly
what she needed, charged it. Luckily Tan knew no
more than the necessary medic first aid. Correct dosage of this meant nothing to him.*

*"I will give your leader"—she would not look to
Oudu—"sleep that he may rest until the machine is
proven."*

*"Not so!" Oudu's harsh protest shook her, though
she hoped not to open betrayal. "Prove no harm—
Mog!"*

One of the guard came forward.

"Prove on Mog."

*"Very well." She held the injector to the Ratton's
forearm, pressed the plunger.*

*He blinked, gave a little sigh, and crumpled to the
floor. Oudu bent over him for a moment.*

"Truth. Mog sleeps. Let Shimog also sleep."

*Ayana bent to that task. The easiest part of her
plan was over. She screwed at the cap of the injector
as if closing it. But instead she opened it to full. Now
she held a weapon of a sort, one meant to handle perhaps even more than one difficult patient at a time,
ones who could not be closely approached.*

What she had used on Mog and Shimog had been

but a small portion of the dosage with which she had charged this. The trouble now was the difference in height between her enemies—Tan so much the taller.

Because of his superior height and strength, she decided he must go first. Ayana arose, still watching Shimog, as if she wished to be sure of his condition. Then she turned swiftly, the injector ready.

Straight into Tan's face went that subduing spray. She had no time to see its efficacy as she went on to aim at the Rattons.

"You—you!" Tan's hands came at her. His fingers actually closed on her arm, then loosened as he went down. Around him the Rattons, bewildered by her attack, also wilted.

Ayana caught up her kit. She did not know how long they would be unconscious. By the time they recovered, she must be well away from here—perhaps even back to the ship, if that were possible. But before she left she had one more duty, to make sure those poor things in the chamber were safely dead, their suffering over.

Down one aisle, up the next, then she was at the chamber where the motor purred on. She looked in—

It was not possible!

With both hands flat against the glass Ayana watched something out of a wild dream. Lost, mangled limbs, mutilated bodies—they could not regrow—heal—in this fashion! She had turned the power to full force. Had she, in hopes for a swift death for the wreckage the Rattons had dragged there, done just the opposite—given them not only life, but healed such hurts as she had thought no living thing could long survive?

If—if this was happening as her eyes reported—then she could not go and leave them. Once the Rattons recovered, knew she was gone, then the vengeance they would take on these—! She would have condemned them to far worse torment.

But the changes, the healing, although already spectacular, would have to be complete, and how long dared she wait?

Ayana opened her kit. She had one more charge of the sedative, but it was less than the full one she had just used. Her only chance would be to keep watch on those she had left with Shimog. What if others came? Shimog was their leader. Would there not be visitors, a changing of guard?

Tan's weapons—the blaster—her stunner!

Ayana ran back. She rolled Tan over, plundered his belt of everything which could serve as a weapon. Then, as she passed that terribly stained table, she swept off the instruments, the things which had been used to maim and not repair.

Back before the chamber she piled up her strange assortment of armament. How long would she have to wait? Waiting was harder to face, she discovered, than open attack.

In the time which followed she prowled back and forth between the cubicle and the renewal chamber. On her second visit to the cubicle she heard a scuttling and stood ready with the stunner.

Moments later five more Rattons were laid out with their fellows. But how long before someone took alarm and sent a larger force, perhaps one even a blaster could not rout? There was no hurrying the healing, but every time she checked the process, Ayana

247

was amazed at what was happening. What wonders her ancestors had been able to do! But if they could produce such miracles of life, then what had brought about the death of this city, the flight of the First Ship?

The Rattons boasted that they had been the companion-aides of the men who had once lived and worked here. She knew that degeneration could cause awesome changes in both physical and mental states. But she did not believe that man and Ratton—Ratton? There was a familiar sound to that name—she frowned and began to search memory.

Those others, too, the animals— Once more she went to study them. There was still the teasing resemblance to Putti— If she could only remember!

"Ratton—" She repeated that name aloud. "Ratton—rat!"

Rat! A tape picture came to vivid life in her mind. Rat—a creature used in lab experiments! But those had been small! What had happened to bring a four-footed, small rat to the size of the erect-standing, intelligent Ratton? Had this been the result of experiments? But rats had been tools used by men, never his aides—unless something had gone wrong. If they could only learn the truth!

"Rat!" Ayana said again. The word was ugly, as ugly as the things it named. She looked once more to her patients. They lay as if asleep, but they breathed easily, mended steadily—if perhaps too slowly for all their future safety.

They were akin to the creatures Tan had recorded on the bridge. Then they had gone armed. It was apparent that they walked erect and were not animals.

About them that elusive memory— Putti—but not really the soft-bodied plaything of childhood. More pictures on learning tapes? Ayana tried systematically to recall what she could of those. If the Rattons had been rats—then these must also have had another beginning.

Like a flash on a visa-screen, bright and sharply clear, she remembered at last.

Not Putti but cat!

"Cat!" Ayana called that name as if to awaken the sleepers.

Cats! So the Rattons had lied. For the cat on the ancient tapes had been truly a companion of man. So much so that his children had lovingly cherished their Puttis when they could not have the real creature to solace their wandering days.

Though these, in turn, were not cats of the past. Ayana could trace the likenesses, perhaps most in the heads with the stiffly whiskered faces, in the upstanding, pointed ears, and in the tails.

But one of the sleepers was again different—another species. She studied him now. There were no whiskers, though he was tailed. But the tail did not lie in as limber a way. His "face" had a longer muzzle, and his ears, larger, were in flaps.

The others were cats, or they had come from cats. But what was this one? Again Ayana returned to memory pictures. And she found what she sought— canine—dog! Again an old companion of man.

Cat-people, dog-people, still here in man's home, carrying on war with Rattons. But where were the men? How long since they had disappeared? And why had they gone? Were the Rattons responsible? Ayana

249

could hardly believe that. Even though those horrors might be able to muster whole armies, they could not have cleared out their masters, masters who were equipped with the weapons she knew existed here— the kind she had seen the cat-person wearing.

One of the patients stirred, opened his eyes. Large and green, they stared straight into hers. His ears flattened to his skull, he drew himself up against the wall of the chamber, his clawed hands coming up in menace.

He must believe she was one with the Rattons! But now they had a common cause. How could she explain? Unless by understanding where he was, what was happening, he would know—

The look in those green eyes, cold and measuring, daunted Ayana. She edged away from the window, decided it was time to check again on the sleepers. But this time went more slowly. If the cat-people, the dog-person, should turn on her, too— She could use the weapons, but if she did she would never learn the truth, perhaps never herself escape from this place in which the inhabitants apparently hunted each other with ferocious zeal.

Ayana stood looking down at Tan. When she left he would remain. So she must give him a chance. He was no longer one with her, if he had ever really been so, but he was one of her kind. And she believed that these filthy new allies of his would turn on him viciously when they discovered what had happened. She should return the stunner to him, give the rest of the sleepers an extra spray so they would still be under when his sedation wore off. In the meantime she would try to prevent any more arrivals.

The door at the end of the hall had no locks that Ayana could understand. But she closed it and then piled there all the loose and heavy objects she could turn into a barricade.

When she had finished Ayana stumbled back to the renewal chamber so tired she could barely urge one foot before the other. She had Extend pills, enough to renew her energy for the final dash out of here. But she would not waste those by premature use. There were E rations, one tube, in her belt loops. She turned the cap to heat and waited until she could twist that off and squeeze the semi-liquid contents into her mouth.

Having eaten, she went to look in the chamber. Time was passing far too fast, she might be pushed to a move soon.

Those inside were all conscious. The one cat-person who had first revived was standing. As she watched, he reached down to draw another up, a female, the scars of her wounds still rawly red but closed. There was another male, and the dog-person, who, Ayana saw, had moved away from the other three, fitting his back into a corner as if he expected to be attacked.

There came a sudden sharp sound, enough to bring a weapon into Ayana's hand, set her looking about wildly. Then she realized that the light on the control board had gone out, the hum of the machine was subsiding. Apparently the chamber had turned itself off. Perhaps some indication that the work was done.

Now that the time had come to release the captives, Ayana found herself hesitant. The manifest anger in the male's expression— But they were weak, helpless, and she was armed—

With the stunner ready in her right hand, she spun the lock with her left. The door opened.

They were gathered just within as if ready to bolt for freedom, the three cat-people to the fore, the dog-person behind. Ayana heard hisses—a rumble of growl. She did not want to use the stunner, it might plunge them all straight back into captivity.

"No—" But they could not understand her, of course. However she babbled on as if they could. "Friend—friend!"

Their ears were flat to their skulls, their fangs exposed, their hands up with claws extended. If they came at her she would have no recourse but to shoot.

"Friend—"

A louder growl in answer. Ayana moved aside, retreated slowly, step by step, leaving a clear path between them and the door through which Tan and the Rattons had earlier brought her. Though she still held the stunner at ready, she waved them on in a gesture she hoped they would understand.

They moved slowly, stiffly, but gave no sign of pain. They moved with their heads turned toward her, their eyes watching. Then they reached the door and were gone, though for a moment or two she could still hear the shuffle of their feet.

Ayana breathed a sigh of relief. Her waiting was done. Now she must make good her own escape. She went for the last time to the huddle of the Ratton party, giving the Rattons a dose of stunner ray and then laid the weapon in Tan's lax hand.

He groaned and she jerked back as if he had made to seize her. He must be close to waking. She must get away fast— Ayana turned and ran, stopping only by

*the renewer to catch up her kit, following the path of
the released captives.*

She was afraid to use her torch. Luckily there
seemed to be a very dim light here, enough to show
the way. She must concentrate on the route she had
tried to memorize when they brought her in. But first
the Extend pills. Her chest hurt as she breathed after
that last spurt of speed. Ayana groped within the kit.
Two ought to be enough. She mouthed the tablets.

They were bitter and she had trouble swallowing
them dry. But she hurried on even before they
worked, so she was in another passage when that aching fatigue lifted. Ayana felt not only completely rested, but alert of mind, able to do anything. The eu-
phoria which was a side effect of such a large dose of
Extend gripped her and she forced herself to remember that this feeling of superb well-being was
only illusionary.

This passage—had they come this way? But they
must have— The trouble was that one of these ways
looked exactly like another. Where had they left
Jacel? She had tried to establish landmarks on the
way in but had found few. And there were several
places of forking corridors. She must remember—she
must!

She had no warning. Out of some shadowed way
she had not even glanced into, they sprang. Furred
arms closed about her thighs as one attacker struck
with force enough to crash her to the ground.

17

Furtig studied their captive. So—this was a Demon!
Though a female, not a warrior. But still a Demon
and as such to be feared. He heard a soft hiss of
breath. Eu-La, somewhat accustomed now to the
wonders of the legendary lairs, had moved beside
him and with her Liliha. While behind them came two
of the In-born males carrying a box with a coil of wire
laid on its cover.

The Demon was awake. When they had taken her
captive, she had fallen heavily and struck her head, so
they had taken her easily enough before she could
reach for weapons. And now here came Jir-Haz, to
whom they owed the capture itself.

"You can do this?" Furtig asked Liliha. "Speak to
the Demon in her own tongue?"

"We hope to do this thing. By listening to Demon
voices on their tapes we can understand their words.
But we cannot make those same noises ourselves. But
perhaps with this"—she laid a proprietary hand upon

the box—"we can twist our speech enough for her to understand our questions."

But the Demon spoke first. She had been looking from one to the other of them, first in what Furtig relished as open fear (thus proving that the warriors of the People *could* strike fear even into Demons) and now with something close to appeal. For she spoke to Liliha, at first so fast and in such a gabble of sound, Furtig could make little of it.

However, Liliha, her ears attuned from very young years to the teaching machines, did sort out enough of those uncouth noises to make sense.

"She wishes to know where she is—and who we are." Then, the In-born having set one end of the wire into the box, Liliha took up a disk fastened to the other and held it close to her mouth, speaking slowly and carefully into it.

"This is the lair of Gammage. We are the People."

It was weird, for they could hear Liliha's words. But also there was a secondary gabble, like a blurred echo following.

The Demon's face was so strange, so unlike that of a rational being that one could hardly hope to learn anything from her expression. But Furtig dared to imagine she was surprised.

"Speak slowly," Liliha was continuing. "We can understand Demon speech, but our tongues cannot twist to answer it."

He saw the Demon's tongue tip on her lower lip. She could not move; they had bound her after peeling off her coverings. For it seemed that the Demons had no fur but wore loose outer skins to be stripped off.

"You–are–cats—" Even he could understand those queerly accented words.

"Cats? No, People," Liliha corrected her. "Why come you here?"

"What–are–you–to–do–with–me?" The Demon looked beyond Liliha to Jir-Haz. "He–was–in–the–healing–chamber. I–let–him–go—"

"Who knows a Demon's purpose?" Jir-Haz demanded of them all. "Yes, I was healed, as was Tiz-Zon, and A-San and the Barker. After we were near to death, she had the Rattons put us there. That they might return us to life and then once more rend us for their pleasure! Is that not so, Demon?" He leaned closer to hiss at her.

"I–could–have–killed—" the Demon said. "But–I–let–him–go."

"That is the truth?" Liliha asked Jir-Haz.

His tail lashed. "We told our story to the Elders. Yes, she let us go. Doubtless that the Rattons might have the sport of once more hunting us! Why else would a Demon heal our bodies and then release us?"

Liliha spoke into the disk. "Jir-Haz says that you did this for the Rattons, that they might once more torment our people. Such was what the Demons did in the old days."

"The–Rattons—" The Demon's face was flushed. She tried to loose her hands, struggled against the ties. "I–was–with–the–Rattons–against–my–will—"

"There was another Demon, a male," Jir-Haz cut in. "He was not with her when she came to look in upon us during the healing. Nor was he there when she loosed us. Ask her concerning him!"

Liliha relayed the question. The Demon lay still as if she knew the folly of battling those bonds.

"I–left–him–with–Shimog. I–put–them–all–to–sleep –so–I–might–escape–and–your–people–also—"

"Why?" Liliha asked, almost, Furtig thought, as if she could believe what *must* be a false answer. For why should a Demon turn against one of her own kind to aid the People? No, she was false and would betray them if they believed her.

"Because–I–saw–Shimog–and–what–they–had– done–to–your–people. I–am–a–healer–of–hurts–not– one–to–give–them!"

"All Demons are false!" burst out Jir-Haz. "The other Demon, the Rattons, stayed out of sight that she might play friend and later point out our trail."

Fur Furtig had been thinking, and Jir-Haz's last accusation bothered him.

"When you captured this one," he asked, "was she not alone? Were there any Rattons or the other Demon with her?"

"Yes," Liliha added. "If she was alone, why was that so, supposing that she hunted you? Your story is that you had sent A-San ahead, and the Barker had gone his own way. She had three trails to follow, which did she seek?"

Jir-Haz's tail twitched. "None," he said slowly. "The Demon was taking a fourth way, going from our part of the lairs. And it is true she was alone. Also, after we had taken her we waited for a space, but none followed."

"So, we can believe that this Demon was not hunting you. She was alone when she watched you in the healing chamber, she was alone when she opened the door of that and bid you go. These are all the truth?"

"It is so," Jir-Haz acknowledged.

"Then what you yourself saw and report being so much the truth, must we not begin to believe that this Demon was not engaged in any hunt devised by Rattons, and that perhaps she too speaks the truth?"

"But she is a Demon!" Jir-Haz protested.

For the first time Eu-La broke silence. She had gone to stand close beside the bed on which they had laid the Demon.

"She does not look like one who kills. See—" Eu-La leaned over to set claw-tip to the Demon's middle. "She is all softness, easily torn. And, though like all Demons she is large, yet I do not believe that our warriors need look upon her as an ever-ready enemy. If she loosed Jir-Haz and the others from the Rattons, perhaps she had some reason. Why not ask her? She said she heals not harms, ask her how she does this and why. And how she came among the Rattons—"

"Also, to some purpose," Furtig cut in "ask her why she came to the lairs and if more Demons are on the way." Of course the answer to that might not be true, but it would do no harm to ask it.

He wished Gammage was here. Of them all, certainly the Ancestor was best suited to deal with a Demon and weigh truth against not truth. But the lair leader had departed to a truce flag meeting with the Barkers —since that hard-voiced people had sent a message and a flag to stand beside the first, thus agreeing to the meet. The second Barker, whom this Demon had freed, was he another scout of the same pack? And if so was he now making his way back to his people?

What influence would his report have on the negotiations?

Slowly the Demon answered their questions. Yes, she had come from the sky—she was one of four—

All that they knew. So they were learning nothing. But when they questioned her about the Rattons—then they could not check her story. She had come from the ship at a call for help from one of her companions. She had found him injured and had treated him. Then the other, the Ratton friend (if anyone could friend that scum) had ordered her to treat a Ratton leader, had threatened her if she did not.

The longer Furtig listened to her halting, slowly spoken words, the easier it was to understand them. And somehow they sounded true. In spite of Jir-Haz, his own inborn distrust of Demons, everything, he could not say this was false.

When she spoke of Shimog the very tone of her voice (now that he was more familiar with it) bore out her aversion to the Ratton leader. But it was Liliha who brought home with a question the strange point in the whole tale.

"So they told you that Rattons were the comrades of Demons? But we have not learned it so. In fact, it is recorded that until the final days when the Demons went mad, Rattons were enemies to all. My people, the Barkers—we once lived in friendly company with Demons. Then the evil which the Demons themselves wrought seized upon them. They turned against all other living creatures, hunted them—".

"This evil." There was such urgency in the Demon's voice as made them all stare. "What manner of evil? I tell you—we came searching for the reason we

left this world, why my people long ago lifted to the
stars and then hid all mention of the past from us.
Tell me, if you know, why did they go? What happened to them here, to you—to this place?"

She looked from side to side as if begging one or another to answer. Such was the power of the emotion
which flowed from her that Furtig believed in her
wholly—that she had come seeking just what she
said. Liliha did not answer at once. She spoke to Furtig.

"Cut her loose!"

His hand slipped into fighting claws in obedience.
Then he hesitated. Jir-Haz growled warningly. It
would seem that he still clung to his suspicions.

"Loose her," Liliha repeated. "What do you fear?"
she asked Jir-Haz. "Look, she has no weapons, not
even claws. Do you believe she can overcome us all?"

Furtig went forward and, seeing his hand so armed,
the Demon shrank back with a cry, trying to free herself before he could reach her. Liliha spoke swiftly.

"He will not harm you, he comes to loose you."

She quieted then, and he cut swiftly through the
cords.

"What would you do with me?"

"We can show you better than we can tell. Come."

So they brought the Demon to the room of learning, and there Liliha started the tape readers, those
records which had given them the information concerning the last days of the Demons. Though these
were faulty and lacking in many details, as if those
who had made them had lost the skill to do so properly. Afterward Liliha explained even more of the tradi-

tions of the People and of what Gammage and the In-born had learned.

But that took some time. And Furtig was not long a part of it. He had other duties, and it was true that the Demon female did not need such guarding—she was weaponless and surrounded by Choosers who were certainly as keen-eyed as any warrior.

There was still the matter of the Demon male and the Rattons. How deep into Ratton territory they dared send their own scouts was a question to bother even Dolar. But before night their numbers began to be augmented by an inflow of People. Not Furtig's as yet, but Ku-La's forces.

What these brought with them, as well as their weapons and supplies, was information, some bits held from the days of the Demons, some gathered by investigation in those parts of the northeastern lairs where Gammage's explorers had never done any real searching. Once their Choosers and younglings were established in the safe heart of Gammage's territory, their warriors spread out to join the In-born and the handful of newcomers such as Furtig.

Reports came in now from questing scouts. The Demon who had been injured had crawled out of the tunnels, gone back to the grounded ship, which was always under observation. The ship itself was sealed, no hatch open. It was as if the two within it held it as a fort against attack. On the other hand the fourth Demon, he who had joined the Rattons, had also been sighted.

A young warrior of Ku-La's people, very small and slim and so able to take ways closed to those of larger frame, had managed to squirm through a side duct and look into a very busy place in the Ratton burrows.

There were machines there like the rumblers, and these the Rattons were swarming over, working on, under the leadership of the Demon. It was apparent that the machines were being readied and that could only be to attack.

Armed with this report Dolar, with Furtig in tow, went to the chamber where the Demon female was with Liliha. She had shared food with them, and at her request they had given her back those looser skins she wore. As the warriors entered she was sitting with Liliha exchanging talk, the translating machine on a divan between them.

"Ask her," Dolar said abruptly, "what the Demon does with the machines and the Rattons. We believe that they prepare an attack, and we must know how these machines will work."

Liliha relayed the question. But when the Demon answered, she spoke directly to Dolar.

"There are many kinds of machines. Can you tell me, or show me, the form of these?"

He clanged his fighting claws together. A machine was a machine. How could you find words to describe it? Then he rounded on the In-born who was his at-tail messenger.

"Bring the seeing box."

The warrior had not gone empty-handed into the narrow ways, but had taken with him one of the discoveries of his own people, a box which made a permanent record of what he saw.

When this case was set before the Demon she appeared to know it for what it was, instantly pressing the right button. Across the room, on the wall, appeared a picture, small enough for Furtig's two hands to cover, yet clear in details.

For a long moment the Demon studied the picture and then she spoke:

"I do not know what all these machines may be. See, there are at least three different kinds. But there —that one upon which the Ratton stands—that shoots forth fire. It is like the weapon your people took from me but much more powerful, for the fire spreads wider. I believe that these are machines of war." Her voice died away, and yet she continued to look at the picture as if there was something there to hold her full attention.

"Machines of war, fearsome ones," Dolar repeated as if to himself. "Let those come seeking us and perhaps the Rattons will win."

The Demon female spoke again. "You have showed me much. Also—there is something—if I can only make it plain to you—" She twined her hands together, finger punishing finger in that tight grip, as if she might wring the words she wanted to say out of her own flesh. "I am one who heals. I have been taught to do so since I was very young. We did not know why our ancestors—our long-ago Elders—left these lairs. And we have a trouble on our home world which is bad—therefore we were sent to seek out our old homeland, and aid.

"But when our ship landed here—we—we changed. No more were we as we had always been. We became strangers one to the other—" She looked at none of them as she spoke thus, but ever at the wall pictures. "We seemed to become—no, perhaps I cannot say it.

But you have showed me that there was once a madness here, an evil thing which possessed my kind. I think that the shadow of that lingers still, so that we are becoming enemies, one to the other. If this is true, that illness must be healed, and we must go. And it may be too late." She covered her face with her hands, sat shivering so that Furtig could see the shudders of her body. Liliha put out her hands, laid them upon the Demon's shaking shoulders. Then, as he never thought to see, she drew the Demon to her as she might in comforting a sister Chooser, and held her so.

Ayana pulled away, though the comfort of that soft warmth the cat-woman offered was such that she longed to cling to it. She wiped her wet cheeks with the backs of her hands. All that she had learned was a weight on her spirit. But it was, as these people made much of saying, the truth. No wonder her kind had fled this place. This sickness of spirit was as strong as once had been the sickness of body which had either produced it or been the end product of it. She need only look at that picture of Tan, at his intense, absorbed face as he readied machines to wipe out life, and know how deeply they had been stricken.

These lairs, as they called them, lairs of darkness in spite of all the light within, lairs of knowledge which could kill as well as cure. Knowledge, could one pick and choose among knowledge? A thing which might cure in one form could be used to kill in another. As a medic, who should know better than she? Had she not

*even sought out death dealers herself on board ship,
gathered them together?*

*But what Tan intended—that must not be! And
there was something else, a warning she must give of
another kind. She had seen this Gammage only brief-
ly when they had first brought her in. His urging for
union among intelligent species—yes, that was a step
forward. But his thirst for alien knowledge—his tin-
kering with the scraps and remnants they played with
here—no! That was tampering with that which might
end him and his people as surely as the Rattons and
Tan, equipped with war machines, could do.*

*However, the immediate threat—resolutely Ayana
pushed aside what might happen tomorrow, concentrated on today. Suppose Tan and his nightmare
army of allies did activate those machines of crawling
death? Weapons used by men who had built and inhab-
ited this complex would be very sophisticated. And
Tan would release what he could not control.*

*These cat-people looked to her for an answer. And
she did not have one. Jacel—Massa—could help, but
would either of them do so? She had no idea of what
had happened between Jacel and Tan before she had
reached them. But that comment of Tan's about Jacel's discovery that the Rattons could be dangerous if
crossed lingered now in her mind. There must have
been ill will between the two men, some argument.
Could she build on that?*

*It seemed to Ayana a very thin hope, but it was all
she had now.*

*"There are many machines, and I have no knowl-
edge of them." She made her explanation as simple as*

possible. "But those in the ship still can help. I see no other way—"

She had been long enough with the cat-people now to be able to read expressions a little, and she saw that suggestion was not welcome, especially to the large male with the scarred ears. But she could not help them. Only Jacel and Massa knew the machines. And how much time did they have?

The growling, spitting speech of the People among themselves was prolonged. Finally the males went out together, leaving her once more with the females she had learned to call Liliha and Eu-La.

"You are a Chooser?" Liliha asked, and Ayana saw both the cat-women watching her closely, as if her answer was important.

"What is a Chooser?"

They appeared startled. Then Liliha explained. "There is a time when one wishes younglings. One's body is ready to hold such. As mine—" She slid her hand over her slim belly. "But not yet is Eu-La so." She pointed to her companion's slighter figure. "When this time comes the warriors display their strength so that we Choosers may look upon them, judge their skills, select one to father a youngling. You have so chosen?"

Ayana looked down at her own hands. Not to get a child had she chosen (or rather had had the choosing done for her) but rather that a certain needed series of traits could complement and perhaps fill out another's character. Had she been subtly conditioned to accept Tan so readily? Now she suspected that. He had become a stranger so fast, as if the sickness which clung here had broken through that shell of acceptance.

"I did not choose, he was chosen for me." She felt an odd shame at making that confession.

"This then is the custom of the Demons, that a Chooser may not choose for herself?" Liliha asked after a long moment of silence.

"Because there were but four of us in the ship, and we must each know certain things, yes, we were chosen by others."

"Ill doing." Liliha's voice was a hiss. "For when a Chooser chooses in truth, she knows the worth of a warrior and he does not later become an enemy. I sorrow for you that this was so, that now you must eat bitterness and ashes." Her hand rested over Ayana's. "It is well you do not have a youngling within you."

"That is true," replied Ayana.

She was not left alone, nor was she still outwardly a prisoner. Oddly enough, she had no desire to leave. Liliha, Eu-La, the other cat-women who drifted in their soundless way in and out, brought food, or simply came to sit and look at her (though she never found their curiosity rude or disturbing) were somehow comforting, though she could not have told why. Several brought babies, purred them to sleep or played with them. But after a space Ayana began to worry.

The memory of Tan and the Rattons, busy with the war machines, was never erased from her mind, though she did sleep at last. And she drifted off to a purring song Liliha seemingly sang to herself as the cat-woman brushed the shining length of her tail.

There was only the gray light of early dawn coming

through the windows when they roused her. Liliha was there, and, by the door, the cat-man she had seen with the scarred older warrior, the young one who had been present before when they had questioned her. He was making the small, almost yowling sounds of their excited speech, and Liliha used the translator.

"The Ancestor would speak with you—it is very urgent."

The male crossed the room with lithe strides, holding the translator. Ayana noted that his strange claw weapons hung from his belt, that belt which was his only clothing. For, though the cat people appeared to vary in the amount of natural fur on their bodies, nearly hairless like Liliha in some cases, or as deeply furred as this male, they wore no coverings.

They went along the corridors, down two ramps, and then climbed another for some distance, until they reached a room where there was a gathering of warriors, a sprinkling of females.

All were grouped about one male. He was a little stooped, his muzzle fur frosted, his arms and legs thin and shrunken. About his bowed shoulders was a cloak of shimmering stuff, which set him apart from the others, though his very air was enough to do that. She recollected having seen him much earlier, in that time she had been a bound prisoner.

This was Gammage who was their leader, or ruler, whose dream it was to reclaim the Demon knowledge for his people.

He stared straight at Ayana as she entered. In one hand he held a translator disk, the box resting before him on the floor.

"They tell me," he began abruptly, "that you be-

lieve those in the ship have more knowledge of these war machines."

"That is so." Cat—man—mixture—there was something very impressive about this Elder. Ayana could understand how he had managed to gather together seekers after knowledge and inspire them through the years.

"Will they support the Rattons, or will they aid us?" He came directly to the point.

"I do not know, I can only ask," she said simply, as directly as he had asked.

Gammage made his decision. "Then that you shall do."

18

Furtig crouched in the shadow of the doorway, one of
the party that had escorted the female Demon out of
the lairs. She stood out there alone now, in full sight
of those in her ship. And the People had given her
back the device to signal her companions. Furtig held
one of the lightning throwers. He could send the
crackling lash to cut down the Demon at the first suspicion of betrayal.

Liliha, though she was armed—so close to him now
that when she moved the thin ruff of fur on the outside of her rounded arm brushed his—made no move
to draw her weapon. She had insisted that the Demon
was to be trusted, that she wanted indeed to halt the
Rattons and her own male. Though it was hard for
the warriors to accept such a turning against one's
own kind.

It would seem that this was a Chooser thing, allied
in a way to whatever moved them when they made
mate choice. Liliha had sworn before the Elders, and

it was very plain she believed what she said, that this Demon, though she had chosen the male now preparing to send fiery death against them, had not done that by her own willing and that she wanted no youngling of his.

Strange were the ways of Demons, strange even were the People's ways now. For their party had not only been augmented by Ku-La's warriors, but, in addition, by those from the caves, who had finally arrived. And—in an opposite doorway—were Barkers!

Never had Furtig believed he would be allied in any way with those. Yet Gammage and the two scouts rescued from the Rattons had convinced the Barkers to send in a small pack, perhaps as observers only. Still they were warriors, and no real fight would leave them lurking in the shadows.

A strange sound from the field—the bridge into the sky-ship was now dropping from the open hatch in its side. The Demon need only to run up that to be safe. Furtig was not sure any of them could use the strange weapons quickly enough to cut her down.

Liliha held to her ear one of the coms—as the Demon called them. Through that she could hear what the Demon said to her own kind. And she was not running, not moving at all. For some very long moments nothing happened. No one appeared in the hatch. All through those dragging minutes Furtig fully expected some awesome weapon to come into action, to their finish.

However, it would seem Liliha was right about the female Demon keeping to her word. At length a figure appeared on the ship's bridge, advancing slowly. It was muffled in clumsy wrappings so it hardly looked

272

like a living thing, more like one of the unreliable lair servants.

It tramped down the ramp, strode ponderously toward the waiting Demon. While it was still some paces away, its thick-fingered hands, almost as clumsy as Furtig's own when he tried to use some delicate lair tool, thumbed something at throat level. The head covering rose and flopped back on its shoulders.

"That is the other female," Liliha reported. "The one Ayana calls Massa—"

Furtig supposed that among themselves the Demons had names as did the People, the Barkers, even the Rattons. But he had never thought of the enemy as living normal, peaceful lives—only as the evil creatures of the old tales.

Dolar was beyond Liliha. "What do they say?" he rasped.

"The one from the ship asks questions— Where has Ayana been, what happens here. Now Ayana tells her there is much danger, they must talk. She asks about the other Demon—Jacel. Massa is angry. She says that he is ill, that Ayana must come and see to his illness. She asks where is Tan—there is anger in that. Now she says that Tan is the one who allowed the Rattons to wound her mate. That he must be wrong in his head—"

"Twist-minded like the Demons of old," cut in Dolar. "Mad—then dead. We must see to it that this time we are not also caught in that death! What say they now?"

"Ayana tells Massa that there is great danger, that Tan will bring death unless he is stopped. Massa says let Tan do as he will here, let them get on the ship and raise it into the sky, return to their own world—"

How easy that would be! Furtig growled, heard a similar sound from Dolar. Easy enough for these Demons to lift, leaving the evil one to finish here. And how could any of the People stop him? Oh, they might be able to blast these two females now. Then the one left in the ship—if he were sick perhaps he was also twist-minded—might join the one in the lairs in loosing the weapons the ship carried—

"Ayana says 'no,'" Liliha's voice quickened with excitement. "She says that the one called Tan must be stopped. That they can never learn what they came for—"

"And what is that?" demanded one of the warriors crouched behind them.

"They came here—Ayana spoke with Gammage of it this morning," Furtig answered, as Liliha was plainly intent on the com to her ear, "hunting two things—the reason their Ancestors quit this world, and an answer to an evil now destroying their new home among the stars. Gammage has promised that when we have beaten the Rattons she may seek such knowledge."

"When we beat the Rattons—say rather if we beat the Rattons!" commented someone else. Furtig saw that speaker was Fal-Kan.

"Be that as it may, there is knowledge here that they seek," Furtig answered with not quite the deference due an Elder. "Gammage made a bargain with this Demon. But she must persuade those in the ship to honor it."

"The one called Massa"—Liliha signalled for silence—"says she will do nothing until Ayana aids the sickness of her mate. If he is helped, then she will think of this."

"If the Demon goes inside the ship we shall have no way to watch her!" Dolar instantly objected.

"She will not go alone." Liliha arose. "I go with her."

Into the private lair of the Demons? Furtig moved. He had already slipped his left hand into his fighting claws. And in the other he had the lightning thrower.

"Not alone!" He thought his tone was not his usual one, but no one seemed to notice. Dolar twitched tail in assent.

Liliha handed the second com to the tough old Elder. "Set it so." She fitted it into his ear. "I do not know whether it will reach into the ship for you to hear. We can only hope it does."

Without glancing at Furtig, she stepped gracefully out of the doorway, her tail curled upward a little as if she went with pleasure. Pride brought him level with her, trying to assume the same appearance of unconcern.

The Demon Massa saw them first, gave a cry, and Ayana turned her head. Liliha, having no interpreter box, pointed to her, the ship, and used hand language.

Ayana nodded her head. Furtig, with the other interpreter, caught fragments of speech. She spoke much faster than she did with the People, and so was difficult to understand.

"We will go to Jacel."

Massa turned, all those extra layers of loose skin making her move slowly. Ayana walked behind her, Liliha and Furtig keeping pace. So they climbed the ramp to the ship.

Furtig's nostrils expanded, took in the many odors, most of them new, some disagreeable. There were strange pole steps one must climb. He set the lightning thrower between his jaws, for he must use all four limbs here. He hated the closed-in feeling of a trap which the cramped interior gave him.

Yet he stared carefully about him, intent on making good use of this chance to see the marvels of the Demons, wishing he could understand it all better.

In the small side chamber where the other male Demon lay in a niche within the wall, there was room for only the two females. But Furtig and Liliha could watch through the doorway. The Demon's face was flushed, his head turned restlessly from side to side, his eyes were half open. But, though they rested on Furtig, there was no sign that the Demon really saw the warrior.

Ayana was busy. She used a box from which wires ran to pads she held against the Demon's head, against his chest, watching the top of the machine where there sounded a steady clicking. Then she took up two small rods, opened them to slide in even thinner tubes in which liquid moved as she turned them. The ends of the outer rods she pressed to the bare skin of the Demon, on his arm, on his chest, at one point on his throat.

Before she had finished, his head no longer rolled, but lay quiet, his eyes closed. Then she spoke to Massa, slowly, as if she wanted the People to hear and understand.

"He will sleep, and wake all right. It is an infection from his wound, but not serious. This place is poisonous in more ways than one, Massa."

Massa had settled down beside the sleeping male, her hand over his, watching his face intently.

"Tan—Tan did this to him," she said. "What happened to Tan?"

"The same thing which destroyed those who remained here." Ayana put away the instruments. "Madness. And now Tan is about to destroy even more. You will have to help stop him, Massa, help us—"

"Us? *Us*, Ayana? You are helping these—these *animals?*" The Demon Massa looked to Furtig and Liliha, and there was fear in her eyes.

"Not animals, Massa—people—the People. This is Liliha, Furtig." She motioned from one to the other. "They have their lives and more than their lives at stake here. Our ancestors made them—"

"Robos?"

Ayana shook her head at that queer word. "No. Remember the old learning tapes, Massa? Remember 'cat' and 'dog' and 'rat'—and Putti, a dear friend?"

Furtig saw a little of the fear fade from the other's eyes, a wonderment take its place.

"But those *were* animals!"

"Were once. Just as *we* were once also. I do not know what really happened here, besides the spread of a madness which wrecked a whole species and altered others past recognition. But whatever our ancestors loosed, or tried to do deliberately, out of it grew the People who were cats, the Barkers who were dogs, and the Rattons—rats. And it is the latter Tan deals with—the filthy, merciless, torturing latter! He uses their aid to start old war machines, planning to wreck this world. Our ancestors left the company of those who began this grim wastage; we must stop it now."

"I do not know how you have learned all this." Massa raised the hand of the sleeping Demon and held it to her cheek. "But Tan—he turned those evil Rattons on Jacel. I owe him for that!"

Beside Furtig, Liliha stirred. She spoke in a small whisper. "This one did not have a mate chosen for her, or if she did, then her choice was the same. She will join us, I think, because she hates the ones who harmed him."

Thus when they came forth from the ship again they were not three but four. And all of them carried boxes and containers Ayana and Massa had chosen from supplies.

They transported these to the place where Gammage had gathered his battle leaders. Not only were Elders of the Barkers there, keeping to themselves, watching the People from eye corners (as the People surveyed them in return), but also Broken Nose brought in the pick of his warriors and they stood snuffling and grunting in one corner, their heavy-tusked leader in the circle about Gammage.

While the Ancestor made hand and speech talk, deft-fingered In-born moved small blocks here and there on the floor.

"The passages run so." Gammage gestured to the collection of blocks. "Walls stand thus. They can bring out the war machines only here, and here. We have scouts at each exit to warn of their coming—"

"But will we have time for such a message to reach us?" The Barker Elder's hand signs were awkward by the People's standard but effective enough to be understood.

"Yes—he will do it." Gammage pointed to Furtig.

"He is here—the scouts are there—" The gestures of the Barker were impatient.

"He can see—in his head—"

Furtig only hoped that Gammage was right, that his ability to contact the scouts would work. Foskatt was one, having with him the box to step up their communication. A second warrior, a small, very agile follower from Ku-La's tribe, had tested out well in box–Furtig contact too. It was the best they could do, for Foskatt could not cover both exits at once.

The Barker chief stared at Furtig. If he did not believe Gammage, at least he did not say so. Perhaps he had been shown enough inside the lairs to lead him to accept any wild statement.

"Only two ways for them to come," Gammage continued vocally for his own people and the Demon females. "And it is near to those that they must be stopped. We have taken all the servant machines and set them at the beginning of each way, ready to put into action. Though those will only cause a little delay. And with such fire shooters"—she looked now to Ayana—"as you say those are, perhaps the delay will be a very short one."

"Massa?" Ayana spoke the name of her sister Demon like a question.

The other was studying a picture projected on the wall, the one showing the details of what Tan and the Rattons were doing. "Those are storage powered." Her words made little sense to Furtig. "If the power could be shorted, or stepped up by feed radiation—"

"They would blow themselves up!" Ayana joined her. "Could we do that?"

"With a strong enough transmitter hook-up. But to do it underground— The backlash would be so powerful—there is no way of measuring what might happen."

"Yet if they bring those out—use them—"

Massa looked from Ayana to the mixed company of allies. "To whom here do we owe a debt? And remember, Tan would be lost, too."

Ayana turned her head also, looked from Liliha to Furtig, to Gammage, old Broken Nose, the people of Ku-La, those of the lair, the caves, the Barkers. It was as if she studied them all to make sure she knew them.

"Tan has already made his choice," she said slowly. "The debt is owed to all these. It is an old debt. Those of our blood started them on the road which they now travel. Our blood did ill here, and if we do not halt Tan, it shall do worse. Since we were responsible, these must have their chance. There is our old madness—and here is new life beginning. If we allow this war to break loose, we shall have to face a second failure for our kind. We must do what we can here and now."

"*You* then accept the full consequences of what will happen?" Massa spoke solemnly like one giving a challenge to battle.

"I accept."

"So be it."

Under the guidance of Massa, who went through the storerooms of the In-born (pausing sometimes with exclamations of one finding treasures until she was hurried on by Ayana), the lair defenders drew out many things they did not understand, placed those on carts which could be driven down into the lower levels.

They finally chose a single point, where the attackers must pass if they would reach the key entrance to Gammage's territory, and there they erected the barricade. Massa crawled in and out laying wires, placing boxes, those she had brought from the ship, others from the stores.

Furtig saw none of this. Against his will he sat in Gammage's headquarters, trying to keep his mind receptive to scout reports. Squatting on their heels before him were two younglings selected for their swift running, ready to carry warning to those who set up the final line of defense.

Meanwhile, out of this section of the lairs in which Gammage's people had so long sheltered, that tribe and the more recently joined kinsmen were moving not only their families and personal belongings, but load after load of the highly useful discoveries. For Massa had warned that when attack came, and if the counteraction she planned worked, there might even be an end to the buildings themselves.

Warriors, shaking with weariness, started appearing from below, stopped to pick up and stagger on with some last loads of discoveries. At last came the final party of all, Gammage, Dolar, the two Demons, three of the People, and two Barkers.

"We go—" Gammage staggered. He looked very thin and frail and old, as if all his years had fallen on him at once. Dolar was supporting him as he went.

"The Demon says this is a distance weapon, released by what she has in her hand—"

Furtig did not rise. "I cannot receive the alarm from below at any greater distance than this." As he said that a hollow emptiness was in him as if he hungered—but not for food, rather for the hope of life. He had tested the limits of the mind-send—and had accepted the fact that he could not retreat with the rest, any more than could Foskatt or the young scout of Ku-La's band, who were at their posts below.

"But—" Ayana paused after that one word.

Slowly Dolar made an assenting tail sweep.

"How long"—Furtig hoped his voice was reasonably steady, the proper tone for a warrior about to lead into battle—"must you know before you use this machine of yours?" He was using the interpreter and spoke directly to the Demon.

Ayana pulled at her wrist, loosening a band holding a round thing with black markings. One of those markings moved steadily.

"When this mark moves from here to here—that long do we have between alarm and when we use the weapon."

She slipped the band off, gestured for Furtig to take it.

Furtig turned now to Gammage. "How long before the Demon war machines can reach the place of the trap after they are sighted coming forth?"

The Ancestor bit at claw tip and then went to look at the blocks which stood for the level ways. "If the war machines go no faster than rumblers, and if those we have put in place do hold them back for a space—" He broke off as Liliha came running lightly across the chamber. In her hands was a wide dish of metal and in its center a cone. Furtig recognized it as what the In-born used to measure time. Gammage took it and spanned the cone with two claws.

"Light this at your first warning. Let it burn as far as I have marked it—then give us your signal."

So at both ends there was a small length of time— time for Foskatt and the scout below—time for himself.

"These go with you." Furtig pointed to his messengers. He caught up the covering on the divan, ripped it apart, and went to a window.

"See, when the scouts' signal comes that they move out below, and this burns to the line—I shall fire this with the lightning thrower. It will blaze in the window, and you, seeing it, can set off your weapon."

He hoped it would work. At least the arrangement gave him a small chance. The others left, taking the last of the bundles with them. If Massa was right— how much of the lairs would be lost? But better lose all than their lives and have the Demon and Rattons rule.

Furtig went back to the divan and sat down. Now he must concentrate on the messages. His skin itched as if small bugs crawled over his body. He licked his lips, found that now and then his hands jerked. With all his might he strove to control his body, to think only of Foskatt and the other scout—think—and wait.

It had been two days since the Demons had agreed to aid them. What had the Rattons and the other Demon been doing all that time? Putting machines to work—? All the pictures the hidden scout had taken were essentially the same. Apparently some machines had been discarded—others chosen—

How much longer—a night, another day? The longer the better as far as the rest of the People and their allies were concerned. They would be on the move away, back from this whole section of lair which was now a trap. Only the Demons and the war leaders would stay with the power broadcaster.

Periodically Furtig contacted the scouts. Each time the report was the same—no sign of any attack. Night came. Furtig ate and drank, walked up and down to keep mind and body alert.

He had returned to the divan when the long awaited signal came—from Foskatt.

Instantly Furtig ordered the other scout to withdraw, then touched the cone on the plate with a drop of liquid. There was a burst of blue flame, followed by a steady burning.

Furtig drew the lightning weapon, hurried to the doorway, his attention divided between the cone and the bundle of stuff in the window.

Longer than he had thought! Had he mistaken the markings Gammage had made on the cone? He held the dish—no, there was the line clear to be seen. Now he looked at that other measure which Ayana had given him, ready to depend upon it when the dish light marked the time.

Now!

Furtig hurled the dish from him, aimed at the bundle in the window, pressed the firing button. A long shaft of lightning crossed the chamber. His aim had been good, striking full upon the bundle. There was flame there which certainly the watchers in the next building could not mistake.

He was already through the door, running at top pace down the corridor, coming out on one of the bridges lacing building to building. And he kept on, intent only on trying to put distance between him and the place he had just quitted. Another corridor, one of those shafts for descent. Not daring to wonder if it worked, Furtig leaped into it as he might into a pool of water.

Then he floated down, his heart pounding. The tremor came. And that almost caused his death, for the soft pressure which supported him failed. It was only that it strengthened again for a moment that saved him, gave him a chance to catch at a level opening.

He was swinging by his hands and somehow scrambled up and through. There came another tremor. The building about him shook. Furtig ran, wanting only to gain the open. The rest of his flight was a nightmare. He kept picturing the whole of the lairs about to crash down on him.

Only when he reached the open did he turn to look back. There was a change. It took him several half-dazed moments to realize that the outline of at least one tower against the sky was now missing. All the buildings were now dark, no lights showing.

Liliha, Gammage, the Demons, the party who had remained to set off the trap—

Furtig, his panic gone, turned around. He dared not trust the interior of the lairs now. In fact the conviction was growing in him that, knowledge or no knowledge, he was through with the lairs. But he must know if the others had escaped. And Foskatt—underground—

He could not search the lairs— Why had he not thought straight? Furtig hunkered down on the ground, began to use his own talent.

Liliha! It was like looking into her face and she—she felt his questioning—understood! Foskatt— Furtig began again—but perhaps they were too far separated. He hoped that was the answer when he could not raise the other.

Morning came and they stood on the edge of the site where the sky-ship pointed up and out. Foskatt and the other scout were still missing. They were all there but one—and without that one—

"He was very old." Ayana's eyes held a tiredness in them as if she needed to rest a long, long time. "And he was weaker than he let you know. He must have been. When the explosion came"—she raised her hand and let it fall with a small fluttering gesture as if she tried their sign language—"then he went."

Gammage, the Ancestor, the one who had always been—a living legend. A world without Gammage? But now Ayana spoke again.

"In a way he was wrong. He wanted you to be stronger, more intelligent with every generation. He wanted you to, as he thought, be like us. So he sought out our knowledge for you. He did it, wanting the best for his people. But in a way he gave them the worst. He wanted you to have all we once had but that was not the answer. You know what happened here to us. Our knowledge killed, or drove us out.

"You have your ways, learn through them. It will be slower, longer, harder, but do it. Do not try to change what lies about you; learn to live within its pattern, be a true part of it. I do not know if you understand me. But do not follow us into the same errors.

"One thing Gammage did for you which is right and which you must save more than you save anything you have taken from the lairs: He taught you that against a common enemy you can speak with Barkers under a truce flag, gather and unite tribes and clans. Remember that above all else, for if he had only done that much, Gammage would be the greatest of your race.

"But do not try to live as we. Learn by your own mistakes, not ours. This world is now yours."

"And the Demons?" Dolar growled into the interpreter. He moved very slowly, as if with Gammage's death some of the other's great age had also settled upon him.

"We shall not come again. This is no longer our world. We have found in the lairs the knowledge which will perhaps save us on our new home. And our people will accept that, after hearing what we have to say. Or if they do not accept—" She looked over their heads to the lairs. *"Be sure in my promise—we shall not come again!"*

Even, she thought, if we have to—to make sure that the ship does not return to Elhorn. This promise must be kept. She did not look back to the People as she drew herself wearily up the ramp. If matters had *been different, if the old madness had not gripped them—if Tan—resolutely she closed her mind to that. But if the madness had not struck in the beginning perhaps the People would not have existed either. Did ill balance good somehow? Now she was too tired, too drained to think.*

Those on the field scattered back to the lairs. There were warriors questing about the ruins, hunting signs of Rattons, but so far none had been sighted. They had, though, brought back a dazed Foskatt, who had been struck on the head and was now closely tended by Eu-La. The other scout was still being sought.

Furtig and Liliha stood together, watching fire sprout around the sky-ship. They hid their eyes then against the glare as it rose, pointing out. The Demon had promised—no return.

But the other things she had said—that Gammage had been wrong, that they must find their own kind of knowledge— How much of that was truth? They would have time now to discover.

"They have gone," Liliha said. "To the stars— where someday, warrior, we shall follow. But before then, there is much to be done—even if we are no longer Gammage's people."

He would follow her willingly, even back into the lairs. Furtig had a feeling that henceforth wherever Liliha light-footedly trod he would follow. No—not follow—for she was waiting for him to walk beside her. He purred softly, and his tail tip curved up in warm content.